—— THE ——
GRIMACE

THE
GRIMACE

A Novel

NICHOLAS SALAMAN

GRAFTON BOOKS
A Division of the Collins Publishing Group

LONDON GLASGOW
TORONTO SYDNEY AUCKLAND

Grafton Books
A Division of the Collins Publishing Group
8 Grafton Street, London W1X 3LA

Published by Grafton Books 1991

A CIP catalogue record for this book is
available from the British Library

ISBN 0-246-13770-3

Printed in Great Britain by
William Collins Sons & Co. Ltd, Glasgow

. . . The mind, that ocean where each kind
Does straight its own resemblance find.
Yet it creates, transcending these,
Far other worlds and other seas . . .

Thoughts in a Garden
Andrew Marvell

1

At this time, a particularly horrible murder was reported in Pressburg.

Johanna related the details to me the morning after I had completed the bust of myself which I have named the Shrewd Moneylender, No. 65.

The crime seemed apparently purposeless. No money was stolen, no passions seemed to be involved.

The victim was a youth of seventeen who was working at the maltings and who was on the early shift to turn the malt. He never showed up, and his remains were later found down a little alley beside the grain store.

'Imagine,' said Johanna, 'his poor mother, that's Mrs Jellinek, and I was talking to her only the other day.'

I clucked and tutted. Jellinek did seem an unfortunate name for the boy.

'We're none of us safe,' Johanna continued, shivering. 'Just think . . . he could be watching me as I come and go.'

Violence and the spilling of blood, when it is other people's blood, has a strange effect on some women. It is said that Casanova went round touching up the ladies while they watched executions. Johanna seemed quite fidgety about the whole affair.

In a professional sense, I must say, I was quite intrigued by Johanna's story. The connection between the trunk and the head, with all those appropriate couplings for food, blood, breath and nerves, to say nothing of the vertebrae themselves, is one of the most dazzling manifestations of the Creator's ingenuity.

'Have they any idea who might be responsible?' I asked.

'The Watch say they saw a crazed vagabond, almost

naked, running through the town around midnight. They couldn't catch him. So far they can find no trace of him. The whole place is searching. I wouldn't like to be him when they find him.'

Strange, I reflected, that a youth should lose his life just, as it were, on the threshold of mankind's new dawn. Even more ironic that the method of his death should have been decapitation.

Did I not mention that?

'The poor lad's head was taken right off with one clean blow, that's what they think,' said Johanna, fidgeting excitedly, 'and they haven't found his body yet neither. Just the head, like.'

She hurried off, eager to catch the latest developments in the grisly affair, while I started blocking out the details of my sixty-seventh head: the Wily Machiavel.

As I worked, my mind kept turning back to what she had told me. It was not so much the murder itself. In these violent times we become used to the horrors served up almost daily in the journals. It was the thought of the vagabond that affected me. He, after all, was still alive. What if he were not guilty and they caught him?

What if no one came forward and the man were executed? There would be two murders then instead of one.

In these strange, heavy days of early winter, the questions flickered about my head like the flurries of first snow around the cemetery wall outside.

2

Let me adjust the mirror, so.

You can see admirably with the light shining from the window in front.

We have an almost perfect equal light, from either side, provided by a day that is thinly clouded with the sun hidden behind a satisfactory gauze.

It is the ideal light. And the mirror is suitably tilted thirty degrees from the vertical which I have found the optimum angle for the time of day. It is an old looking-glass of my grandmother's. They made mirrors better in those days, something to do with the quality of mercury employed. I will look the details out for you some time.

Now I have reassured you on these points, come a little closer and let us examine the face.

The face is oval-shaped, not bony. From the crown of the head to the point of the chin, and from ear to ear, I have an identical measurement of 13½ inches. This is an excellent proportion and one that is recommended by no less an authority than Praxiteles himself. You are impatient to get on to the eyes and nose, the hair? You wish to see the *tout ensemble*? I'm sorry but you must contain yourself. You don't expect to see the gallery in one whole swoop. No, you shall look at the face by degrees, for a face is indeed a gallery of a kind.

Excuse me, there is someone at the door.

3

I have always had a horror of things growing on my face. Even the hairs of my beard seem to be an unwarrantable intrusion.

Spots are of course anathema. How many miserable days did I pass as a youth examining those molehills which were to me great throbbing ranges of shame and self-disgust! To rid myself of them, I squeezed too soon, inexpertly, with grimy fingernails, raising what crusts and weepings. These I would examine intently in the mirror, from every angle, screwing up my face so that the offending area would be raised to catch the light.

My mother would sometimes try to reason with me.

'Nobody is going to notice them,' she would say.

'But, Mother, I notice other people's.'

'That is because you are over self-conscious. You look for your own faults in others.'

My mother was under self-conscious, and she was wrong. People did notice my spots. A cousin called Johanna, whom I went to kiss merely in the way of friendship, said, 'Oh, I didn't know you had spots.' Nobody wants to kiss spots. But all this was small stuff, simply Nature making the blood too rich, the soup boiling over as it were. Spots were nothing.

It was the naevi – what people call moles – that seemed to me infinitely more disturbing. At around the age of forty, the naevus can become, as it were, activated. Flat brown patches can suddenly rear up from their long sleep and become protuberances. Scaly pale naeval warts can manifest on the scalp. Harmless little blobs can grow into nasty black slagheaps. And, of course, the naevus is harder to deal with. Once arrived, it does not in time depart like a bed-and-breakfast spot. No, the naevus is long-term residential.

4

Franz had been Assistant Teacher of Drawing and Anatomy at the seminary for four months when he suddenly developed a cold sore.

He had been dreading this eventuality ever since he could remember for he had always had a horror of it on others.

5

You see. I have started my story in several ways. I was told once that a story should be related in the third person. But after two attempts at it, I must give up, for this is so intense, so personal a story that to relate it in the third person would be like trying to do a pirouette in a straitjacket. I must be singular.

The facts, then.

I have left my job at the school and am living in a small studio in Pressburg.

I see no one. No, that is not true. I see myself – or that mirror-image of myself – or that thing which is both us and not us and which is called a face – I see that all the time. I am imprisoned by my face but I am not my face.

Occasionally, it is true, I huddle on a coat and go out to the shops to buy the necessities of life: bread, a little wine, perhaps a sausage, apples. But this is undertaken at a gallop. I rush through the shops. I have a terrible dread that when I get back to my mirror, my face will not be there. Ridiculous, of course; but there are always reasons for our fears. I think I will not go out so much in future.

It started with a cold sore.

Where will it end?

<hr/>

6

My wife and children were fine people. But sometimes it seemed to me that I was becoming invisible to them. It was the same at the school.

'Hullo, Franz,' they would say. 'Good weekend?'

'Yes, thank you. And you?'

'Very nice, yes. Very quiet. You do anything?'

'Very quiet.'

'Nice.'

We all liked it quiet. Don't ask me why.

It was suddenly borne in upon me that I was getting near having no interest in anything.

And then I got this cold sore; that, I must say, interested me strangely.

In spite of all the advances in medicine, very little is known about the cold sore. It is beneath the learned doctors' dignities. For sheer drama, it is not in the same league as cholera or leprosy. Smallpox beats it into a cocked hat. You do not see headlines proclaiming – 'Outbreak of cold sores in Moravia.'

A cold sore is rather like love.

It starts with an itch, it progresses to a blister, it turns into a scab, and it finally drops off. No, I am not anti-romantic. That was just a joke. I enjoy a little amorous jiggery-pokery. More pokery than jiggery if I have the choice, but that's only to be expected.

14

It is not that I am anti-romantic. Nor am I a realist. I am more of an unrealist. I would like to be romantic but every time I fall in love I think pussy.

I think there is a daemon in the cold sore trying to get out. Or deeper.

7

But what is a face? Are we our faces? Surely we are more?

People who have had their faces badly disfigured are often acutely changed in personality. So, our faces affect us. Do we affect our faces?

I am trying to draw as I think. A little line here, on the chin. No, too much. That is better.

Yes, one can say that bad temper leaves its mark, a sardonic personality, even good humour. They all etch the face. But is it not rather like living with another person? We affect each other; but we are not each other.

My wife, she calls herself my wife, still visits me. We still affect each other.

My daughter Johanna is down with mumps. She is doing well at school. Money is short again. That affects me too. My face remains impassive.

8

A conversation with the face.
'Hullo, face,'
The face looks at me.
'Hullo, face.'

The face looks at me further.

'Come on, pudding.'

That usually sets it off.

'Don't call me pudding. At least I am there. We cannot even see you. We do not even know you exist,' it hisses.

'I think therefore I am.'

'Shit.'

The face is not very subtle.

'You are just animated meat,' I say to the face. 'At your very best, as Pastor Lavater has it, you are but the mirror of the passions.'

'And you,' says the face, 'are just grey soup.'

'I think we'd better stop this,' says I.

'Nah-nah-nahnah-nah,' says the face.

'If we add one vowel to the word faces, we have faeces,' I say.

That usually shuts it up, though it may make some weak remark about Lavatery jokes, ha ha.

Of course, when I am talking to someone else, a pretty girl, for instance, I am conscious that the conversation is now a three-way affair – possibly four-way if the girl has the same problem with her face as I do. But on the whole I think not. Girls and their faces seem much more firmly glued together; though I did know a girl who knew a girl who said she had the strangest feelings about her face; it was on holiday in the mountains. This girl kept complaining of pressures; said she felt she wanted to take her face off. I was curiously intrigued by the tale until her friend told me that the girl had a slight hare-lip. It then became, of course, perfectly straightforward. She wanted to take her face off and put a new one on. That's rather like wanting to take your pussy off and put on a penis because you think it might be better – or vice versa – which I have heard is current among the Mameluchi.

But my problem with my face is not like this.

16

Let me tell you a little about myself. No, why mince words? Let me tell you a lot about myself.

9

As small a thing as a smell has the power to halt the galloping horses of time; yes, and send them racing back. I remember little from my early years unless I smell something now that reminds me of them.

Pictures cannot do it half as well. Statuary is left standing. Even music has not that gift of backwardgoingness. But a fragrance . . . that particular Hungary Water that my mother used to wear on special occasions . . . the peculiar smell of hot metal when the stove had been blacked . . . a kind of tobacco my father used to smoke which you hardly find nowadays . . .

All these recall for me that I was once a shy little boy with fair hair who was beaten for eating a neighbour's fig; who used to get into my mother's bed and be rolled up in the sheets like a sausage roll while she sang 'I had a little sausage, a bonny bonny sausage, I put him in the oven for my tea, I went down to the cellar, to fetch my umberella, and the sausage he did run away from me'; who took a musical box to pieces because he wanted to see the baby man inside . . .

I went out today and smelled wallflowers. Immediately I was back in Wisensteig, eating biscuits with my brother on the lawn. Take me apart and you will find a baby man inside, eating biscuits. We do not change. We grow like Russian dolls.

10

I was born in the small town of Wisensteig near Munich on February 6th 1736, forty-eight years ago. My family was artistic, as my mother would say, though whether they were artists or craftsmen, I wouldn't really care to be put to the stake upon. Both upon my mother's and my father's side, there were sculptors and woodcarvers who would decorate churches and suchlike impressive haunts with flowery curlicues and gilded whatnots.

I can't bear the style now, but in my grandfather Johann Georg's workshop in Wisensteig, and later in Munich, I thought it was gorgeous stuff.

My father died when I was six. He spent so much time on his travels, carving in those little churches, that I hardly knew him; but Mother was upset so we were all upset too.

One of my few memories of Father was of him lifting me up to see soldiers in the square. A war had broken out.

'It is about the new Empress,' my father told me.

'Are they our soldiers?' I asked him. 'Friends or foes?'

'They are grenadiers from Württemberg,' he said, 'they are friends.'

They all looked exactly alike, like toy soldiers. Their hair was dressed in innumerable curls, combed and powdered snow-white, and every beard was greased coal-black, and shining like wet paint. They were so pretty I wanted to put them in my cupboard.

Weeks later we saw other soldiers who weren't so pretty, coming back from the distant battlefield. One of them had what seemed like half his face missing, done up with a bandage. You would think it would have killed him. I was fascinated to know what was behind the face. I asked my father.

'Can we see his soul when he takes off the bandage?'

I was told not to be disgusting.

Soon after my father's death, Mother, brother Joseph and I moved to Munich because money was short, and my mother's brother, Uncle Johann (another woodcarver – naturally Mother called him a sculptor), said he could use me in his studio, and teach me the ropes. I learned the ropes well, I believe, for after seven years, when my apprenticeship was up, he sent me to Uncle Philipp at Graz to find out about gilding. Thus, by the end of my nineteenth year, I had learned my trade at two of the greatest centres of the art (yes, why not art?) in the world. A good start, wasn't it? And to tell you the truth – and why should I want to tell you lies? – I was a talented chap. If I'd been a musician, I'd have been fondled and dandled and taken up by great lords and fine ladies, and travelled to London and Paris and Prague and Vienna, and all in all I would have been a pretty coxcomb.

But I was a woodcarver with a talent for making figures. However, at the age of nineteen, I did in fact go to Vienna at my uncle's urging – he had friends there who could help me – and there I enrolled at the Academy of Arts. The Academy stood in one of the pleasantest squares in the city. It was an imposing pile built about fifty years before, and the professors seemed equally august to a youth up from the provinces.

The course itself was arduous both in theory and practice but I had never been happier. It is always congenial to add to one's talent. I enjoyed my fellow students, and they were, it seemed, agreeably amused by me. I was a droll fellow in those days. I began to play the flute – a whimsical instrument. It was the springtime, before the shadows of unrest and the menace of the years.

True, another war had now started up, much on the same matter as the last one. This time the enemy was Prussia. I should not have liked to have been a Prussian at the Academy, but a mere South German was seen to be a harmless sort of creature.

Occasionally we would see a detachment of troops marching off in their pretty Austrian pinks or greens; and as the war progressed, there was a slight increase in the appearance of crutches in the streets, particularly among the mendicants (this could have been opportunism). Otherwise there was little to suggest that Vienna was at war with anyone. It was generally assumed that the Empress would sort it out. That is one of the advantages of absolute monarchy.

I remember only one serious furore at the time. That was when the silk weavers went on strike and the courtiers thought they weren't going to have enough silk to cover their hides. So the Empress had all the weavers arrested.

11

The pains have been bad today. I cannot make out exactly what they are. It feels as if they are gut-ache, but I have eaten nothing that would precipitate such an attack. The old woman who comes in makes soup, but I hardly touch it. Fasting somehow seems to heighten my perceptions. I take very little wine. Why then should I be tormented in this way? It is like a devil with a corkscrew, pulling out my giblets.

It makes me think of death. Perhaps indeed it is the beginning of cancer. Uncle Philipp died of it. Uncle Philipp died a ghastly death. I wouldn't like to go like that.

The odd thing was that Uncle Philipp's pains, though intense, at least seemed to come from one well-defined spot: his bollocks. Mine seem to be much more peripatetic. The week before last they were in the stomach. Before that they were in the chest. Now they're just below the navel, so.

At least I can employ my grimaces to some advantage. When the pain comes, I switch from one face to another. If I am working on, say, the Childish Weeper, I put it aside and move to the Wounded Soldier. It does not relieve the pain but it gives me something to think about.

These heads I am doing are going to create something of a stir. Not just for their style – already those pompous old farts who used to sit for me on their gilt barocco thrones know that they must now be seen in the light of Nature (though of course the light of Nature can be infinitely flexible) – but for their subject. Instead of the pompous old farts and their flexible light of Nature, the subject is . . . myself!

If such an enterprise lacks funding, at least I can be my own man; patronage is a prison. Who is his own man – or what passes for it – these days?

My idea is quite simple. I propose to explore, like an intrepid traveller, the uncharted continent of my face. I have reasons for doing this which will become clear. However, there is something that does not wish me to engage.

Ah ah. That was a bad one.

There are secrets, such as those of the Freemasons, which are better left unrevealed. There are unscrupulous people about who profane and subvert such secrets.

There are secrets locked in the face – mine and yours – which can hold the key to our very existence. One has to be careful with this kind of secret.

12

I had found lodgings in the Schönlaterngasse – or rather my Uncle Philipp had found them for me – with a kinswoman of his wife's. She was a widow, a decent old biddy, with three daughters, each one more beautiful than the last. I had the room right at the top of the house; it was an attic really, but I had the most wonderful view between the geraniums of my window-box, across the spires and turrets of Vienna. The sisters called me their bat in the belfry. I was in love with all three of them. They were called Anna-Maria, Johanna, and Eva.

How happy were those days! My work progressed well. I had energy and talent. My masters were pleased. And Vienna was such a pleasant place to be young in. My friends and I would walk in the woods, or stroll by the river, or sit in the cafés drinking coffee and eating those chocolate cakes, and we would be always talking; of love, art, politics, religion, love again, and more art. And sometimes in particular of Anna-Maria, Johanna and Eva who would come with us and who would make me horribly jealous as they flirted with my friends.

The Widow Mohler, their mother, asked me if I would do a portrait of each of the girls, and I set to with a will. I did Anna-Maria first, as befitted her seniority. She was a tall glorious girl with a fine figure and brilliant blue eyes which shone like twin glimpses of the heavens caught between creamy clouds. Though paint was not yet my real medium, I contrived to catch her likeness well, and I presented her as an Empress with bright sky and puffy cloudlets behind her, complete with gambolling putti. She was so enchanted with the result that she kissed me and showed me one of her bosoms.

Eva was the youngest, only fifteen, and though she was so beautiful, she was too young for any serious frolicking. I painted her as a Diana, splendidly, almost provocatively chaste, in a hussar's tunic which served very well as a hunting dress, lugging along a greyhound which belonged to a gardener I knew. The whole effect was tremendously jolly.

As for Johanna, she was my favourite and I resolved to make her love me for my efforts. Johanna I painted as the very Queen of Love, and I told her mother that she would

22

have to be dressed in little more than a fog. It was an extreme impertinence of me, but Mrs Mohler was so proud of her daughter that she agreed, and Johanna and I were left to our devices in my attic.

She was darker than her sisters and had a face of grave beauty, a slim figure, but with the most beautiful breasts I have ever seen and, believe me, we sculptors see breasts. I made her lie down on a couch. She seemed not in the least disturbed to be seen without her clothes, and made little use of the muslin that I gave her for modesty's sake. I painted her as Venus Observing – for Love is a Voyeuse, peering at our mortal junctures. When she was finally satisfied that I had done her justice – she was a very vain girl – she allowed me to look at her all over. I shall never forget that first crossing of the divide between art and carnality. Her body had that sweet milky smell that young girls distil, and between her legs was something beyond the capacity of any fruit of Paradise. I wanted to undress and leap upon her, but all she wanted was to be looked upon.

'Just look upon me, Franz,' she wrote to me. She did not speak. She wrote to me.

They were strange afternoons at No. 8, Schönlaterngasse, and it was the strangeness of an enchantment. You did not know such rogueries went on in the Vienna of the 1750s? You thought all the smut was in your own day? You are wrong. It was in Schönlaterngasse, I think, that I first came to be interested (obsession came later) in another characteristic of humanity; in the difference between the real self in a person and the semblance – that is, the external manifestation; what the priests would call the outward and visible sign, the body; and most importantly the face. Or was it there? Or somewhere else? Or have I not always studied that skull, upholstered with flesh and covered with skin, with those twinkling bits of jelly peeping out that we call eyes, from my very earliest days? I seem to see the schoolboy now, intent, grave, peering at his face in the twilight room until he almost seems to merge with the mirror and disappear although his face remains.

Where am I? And who?

13

Mesmer has called again. Confound the fellow! And yet I must not confound him too much because if it were not for him and one or two odd visitors like him who buy things from time to time, or come with commissions, I should be sunk. But I don't like Mesmer. It makes it all the more galling that I should have to depend on him.

Mesmer has thick lips, a lecher's face. He *is* a lecher. I believe his prime motivations are self and lechery. Now we all like lechery. I have been a lecher myself. But there's no need to let the thing get out of hand. Mesmer has let it get out of hand.

He's hit on magic as being the best method of influencing the ladies and of making money at the same time. Money of course is the lubricant of lechery.

Mesmer, they told me when I first met him, has concocted a whole farrago around electricity and magnetism. He prepares a bowl of dilute acid and makes quaint passes over it towards his subject, usually a lady, while wild music plays and the rest of the gathering hold hands. He waves his hands, and the music plays, and the subject falls asleep or mumbles, or both; and he calls it Animal Magnetism; and everyone just about has an orgasm. That is what they said. The truth is rather different as you shall see.

Exactly why he should want my heads is still a mystery to me. He doesn't understand my search. Truth could not be further from his mind. The man is an illusionist. Correction: the man is a rich illusionist. He has a house in Vienna as well as a villa not ten miles away. It has a theatre in the grounds where he puts on operas and magic shows, and steals the hearts of young ladies.

Ow.

It was Mesmer, however, who brought me the Egyptian. Where he obtained the bust, he would not say. Doubtless it was illicitly.

'I have no use for this, Franz,' he said.

'No use,' I cried, examining the head. 'But it is very ancient. And it is superb.'

'It is Egyptian, I shouldn't wonder,' said he, carelessly.

'It could well be. It is perfect.'

I was seduced by the thing. The face had an enigmatic smile, or was it a frown? It was hard to read the expression, as sometimes it is upon a living face, but the proportions of the piece were impeccable. It was full of weight if you know what I mean, with the utmost lightness. The meaning was heavy, the execution irresistibly graceful.

'It is for you,' said Mesmer, offering it again.

'I could not afford it, Mesmer,' I said.

It was strange how commissions had fallen away recently. Had I been too preoccupied with my face, my heads?

'I am not selling it, Franz,' he lisped – lisping was one of his affectations, 'I am giving it to you.'

'But . . . but why? The head is worth hundreds of florins.'

'I value your friendship, my dear fellow. Besides, I should like two more of your own heads. They have so much latent electricity, a séance would be a sorry thing without them.'

I needed little persuasion. The Egyptian head was the most beautiful thing I had ever seen. I gave Mesmer two of my worst heads – which in fact I was intending to recast – and set my Egyptian on a plinth in the corner where I could watch him as I worked.

The funny thing is that since that day, Mesmer, who

had previously behaved like a supplicant, adopted a much more patronly manner towards me, half condescending, half hooded. I fear that one day he is going to want my Egyptian back. He is going to say, 'But I only lent it to you, Franz.' That would be the finish of everything.

14

I worked hard at the Academy of Arts, and I was rewarded by the kindness and encouragement of the Directors. One in particular took a special interest in me, a man by the name of Martin Van Meytens. This gentleman was a Court painter much in favour, who specialized in sumptuous scenes and noble postures. He used to come by the studio where I worked with my classmates and pause at every easel; but I noticed that he would particularly pause at mine. I later realized that his interest in me was not purely artistic but I was unversed in the ways of the world at the time, and I was flattered.

'Good, very good,' he would say. 'Perhaps a touch of carmine here. And that line a shade stronger. So! You are a most promising student. But your colour lacks something yet. How would you like some special tuition?'

'Very much indeed thank you, sir.'

'Excellent. Come to my office after your classes finish and we will see what we can inculcate.'

One or two of the other students exchanged glances, but I went along feeling well pleased. Van Meytens had a pleasant room overlooking a little quadrangle lined with flowerbeds and adorned with green creepers. He poured me a glass of wine and we sat and talked for a while.

'How old are you, Froberger?'

'I am twenty, sir.'

'Ah, a magical age. Make the most of it, young man. "Youth's a stuff will not endure".'

'Sir?'

'Shakespeare. Have you read his plays?'

'No, sir.'

'You should. It is always good for one art to be aware of another.'

'I will try to find a copy.'

'You can borrow mine. It is only a translation, but I imagine you do not speak English?'

'No, sir. Though I hope to travel to London one day and must learn a little.'

He rose and went to his bookshelf, returning with a stout volume.

'There,' he said, handing it over. 'That will do for a start.'

I accepted the tome with proper gratitude and waited for the lesson on colour to commence. He settled himself into his chair, sipped his wine and looked at me reflectively. I returned his gaze. He was, I suppose, in his early fifties – a man of the world – well dressed without being precious – perhaps a little over-fastidious about appearances – bushy greying eyebrows betraying iron-grey hair under his short wig – blue-grey eyes the colour of some of those Dutch seas – thin but well-formed lips – a quizzical, watchful expression. If I had been painting him, I should have concentrated on those eyes and lips. Always watch the lips.

They were the key to his character; not that it was done at the time to reflect too much character in a portrait. 'Position', that is to say importance, and likeness were the thing, and plenty of red and gold.

Van Meytens finally leaned over and patted me on the knee.

'Good,' he said. 'Well done.'

'Well done?' I asked.

'You will make a good sculptor. You feel through the

face to the man within. But are we our faces? What are we without our faces? Do we survive as characters if our faces are ruined by war or disease?'

He raised a subject that had already started to exercise me.

'I think we are our faces, sir, but our faces are not completely us,' said I, feeling the smoothness of my nose and cheekbone.

I could not imagine myself without my features. I was a handsome enough lad with reddish-brown hair and bright blue eyes, and a golden-brown skin now uncorrupted by pustules. I was pleased with the frame God had given me, whatever lay behind it.

'And yet,' I went on, 'there must be more to it than that.'

'There must be more to it, or we should die when our bodies do,' he agreed.

Then he asked me another question that unsettled me for I had always tried to subscribe to my mother's philosophy of relentless optimism that she used like a curtain to shut out the dark.

'Do you think people are generally better or worse than they seem?'

'Well . . . er . . . I should think they should try to seem what they are, sir.'

'That is all very well. But supposing they are shallow, greedy, venal little shits. What then?'

'I should think they should try to improve their characters, sir, with God's help.'

'Do you think it is possible for shallow, greedy, venal little shits to improve their character, or even to want to improve their character?'

I floundered.

'I . . . I don't know, sir.'

'I know,' he said. 'I know very well. They don't want to. They don't mind being shallow, greedy, venal little shits.

The only thing they mind is for a portrait painter to exploit it in a picture for all to see. So a portrait painter, a successful portrait painter or a sculptor such as you wish to become, Froberger, must study the art of likeness, of individuality, of animation, but not always of truth.'

'But what is beautiful must be truthful, sir.'

'Who's talking about Beauty, Froberger?'

'But, sir . . .'

He rose. It was clear that the conversational part of our evening was over.

'Come,' he said. 'I will show you how I mix my colours.'

15

But I was talking about Beauty. I have always, whatever the vicissitudes, in success and in rejection, I have always believed it was the work that mattered. I still believe that, even though I am fallen on hard times in my middle years – in what should be my greatest years – I am deserted, mocked. Only the ideas of Beauty and of Truth sustain me.

Grand words, of course, and fiddlesticks. What sustains me is the very small income got from the sale of my home in Vienna, and commissions from Mesmer and his funny friends. I am, at the end of the day, a soft engine. I must have my stoking.

I hear that Mozart is beginning to be out of favour. I am not surprised. No one of any merit can be in favour long in Vienna. The shallow venal little shits will do for him soon enough. They can't bear to see the ugly shadows they cast in the light of genius.

But come, come; come, come. To the matter in hand. Let me advance the mirror, so. They used to make heads an exercise, like scales on a forte piano. Do a merry fellow, they would say in the art schools. Do a melancholy girl. Do a witch. Do a sly trickster. It was Le Brun who made it so popular. But it is through scales that I am finding scale. Look.

I have completed sixteen heads. Let me remove the drapes. Yes, they are all of myself. See the gradation of expression? I believe that if I can catch the exact gamut of all my expressive possibilities – then I can free my spirit from its house for I will have undone Nature. What do you think of that?

What started as an exercise has become a labour of love.

I have given them titles. Yes, the Childish Weeper, the Constipated Man, and so forth. I fancy Mesmer intends to make capital out of them but it will be over my dead body. I wish Mesmer would not call so often. He is like a vulture sitting on my not-quite-dead-yet body. But he brings money. He needs me.

The Egyptian bust watches gravely. I find myself looking more and more at it. There is a secret in its alabaster. We think ourselves so modern and clever but we cannot match the mastery of the ancients. There is a spirit locked in that face, you can depend on it.

I am working at the moment on what I am calling the 'Old Buffoon'. It involves opening my mouth and screwing up my eyes in front of the mirror for long periods while I make the necessary sketches. Have you ever tried to hold a foolish gape for half an hour? It is extremely painful and makes you realize what habitual foolish gapers must go through to maintain their customary mode.

My mouth has always been a very satisfactory orifice, but I have seldom used it for gaping. It lacks gaping training. Now I am making up for it.

As I gape, I think about my mouth. The upper lip is pleasantly arched but not I hope effeminate. The lower lip rounded and shapely. Within, my teeth are still, I thank God, intact. They are not as white as they were but thanks to my daily applications with larch twigs (my mother used to make us twig our teeth twice a day), they are at least serviceable.

My mouth was fine until I had the cold sore. How I got it is a mystery. I have not kissed anyone in a year, I am sorry to say.

Hold your gape, damn you.

That's better.

Actually, I do not like to hold my mouth open in this way. Who knows what might not force entry?

16

It was at the Academy that I had my first brush with bronze, a baptism of fire that inaugurated a lifelong enthusiasm. I had never seen a bronze cast before. Indeed, I had very little idea what actually happened between the image and the statue. My good Uncle Philipp had been solely concerned with the carving of wood and stone.

Another favourite professor of mine, Balthasar Moll – one of the Court sculptors and a more savoury fellow than Van Meytens – conducted the lesson. He was a kindly old josser underneath his lazy, sardonic air.

'How can you be such a fool, boy?' was one of his favourite lines.

'To be an artist in bronze,' he told us, 'you have to be more than an artist. You have to be an alchemist.'

'You mean with a mummy and a stuffed crocodile, sir?' asked a little squirt called Strodl from Burgenland. 'And a horoscope, like?'

'No, I do not mean that, Strodl. I mean that you have to

know about the behaviour of metal under extreme heat – so that the noble features that you have in mind do not fly asunder in fumo, as the alchemists say, when the metal from the kiln hits them.'

He took us through the process, showing us examples along the way – from the carving of the image in clay to the making of the reverse image in a mould of gelatine or plaster, to the lining of that reverse image with wax.

'Wax, sir?' piped Strodl again, keen as anything but stupidly puzzled. 'But won't it melt when the metal's poured on?'

Moll rolled his eyes.

'Wait, Strodl, you go too fast. You are ahead of us, Strodl. You are headlong. I dare say you rush your young ladies off their feet. Or should I say, off their pedestals?'

Everyone laughed. Strodl was known for his hopeless admirations for young ladies of birth. But the Professor was already doing something strange to his waxen head.

'The wax, as you see, Strodl, has once more made a positive image for us. Just like the noble features you have carved. It is like a mask. And from it we shall build a series of little wax pipes that we call runners and risers . . .'

Strange tubular streamers like stiff papillomas began to stretch out from the head. And now the Professor shaped a cup above them into which they all disgorged.

'What do you think that is for, Froberger?'

'The sculptor's cup of bliss, sir?'

Everyone laughed. I was a wag in those days.

'Always thinking of pleasure, Froberger? How can you be such a sybarite so young? Pleasure is the consolation of the middle-aged.'

'Sorry, sir. Is it for hot air, sir?'

Everybody laughed again, thinking I had made another impertinent jest, which I had not, for it struck me that what I was watching was almost an engine.

'No joke,' said Moll. 'He is very nearly right. Gas, that

is the enemy here. Without the risers to collect the gases, they would pockmark your pretty opus or even break it up altogether. But the purpose of the runners and the cup is to conduct and collect the liquid metal itself. And now for the grog.'

'Grog, sir? But I thought you said . . .'

'Grog, Froberger. That is what we call this mixture of ceramic and plaster that we chuck at the wax to build a deep faithful casing around it. And when that is ready . . .'

Here he turned to show us a completely encased specimen.

'Why, then we pour on the red-hot soup of copper, tin and zinc that we call . . .'

'Brass,' said Strodl, triumphantly.

'That we call bronze, you misbegotten dauber,' shouted Moll.

And he took us down to the foundry to observe the next stage.

'Here we have our casing,' said Moll, picking up the lump of grog, 'and here we have the hot bronze broth about to become a bust.'

A minion (like an alchemist's 'Lungs', indeed) took the lumpen shape and placed it in a receptacle beneath the furnace, opened a door, extracted from the dragon within an incandescent pot with a long pair of tongs, and tipped the whole boiling into the casing. A wondrous hissing and spitting ensued accompanied by clouds of fume.

'That was the wax melting, Strodl. That is why we call this the Lost Wax process. And that smell like a fiend's fart is your hot air, Froberger. All carried along pipelets of wax. A miracle, really.'

And so it seemed – and still seems – to me. A miracle.

'Finally,' concluded Moll, 'we let it cook, we chip away the grog – not too hard, mind – with mallet and chisel. And we are left with a head which has a number of metal tubes and a cup sticking out of it. Like this . . .'

He produced a chocolate-coloured head that looked like a cross between a porcupine and a Medusa with face worms.

'And this,' he said, rubbing and chasing, 'we chase and plug, removing all trace of the pipes. Next we patinate to give a cogenial colour. Each has his own recipe – steeping in vinegar, horse manure or even piss, Strodl. And finally we give it a wax finish. And talking of finish, that is it for the day. All clear, everybody? Pleasure-time, Froberger. Don't strain yourself reaching for food.'

His injunction was unnecessary. I lingered in the foundry after everyone had gone, sniffing the fumes, inflamed with this mystery of heat and its eggs of beauty brought out of flame. Even its language seemed magical, arcane. Runners and risers . . . and, what was it that the old man had called it? The Lost Wax process. Wax, lost like some ancient language or legendary treasure, lost, or like youth and happiness itself.

17

Van Meytens and I used to meet regularly in his room, have our conversation on matters philosophical, artistic and political, and then get down to brushing-up my colour-sense. You may think it strange that I should need such instruction, since I had been singled out for my talent; but remember that I had been grounded in carving and gilding. Anyway, Van Meytens was pleased with me for I learned fast and soon enough had his secrets at my disposal. I became, though I say it myself, a very creditable painter even if my first love was still sculpture.

Just before I completed my studies, in my last week at the Academy, I went to Van Meyten's room to say goodbye.

'So you are off,' said he. 'You have done well here. You will collect your diploma and then what will you do?'

The thought had been exercising me for I needed to earn money. My mother who was not rich had been supporting me with the help of my uncle, and I wished now to be self-sufficient, indeed to pay them back if I could.

'I will go back to Munich,' I said. 'Or Graz. I have relations there. Or even to Wisensteig. I will find work as a craftsman sculptor.'

'That would be a waste,' said Van Meytens. 'You are too good for that. I do not want all the time that I have spent with you wasted on bas-reliefs for provincial latrines. What do you say to a job in the Arsenal?'

'The Arsenal?' I exclaimed stupidly.

'The Imperial Arsenal,' he repeated. 'I know the Director.'

'But I know nothing about guns.'

'At the Arsenal they prepare ceremonial guns. The ceremonial cannons need decorations and ornaments of the highest quality. They will be noticed by people who matter. Soon you will get other commissions. You are as good as made.'

I apologized for having been so slow, and thanked him for his kindness once again.

'Why do you do it?' I asked him.

'It is my pleasure to assist merit,' he replied. 'You are a good person and may go far.'

'Is there nothing I can do in return?'

'Why, yes, as a matter of fact there is,' he said.

'Name it and it is as good as done.'

'You have a young lady friend?'

'Yes.'

'Do you . . . sleep with the young person?'

'Er . . . yes . . . Well, no. She undresses and lets me look at her.'

'Then I should like to watch you do that.'

I looked at him hard. He was sitting as usual, with one leg over the other, smiling urbanely.

'Well?' he went on.

It seemed foolish to refuse such a simple request when my whole career depended upon it. I introduced him into my room, popped him in my wardrobe, and let him goggle at me goggling at Johanna. It seemed to do him a power of good because my interview at the Arsenal was a mere formality. The wardrobe was a bit stuffy afterwards.

18

So there I was. I had a good job in a smart place. I had a beautiful girl to look at. I had friends. I had a little money. I felt the whole of Vienna was at my feet.

Vienna in those years of the late fifties and sixties was a merry place – how different from the suspicious, envious, acquisitive ugly city it became!

We danced, we sang, we played, we ate feasts of fish at waterside taverns, we drank, we drew, we walked, we rode, we boated, we sat up talking half the night and sometimes all of it, we made love – never, alas, to Johanna – but there were other girls who enjoyed country matters (you see, I profited from my Shakespeare reading!). I even allowed Van Meytens along for a peep from time to time.

The whole city seemed bathed in the precious metals I worked in – gold for summer, silver for the snow.

The war ended without much sign of gain or loss (except for the beggars in the square), and there were more cannons than ever to decorate. I lavished all my art and energies upon them for I had now been at the Arsenal four years and had mastered every stage of the practice.

They started as no more than a spindle; and out they

went like popinjays, encrusted with scenes that might be classical, biblical, historical, or simply pure invention; gun castrati for ceremony only. Apart from the Imperial coat-of-arms – and those of the Master General of the Ordinance – nobody seemed to mind what the depictions were so long as they were well done. And though at first I kept to orthodox channels, I was soon urged to be more adventurous by one of the visitors, good old Balthasar Moll, who as well as being a professor at the Academy, was a Court painter and favourite of the Empress.

'Anyone can churn out a Jason and the Amazons or a Hercules and the Harpies or even a David and Goliath. Ceremony can be so stiff, boy, so stuffy. Let us have something gorgeous. Don't worry about the Generals. Nobody looks at cannon ornamentation except cranks like me. Pretend these are the Baptistry doors and you are whatsisname.'

I set to with a will and produced scenes of extraordinary splendour. I gave them Cortés subduing the Incas. I gave them the Rape of Lucrece. But even this was tame stuff. I then did a whole series of scenes from Shakespeare which undeniably covered new ground. My Lear on the heath, raging against the storm with a Fool and a Wild Man beside him, had an animation that was entirely fresh. It was actually a minor masterpiece, and Moll went into raptures.

'Your scenes have nothing to do with Austria,' he said, 'but they have much to do with art.'

As I was working on the second set of these illustrations – taken from the Comedies – I received a message that the Director of the Arsenal wished to see me. Thinking that I had perhaps gone too far with my whimsy or that some of my decorations had used too much gold, I approached his office with some trepidation, but when I entered I was relieved to observe a benignity of expression beneath the whiskers.

'Your work has been noticed, Froberger,' he said. 'It is the first time in my experience that a Field Marshal has ever commented upon a cannon.'

'A F-f-field Marshal?' I stammered.

Moll had assured me that soldiers were art-blind. 'The great Field Marshal Graf Daun, no less,' observed the Director. 'He is quite an enthusiast of yours. It is gratifying, is it not, to know that our efforts here do not go entirely unrecognized?'

I could see that the old lobster was hoping for some promotion or other.

'I am glad His Excellency is pleased,' I said grovellingly. 'I know that you yourself, sir, have been instrumental in allowing this kind of work to go forward by your enlightened attitude.'

If flattery didn't work it wouldn't be so fashionable. He inclined his whiskers graciously.

'You are an excellent craftsman,' he told me. 'We need new decorations for the Great Dining Room. I should like you to supervise them. The Field Marshal will be dining here in November. It must be ready by then.'

This was the chance that all the other artists in the Arsenal had been waiting for – the opportunity had been discussed endlessly at meal-times and over our beers in the evening. It was known that the commission had been coming up, and a dining room or ballroom was of course the optimum way to make one's mark and advance into the fields of gold. Some of the other craftsmen already had the lineaments of defeat upon their faces. When they heard the news that I had obtained the job, they inclined their faces gravely but resignedly as though the cancer that was gnawing quietly away at their hopes had suddenly surfaced with a pain, but some of the younger ones were angry. They had been at the Arsenal longer than I. They didn't see why I, an upstart, not even an Austrian, should come barging in and rob them of what was rightfully theirs. I could see their point but it didn't make them like me any more.

'Who is this Frobugger?' demanded Stadler, a restless, uncomfortable, sneering sort of fellow who was irritatingly not altogether untalented, investing the possibilities of the prancing horse with something approaching bravura.

He was one of those people who seem to dislike you from the first for no reason that you can fathom. He disliked me anyway; and now he had a reason. Others took up the cry.

'Who is this Frobugger?'

I pushed the door open at this point. I saw their faces turned against me, vengeful and truculent.

'I am Froberger,' I said. 'What of it?'

Stadler walked right up to me. He was taller and bigger than I was.

'You,' he said. 'You Frobugger.'

'Don't call me that,' I said. 'You are insulting the name of my dead father.'

'Good,' he said. 'Frobugger.'

I kneed him sharply in the balls.

'Oof,' he exclaimed, and subsided onto the floor.

'Sorry,' I said. 'My knee slipped.'

The others who had been crowding round me backed away.

'I'll get you,' he groaned at length. 'You see if I don't.'

'My knee slipped' passed into Arsenal vernacular. Many of those who had crowded round came to help me with the Great Dining Room. But it is never wise to make enemies. Stadler did not forget.

19

I have spent all day again looking at my face and at my Egyptian head. I have put the head beside me, so, where

I can see it in the mirror. It is almost as though it is my double.

There is something I long for in it, so much so that I have a ridiculous urge to break it open like an egg and find the meat inside. Of course I could not do that. It would be like destroying myself.

The daylight has gone now and I have lit the candles either side of my looking-glass. Sometimes as I sit strange sounds come out of my face which I do not understand, or out of the Egyptian. Sometimes I feel an almost imperceptible vibration.

Today there has been no pain.

I have done no drawing but, this is the most important part, the drawing inward; the art must be to watch, to merge, to submerge. My other heads stand around, waiting. The ceremony has barely started but already I can feel a stirring.

What's to come is still unsure.

20

The Great Dining Room project went triumphantly well. I took as my theme the History of Gunpowder. It seemed a thoroughly proper subject. All around the room the frescoes proclaimed the glory of explosion from the earliest Chinese fireworks to the pot-bellied culverins of the Middle Ages with their barrels like beer butts; on to the great sea bombardments like Lepanto; taking in sieges; gunpowder plots; hopping to and fro across the world to show the Hottentots worshipping the firestick; and the Red Indians dancing around a captured field-gun; then back to sea again to show ships exploding all over the place; back again to land and the Battle of Blenheim, with whole regiments being heroically cut down by chain shot; and finally ending up with a relief showing Mars, God of War, looking very much like Field Marshal Daun, ramming the ball into an Imperial cannon while putti fluttered about holding fuses and firebrands.

It was colourful, it was energetic; it was glorious, it was preposterous. And the whole effect was augmented and, shall we say?, brought down to table-level though naturally not down to earth by a series of busts depicting the Emperor, the Emperor's son, the Emperor's nephews, one or two important Emperor's favourites like Field Marshal Leopold Graf Daun, and finally the Director of the Arsenal, General (retired) von Morbisch himself. I'd have put the Emperor's dog in if I'd known what it looked like.

It was a stupendous achievement in the time – less than six months – but fortunately I had the willing help of many of my comrades in the workshop. Not many cannons were ornamented between April and November that year. Only Stadler continued sneering away on his own with a couple of his cronies, etching his prancing horses into the Imperial artillery, and plotting revenge in the blackness of his heart.

But what cared I for Stadler? When the great day came and I was summoned to be presented to the legendary Field Marshal, and he shook my hand and said, 'Well done, my boy, call on me next week, I have a commission for you,' I knew I was made. The applause of the mighty and the fashionable was ringing in my ears. I craved the jade success. I wanted more. It was all so easy then. And the older men with their sad resigned faces, they too who had perhaps pranced like Stadler's horses in their youth, they looked at me with envy; not with hatred, but with pain; and I was allowed to give them and all my helpers a special dinner in the Great Dining Room; and speeches were made; and I told them that I should be leaving them tomorrow to work on the Herr Field Marshal's ballroom under his beautiful daughter (ribald laughter); and that I should come and see them often and remember them always; and the older men with their grey faces looked at me as though I were about to be taken up to Heaven in a fiery chariot, and thought of their disappointments and their families who knew of their disappointments; and of how little time there is; 'the life so short, the art so long to learn'; it was my toast; and I called for more wine because there was something in their faces that disturbed me; even then, I could read faces too well; and we sang songs and staggered home through the night; and their wives let them in and smacked them on the head and told them to be their age; and I walked alone to my high bedroom under the eaves, and twinkled to sleep like a star.

21

The pains have held off for a week now, but I have another pain to contend with.

Mesmer has invited me to one of his séances. It has thrown me into confusion as I never go out.

'I never go out.'

I said it to him.

'I never ever go out.'

I said it to him.

'Nonsense, my friend. You are too solitary. It is not good for an artist to take no inspiration from outside.'

'Who says I take no inspiration from outside?'

He could see he had touched me on the raw for he now made pacifying noises.

'I need your opinion, Froberger. A séance is above all an aesthetic as well as magnetic experience. I am not sure that I have the right décor, the right colours. You now, with your eye, you will tell me.'

I knew that he was lying. The man was never uncertain about his taste – though to my mind he should have been. What the devil did he want? I had, however, to be circumspect. He was the chief among my patrons, indeed the few others that I had all seemed to emanate from him. To pursue my work, I needed money.

It wasn't difficult to read my face but I was piqued all the same when he did.

'I was telling a great friend of mine about your work the other day, Franz. The Baron Erich von Eckhardt. You know him?'

Of course I did not know him. Do I know every coxcomb with a handle to his name?

'He is very interested in the new expressive movement. And he pays well, my friend. He may even be at the séance.'

There was as usual that insidious, charming-threatening quality about Mesmer, like a chocolate full of atropine.

'Very well,' I said. 'I shall be pleased to give my opinion and to meet your friend. What hour do you need me?'

He gave me the time and the day; and hurriedly departed, casting a long look at my Egyptian. I hope the fellow is not contemplating repossession. I believe I should have to thwart him if he were.

Is this whole séance a farrago, a ruse to get me out of the house so that he can have it stolen? I shall have to find a place of unimaginable security.

I could not now bear to be parted from my Egyptian. He is like my father; my child.

22

The Field Marshal was an elderly man in his late sixties but he had married late, his wife had died, and he was left with one daughter, Isabella, who was as beautiful as he was rich. Isabella was now twenty-five, in the full blonde bloom of her girlhood, and many had come to the palace for her hand in marriage; but, rather like the princess in the storybook, she had refused them all because she said they did not amuse her. She told me all this as we walked round the palace. (I never liked, even then, to embark upon a room without knowing what goes on in the corpus of the building.)

She was a remarkable girl. I fell in love with her immediately, of course, hopeless as it was. Artists were rated no higher than musicians. I was a tradesman. I might as well have been a cheesemonger.

The palace itself was a building of the early years of the century, designed by Hildebrand in the baroque style. He had had to contend with a cramped frontal space (although the building opened up like an umbrella behind!). His façade contained only seven windows! However, by the use of tapering pilasters and a web of flat arabesques – and of course the ubiquitous Viennese white stucco – he had actually made it seem – what indeed it was – the preface to a cool and graceful palazzo.

Inside, it was full of martial statues and dashing vistas. I could sense what the ballroom was going to be like well before we got to it – I had naturally asked that we leave it till last.

I told her I thought it would be a well-proportioned but imposing room, with grandiose reliefs and sumptuous ornaments, some of its decoration doubtless now a little faded –

for after all they wished for a change. She threw open the doors and we paused at the threshold.

I was proved right in my forecast in every particular except the last.

'Why, Duchess,' I said, 'The decoration is in apple-pie order. The painting cannot have been done more than a year ago. It is a ballroom of the gods.'

'That is just it, Mr Froberger. Of the gods but not for the humans. It is a fine ballroom for an old Field Marshal, but Father does not dance. He has told me to create a ballroom in my image. What do you think?'

'It is a very beautiful image, if I may say so, Duchess.'

That was daring of me. She stopped and looked at me quizzically.

'Why, Mr Froberger. I hope your designs will be as pretty as your phrases.'

I answered her that they could outstrip them.

'I am a plain speaker, Duchess. I only say what I see.'

I fancy she blushed a little at that. Had I gone too far?

'It is a pity you're not a Baron or something,' she told me. 'Too bad, Mr Froberger.'

That put me in my place, even though she smiled as she said it. I knew that I was going to be besotted with her before I was finished. I never knew a girl before or since who was so perfect in every particular. Her hair was like golden rain, her eyes were huge and green with little black circles around the edges of the iris accentuating the colour. Her skin was smoothest pink-white like a perfectly blended blushing daisy. Her figure was slender but full, her ankles were of the trimmest, her feet small and slim. Her mind was a mysterious river full of currents and turns; shaded and even haunted in some places; glittering and dancing out of reach.

I suppose she knew I was in love with her but she was kind enough not to comment upon it. It was as if I had come up in boils; or a cold sore.

I resolved to provide her with the most delightful ballroom in the world. Noting her love of folk or fairy stories, I decided to make them the central motif of my designs – not, of course, that the room would look childish but I had discovered from my experience with the cannons that no one really looks at reliefs. Their purpose generally is to create a mood. Thus the motif of the fairy story simply appeared reassuringly ornate until you looked into it – and then it sprang to life with witches, spirits, monsters and trolls, frolicking elves, pied pipers, wicked stepmothers, fairy godmothers, gingerbread houses, dragons, and ice maidens.

She clapped her hands when she saw my drawings.

'Perfect,' she exclaimed. 'Much more suitable than the scenes from Hapsburg history we usually get round here. And yet what a joke! All these grand people waltzing around under the goblins. What about statues?'

'I thought we should have something light but elegant with some family relevance. Your father not as a soldier but at his music, with a lyre. You perhaps as Terpsichore, Muse of the Dance . . .'

How many hours, how many days were spent with her finalizing the design, choosing the materials, supervising the details of the execution. When it was finally over, our collaboration won universal applause. It was the first ballroom in Vienna to be actually enjoyable as a room – gay, easy, gracious, elegant – rather than the usual formidable declaration of wealth and broad-bottomism. The Graf Daun and his daughter did not need to boast. My design, fortuitously, caught the tide of Grand Manner on the turn. It didn't disappear overnight, of course. And even I would be careful not to shed the 'heroic' entirely – the sovereign pose, the resplendent appearance, the pathos – but as well as the required elegance and decoration, I tried to put character into my creations – detail without trivial monumentalism.

I owe that to her, for she would chide me if she saw

portentousness creeping into my work. And indeed she was no mean artist herself. There was an airiness about her drawings and watercolours that I tried to catch and learn from.

We used to go together on little painting excursions while the last touches were put to the ballroom by my craftsmen.

I could not bear to leave the palace and I lingered on, inventing pretexts. There was to be an inaugural ball, a *bal masqué*, to which I was invited. I had to be in residence for that, in case there should be some last-minute hitch.

Her father sent for me one day. I had spent some time with him previously as I took his likeness for the bust. I thought that he might perhaps want another pose. Important people were always fussy about how they would be seen.

He motioned me to sit. It struck me that the old boy was not well.

'You have done good work, Froberger,' said the Marshal.

'Thank you, sir.'

'Don't interrupt, sir. It is time to go.'

'Go? But . . .'

'It's as good as finished. I want you out.'

'Out? But . . . Have I done wrong?'

'My daughter has conceived an affection for you, sir. That is what is wrong.'

Could it be? She had always retained an amused, even slightly detached attitude towards me. I wondered whether to tell him that I reciprocated the tender emotion; but I knew that this was Vienna not Utopia, and his next words proved me right.

'Now I have nothing against you, sir. You have worked well. You have entertained Isabella. You have done nothing to compromise or seduce her. Whatever the cause, you are the first man she has loved. But the fact is, it won't do.'

I could see that the old man was torn between love for his daughter, pleasure at her happiness, and total dismay at her love for a tradesman. As he said, it wouldn't do. In London where painters were fêted it might just have passed, but in Vienna the thing was unthinkable.

It was true, for a moment the thought crossed my mind that we might emulate Antony and Cleopatra, and give up all for love, but the old man's next words put paid to that.

'I do not like to utter threats, sir. It is not in my nature, but I will do anything to protect the good name and future happiness of my daughter. I believe you are a sincere and good and properly ambitious artist. If you attempt to persevere in this connection – for I see you are pleasantly moved by my revelation – and indeed who would not be? – but if you attempt it, if you even dare to think about it again, I shall see that you never get a commission in any country where I exercise influence – and that, as you probably know, sir, is just about every country worth thinking about. If, on the other hand, you agree to leave now, immediately, and never see or communicate with my daughter again, I shall make it my business to further your interests in every way I can. I may add that, if you do hold my daughter's interests at heart, there can only be one course for you to take. Come, sir, your answer.'

As he indicated, there could only be one response. I was ambitious before I was sentimental. I was an artist, as you might say, before I was a heartist. Some of my artist friends afterwards told me that this is not a fault, that the artist must be single-minded. But in his own dealings too as well as in his work, said others, the artist must be true to life. At any rate, however much it may have spurred on my career, what I did that day feels now like a betrayal of life. Perhaps it did to the Field Marshal too, for he died strangely depleted.

I often thought about Isabella in later years, defying the old man's edict, and only once did I see her – by accident – at the opera. She looked grave. They weren't making her

To Franz Xaver Messerschmidt

laugh. She did not, I think, see me. I left at the interval. Some years later, I heard that she too was dead. Vienna was full of strange fitful fevers taking away the beautiful and the bright.

I believe that even now, if she walked into this room, even now, I would leave my faces, yes, and my Egyptian, and walk away with her down that dappled, shady, sunny, mysterious river for ever.

23

Ow. It has started again.

24

Ears have to put up with a great deal in life. They hear some frightful noises, bad music. They get boxed. They blister in the sun and peel in the cold.

I have often thought about that servant of Caiaphas in the Garden of Gethsemane. Peter struck his ear off, but we do not hear about Christ putting it back on as He could have done. He had other things on His mind at the time. But it was hard commons for the servant in a way. He was only doing his job. He thought, 'I had better come along with the High Priest in case he loses his prayer-book or needs his waistcoat,' and swisssh!

How did he feel next day?

Ear today and gone tomorrow.

The ears are features that you can easily overlook if you are not properly observant. But if you examine them closely, you will find them full of fun and character. What odd little flaps they are! And not so little sometimes . . .

The upper part is odd enough with its strange lips and cavities and its curious little rubbery protuberance just in front of the hole; but the lower portion, the lobe, is the piece that makes me laugh. It seems to have no rhyme or reason. And why should some people have those monstrous low gutter-scraping lobes, while others just have silly little apologies, mere lobules?

The whole external ear, it seems to me, is Nature's dress rehearsal for the vulva. She knew it was too silly so she tried again – though to be honest I don't think she made a much better job of it second time round.

My ears, as so often happens with a pair of ears, have totally different characters even though they adorn the same head. My left ear is cheeky, light-hearted, frivolous. It is an aura buffa. It has a short, dapper little lobe and its whorls are as neat as a cut-through cabbage. This is the ear that listens to jokes, gossip, tittle-tattle, scandal, love's whispers, peccadilloes, rhymes, comedies, street-ballads, and smut. It is not much employed these days.

My right ear, on the other hand, is a much more solid affair. It is my aura seria. The lobe sinks lower as though burdened by the weight of responsibility. The gristle is thicker. The little fleshy ante-pod is redder and more pronounced, flushed like an alderman. This ear is the ear that hears tales of woe, tragedies, finances, threats, dire escapades, dubious enterprises, blackmail, funeral orations, and diabolism.

They live on either side of my head like husband and wife – totally different in temperament but forced through lack of funds to share the same habitation. To do justice to them both, as I work on each new head, is not easy for, you know, the ears change as we change our expression.

But ears aren't the only pebbles on the beach. We also have eyes, lips, nose, teeth, skin, hair, jaw . . . All these must have their due proportion and their unassailable but

50

mutable selfness, if I may put it like that. It's like a juggling act. They've all got to be kept spinning at the same time.

The Egyptian thinks I can't do it. That is exactly what he is thinking. Just because someone has got him to spin, he thinks no one else can do it, but I shall unlock the secret, depend upon it.

Then we shall see what is what and who is who.

25

The artist is in some ways like a surgeon. He has the same knowledge of anatomy and his brush is his scalpel. But instead of cutting out the fault, the artist's aim must be to disclose it for it is the faults which make the man. Faults are legion and individual. Virtues are few and the same everywhere. Valour, steadfastness, temperance, chastity . . . we see their silly sameness on a thousand busts. We live, however, in an age which for some reason rates silly sameness above art, and the artist must be wary that his scalpel does not touch the wrong nerve. For this reason, I keep to my own head; I am hardly likely to complain when I see vanity, cowardice, venality and greed on my features. I know that by showing them I can help exorcize them. I do not need to flatter myself. My purpose is to strip away the superficial with the aid of my heads, in order to reveal the something underneath.

Why else did Rembrandt do so many self-portraits? He did not need to exorcize. He was looking for something. You can read it in his eyes.

There are unseen forces below the surface which move us. Signor Galvani has proved the power of electricity. We cannot see it but it can move a frog's leg. How infinitely more subtle are our workings! What is the power that moves?

Where am I under all that fleshy upholstery? And yet . . . when I have lifted the last quirk, the final humour, the ultimate expression, what will I find . . . Nothing?

26

The Field Marshal was as good as his word. Almost the next day, I received a letter from the Chamberlain of the Imperial Court, requesting me to present myself to the Archduke Joseph and his Archduchess with a view to an official commission.

Still heavy-hearted and indeed heavy-conscienced at the loss of Isabella, I nevertheless legged it across to the Archducal Palace with a will. Fame, glory, riches awaited me in the shape of those chubby little children whom their Royal Highnesses wished to capture for posterity.

Now, it may seem to you that for a sculptor, as for an actor, a child is nothing but trouble; and of course this is true in a way. They will not sit still for long. But the great advantage of the little beasts is that, no matter what their blood and title, they do not give the artist some notion of grandeur or dignity to paste over their features, unless, of course, they are Spanish. They are young, they are alive, they are living in Vienna. That was all I had to show. The children did the rest. Actually they were quite pleasant little brats. Daddy and Mummy were overjoyed. They showered me with gifts.

I was soon brought to the attention of the Empress. She was a handsome woman in middle age, a little inclined to stoutness, over-addicted to chocolate and small dogs, but widely read and more knowledgeable about art than her critics would allow. She sent for me and I had an audience of ten minutes. She kept quoting my old professor, Balthasar

Moll, and told me that he spoke well of me, which was nice of the old fart. Presently the commissions came in.

I did a couple of dukes, an ambassador, an archbishop and a margravine. I believe I did them tolerably well – in the baroque manner to which they had been accustomed – but perhaps with a little more of the sitter coming through than usual.

I was like one of those men who undress women with their eyes – I found more and more that I could undress character. It was simply a matter of tact to decide which trait they would like exposed, and which subdued, masked or obliterated. Again, I was reminded of the surgeon's trade. But whereas he can merely cut, I could restructure. Dissimulation is an art in itself.

I made a forceful soldier out of a bully, a statesman out of a sycophant, a grave and reverend Monseigneur out of a silly old piss-artist, and a great hostess out of a trollop. It wasn't lying, it was simply a matter of emphasis. Naturally the end result did not look like a satire. Even in those days, it would have been social suicide. No, I made sure there was something about each one that, as well as having the necessary panache and importance, yet presented at the same time an unmistakable integrity. That was the triumph of art.

27

And of course my skill came from my own awareness of the slippery nature of character.

In the mirror, even from early days, as I say, I was always intrigued by who was this in there? Was I really aware at all? Uncertain of the answer, I used to repeat catch-phrases to remind myself how I thought I should appear to the world. 'Amused and detached' was one of them.

Not a bad catch-phrase as catch-phrases go, and suitable for an artist. I think I had a natural tendency to be sensitive, easily hurt; and 'amused and detached' stopped my flying into rages, bursting into tears, and (later) blurting out my ardours before the *moment juste*, a thing one should never do with ardours.

I remember a girl called Johanna for whom I had an ardour in Munich saying to me once, 'You always seem to be smiling at some private joke.'

I was immensely gratified. It was exactly the impression I wished to create, and she let me undo the strings of her blouse which was a sure sign that I was on the right track. Later, I stopped repeating the phrase only because it had sunk in. I had become amusable and detachable. But was I really like that? Why had I had to say it to myself in the first place? The truth was that I was not amused and detached at all. I was shit-scared and in it up to the nostrils. I realized it at last. That is the meaning of maturity. It is that, rather than the failing digestion and the incipient gout, which makes middle age so untenable.

28

I will not delay you here with details of my early triumphs – my bust of Prince Wenzel of Lichtenstein; my portrait of the prodigiously wealthy Princess Marie Felicitas of Savoy; or even of my crowning achievement and signal of success: the commission for two more-than-lifesize statues of the Emperor and Empress for the Royal Collection no less – concerning the execution of which the Empress was so pleased that she gave me a weighty medal 'for the greater encouragement of all artists'. I sold it years ago. Mesmer tells me it was bought by a fellow called Stadler . . .

Suffice it to say that I was now the first, the only sculptor people thought of when they wanted 'face'. 'Send for Froberger' would go the cry. And I would go along if I thought it worth my while. I could have done with a dozen more eyes and a hundred more hands. But even so, 'amused and detached' as I thought I could be (and in a way my official portraits very much exemplified my motto) I could feel that urge within me growing stronger with my success, to go to the centre of the matter. So I used to get friends to call round for sittings in my studio – I had moved from the Widow Mohler's house to my own little flat in the Lindengasse – and here I could indulge a much freer, and at the same time more penetrating, style. Sometimes I could pay models to let me do their heads, for then they could not complain about likeness.

'Oh that's not like me,' they would say.

'Five florins says it is,' I would tell them, giving them their money and ending the matter.

Sometimes, again, I would turn to allegory and symbolism – heads coming out of heads, men emerging from tree-trunks, birds with women's faces, prancing horses with Stadler's features on them (a private joke), a ballerina with a goblin's head. These I did not show but kept locked in my store-room. Do not ask me what they meant. Five florins says it's allegory and symbolism.

Later that year – which year are we in now? – I went back to Munich where I was fêted as the leading sculptor of the day although I was still only thirty-two and called on my good old Uncle Johann Baptist and did a statue for him and his three young daughters (one was still only eleven), my cousins, which was perhaps the best thing I had ever done – simple, unaffected, full of love and respect – but then you can't feel these emotions all the time, can you? You can't go round repeating to yourself 'Simple, unaffected, full of love and respect' when you're sitting in front of a great fat Hapsburg princess. It's easier to say 'amused and detached' and get on with it.

At any rate, my good uncle and my cousins seemed delighted when I presented them with the piece. I said to them, 'It is simple, unaffected and full of love and respect.' We all hung around each other's necks, and shed tears.

Another commission I had which amused me was for the Convent of Savoy – a fountain in the midst of one of their courts. It was doubtless an excellent convent but somehow I have always found the idea of all those chaste women living together rather forbidding so I resolved to give them something . . .

(Excuse me. The light is going and the face is nearly in darkness. There. What a mercy these new tinder-boxes are.)

. . . that seemed perfectly respectable but was in fact quite racy. We agreed on the classical theme of Elysium. I got in touch with my old friend Johanna who was now a young woman of twenty-seven. Johanna had married a much older man and had no children. It is difficult to conceive if you only allow your older man to run his eyes over you. However, it was all to my advantage for she had still the most glorious figure and all she wanted to do was to be looked at. She undressed and stood in front of me and I ran my hands over her to give her her pose, and she shuddered, yes I have to say this, actually shuddered with pleasure. Maturity had increased her love of exposure, and I have never seen a woman so aroused.

I worked in a permanent state of erection. She stood, or crouched, or lay – according to my direction – with so much pleasure upon her I thought it would swamp us both. I implored her to let me lie with her but she would have none of it. It was like some refined torment of Hades rather than the pleasures of Elysium that we were engaged upon. Finally, the piece was finished. My beautiful Johanna, symbol of the soul's happiness on the fields of amaranth; strolling, reclining, seated, with a look of ineffable bliss on her face; was to become one of the central exhibits of the convent. I attended the inaugural ceremony and, after a prayer or two and a specially composed hymn, they switched on the water. As I watched the clear bright liquid splashing around her belly, I was amused (if not detached) to note that the old stirring in my own loins was beginning again. Life is like Johanna. Something to look at and lust after, something even to touch; but somehow never properly to grasp.

29

Sometimes, too, I would go down to the Spittelberg, running like a boy just for the sheer beauty of the day, and play skittles all morning.

30

I have now completed twenty-four faces. Tomorrow I have agreed to go to Mesmer's séance – a foolish waste of time.

I can feel my Me-ness beginning to stir as the enfolding expressions are laid down in my heads, like a prisoner who can hear the distant opening of a multiplicity of doors.

Imagine, if it is true, how much my discovery will benefit mankind. For, if we can find our true selves, rather than the grimace that the world twists us into, we can look forward to a condition where we are all simple, unaffected, full of love and respect.

I am held back momentarily by my nostrils. I do not have much time for nostrils. I am not a nostril man. They are generally unsatisfactory orifices. Even a pretty woman may be ruined by her nostrils though in every other particular her face may be superb. Her nostrils on either side will suddenly reveal themselves, hairy and bleak. Compared with the ears which are merely amusing, or the mouth which is expressive, or the eyes which are like those bottomless lakes which go straight down to the underworld, the nostrils lead only to snivel. And yet they too are expressive in their way. They cannot be ignored. It is said that the devil enters into us if we sneeze. One cannot dismiss an aperture with that kind of entrée. Does he, I wonder, take the left- or the right-hand nostril – or does he penetrate both, whip through the sinuses, and meet up again in diabolical wholeness at the back of the palate? It has doubtless been the subject of many a treatise.

But if one forgets about the devil – though he is never far away from our minds, walking about like a roaring lion – and if one simply concentrates upon expression, one finds that the nostrils are generally connected with adverse humours. The sneer is very much a nostril activity; pride is certainly expressed nostrilarily; and the flared nostril – although it may be associated with drawing in pleasant aromas – is also a well-known sign of anger.

That is why it is important for me to catch my nostrils correctly when they are called upon to play their part. It is true I do not often flare my nostrils these days. Even sneering doesn't seem as prevalent as it was. But every expression of which my face is capable must be set down; that is the magnitude of the task I have to set myself. By my present estimation, that will make sixty-nine heads. Put that in your pipe and smoke it, Vitruvius.

Albert Magnus wrote that, if you take the image of a man, you take something of his power. Indeed, it is still a common belief among the country people.

It is easy to flare your nostrils (Head No.25, The Insolent Jackanapes) and talk about magic and primitive superstition. But when I have my sixty-nine heads finished and complete we shall see who flares his nostrils last.

Excuse me, while I fetch a handkerchief. That is nostrils for you.

31

And talking of Vitruvius, I should say that about this time, shortly after the episode of Johanna and her blissful fountain and the dear nuns who will never know the joke, I made my pilgrimage to Rome.

Apart from its position as repository of by far the largest collection of classical antiquities, Rome had at the time re-established itself as the centre of classical aesthetics. Students of all nations, even Austria-Hungary, were flocking back to hear the professors and the experts and Winckelmann expound 'Noble Simplicity and Calm Grandeur'.

I got the clap. There was a great deal of it about. I think it was a pretty little tart I met on the Via Veneto but you can never be sure. It was all art by day and tart by night. And I must say that I also got the classical itch. There was something about the Roman stuff that made the old barocco seem absolutely preposterous. The more pomp we piled on our Emperors and heroes the smaller they became. Marcus Aurelius didn't need to pose with his nose thrown up as if someone had farted or turn impossibly on one of Stadler's prancing horses while pointing a sword at some reeking battlefield. 'Noble Simplicity and Calm Grandeur' was the thing. Great effects by simple means. I was already in the classical camp before I ever arrived in Rome, which was why, of course, I went there. But I began to see now that even my work for friends and family was not just unpompous but trifling, even coarse. I had thought I could teach Rome a thing or two. Animation, character. But the sheer renewed effect, every day, of so much grace made me pause. Such a meal cannot be digested in a week or a month. In effect, it took me years.

The clap, I am glad to say, was more expeditiously despatched.

Something rather irritating happened during my stay. Stadler turned up. He had always been the sort that collects a little sneering coterie around him, and so it was now. I became conscious that, every now and then, at some function or other, people were laughing at me. I affected to ignore him. I had other things on my mind. But was he following me? And had he not, in his pink coat, been whisking into a shop just as the little whore accosted me in the Via Veneto? Was my clap his ruse? Or indeed his clap?

One other strange thing happened. As I walked by the Tiber, I was approached by an old gypsy woman.

'Scusi,' I said. 'My Italian is terrible. I am German.'

'Ah, tedeschi,' she said, and lapsed into the most appalling Deutsch.

She had apparently travelled in the country. Would I cross her palm with silver? She would tell my fortune. I obliged with a small coin which seemed to satisfy her, and she looked intently into my face. I waited for the usual dark strangers and travel, but as I watched her, her mouth turned down and she backed off, crossing herself.

'Wait a minute,' I said to her. 'I want my fortune.'

'No, no,' she muttered, warding off the evil eye. 'Face, no face . . .'

I checked my reflection in the water. There it was, amused and, I was glad to see, attached. Wasn't that a pink coat flickering behind the bridge? Or was it the Egyptian in Stadler's garb, another twist to the play?

32

Back in Vienna, I was restless – my Roman interval had given me a taste for further discoveries – and, having some money yet saved from my commissions, I determined to journey to Paris and thence to London – both cities which I had special reasons for wishing to visit.

Travelling by river and road, I reached Paris in ten days and, finding the cost of staying at an inn exorbitant, after one night I took lodgings at a cabinet-maker's in the Rue des Bons Enfants.

In Paris, much more than Vienna, you noticed the effects of the late war. Everyone grizzled about the prices which had risen so much over the last few years. Even firewood was five sous a log.

I had been given an introduction by my flute-teacher to a young musician named Johann Schobert who was in the service of the Prince de Conti. On my calling on him, he welcomed me warmly, and we talked of Vienna which he had recently visited. He gave me some useful glimpses into the French manner of life.

'The ridiculous desire for "mode" in the French,' he said, 'means that they have to continue their magnificence even when they're short of funds – so they take loans from the big *banquiers* and *fermiers* who waddle like nabobs while they grow poor. The mass of the country's wealth is in the hands of a hundred people.'

I expressed astonishment while privately wondering who it was who could be hiding behind the curtains.

'Most of the money is spent on mistresses,' he continued. 'Indeed, it is difficult to distinguish here who is the lady of the house. Everyone lives as he or she likes. It has been said that, if God is not especially gracious, the French state will suffer the fate of the former Persian Empire.'

Could it be that there was a lady of the house – or some other *maîtresse* – behind the drapes? I suppressed my question. Schobert seemed a little starchy for his years, but by no means dull. Was he harbouring a concubine? I did not wish him to think me prurient.

Expanding on his (hypocritical?) theme of the Babylonian luxury of the place, he pointed to some fine gentlemen in the street below, sporting sword-bands, or scabbards, bound round and round with costly fur.

'See,' said he, 'the latest fashion. An excellent idea, for the swords will not catch cold.'

I laughed. The curtains could not have held a full-grown woman. He was an honest musician not a Don Juan.

'Do you have a child in the house?' I enquired.

'The Prince and Princess have children,' he replied, looking at me strangely, 'but, in this town, children of every degree are sent away to the country as soon as they are born. Why do you ask?'

I did not like to tell him what I had seen out of the corner of my eye. I made up some feeble story about my interest in mechanical toys.

Later that day, Schobert introduced me to the Prince de Conti who was good enough to open various doors for me; and in the ensuing weeks I was able to see a number of the finest works by artists considered to be admirable. Boucher was all the rage, and considered very chic. Fragonard, a showy fellow, so-so. Watteau, a young man, dead these forty years, has a strange nervous way as if he too were aware of something fluttering behind the curtains. Quentin de la Tour has some pastels of the nobs.

As for their sculpture, in the works of Clodion, Houdon and Roubiliac (who spends much time in London), I could sense something new stirring (and not just behind the curtains, either), living people, Nature if you please, and Simplicity if not always noble!

All this was incidental, however. What I was really after was Le Brun.

The sculpting or portraiture of Character Heads, that is, heads that expressed a particular trait or emotion – anything from pain and sorrow to inane laughter, ecstasy, or queasiness – had a long tradition in art before Le Brun. The masters of the Renaissance had practised them. Rembrandt himself and Rubens, too, had exercised themselves upon these subjects. But Le Brun had formalized and indeed reformulated the disciplines in a series of drawings and engravings which I felt could be, for me, like the point of entry to some magical cave.

When the Prince heard of my interest, he kindly obtained for me the entrée to the gloomy Palace of the Louvre where the drawings of the Roi Soleil's drawing-master, and much of the rest of the King's art collection, are to be found.

I was allowed to enter – paused in front of the Mona Lisa – one must pay one's dues to celebrity – and at length conducted to one of the great galleries where I was left alone with the books and engravings that I had come four hundred miles to see.

I poured over them for many days, sometimes copying, sometimes making notes. I would have travelled twice the distance to have been in that room. The old man is a fox. There is more to these faces than exercise. You will find my notes and copies in the right-hand drawer of my table.

But there was one omission; a drawing he himself referred to in a note I saw, in a margin, almost deliberately elusive, as *his* Gioconda, his Perfect Love; instead of mere enigma, what it portrayed was an expression of surpassing sweetness and grace, without sickliness, an expression that only a Madonna might have worn and that no artist had yet quite been able to bring off. It was in his margin but it was not here.

So later, when I had at last finished, I prevailed upon the good Prince to give me an introduction at Versailles where there are more of the Master's works. Of course, I also wished to see the palace of which so much has been written. (Anyone can walk in as long as you hire a sword outside – it shows you're a nob!)

I will not detain you with the palace of which so much has been written. It is a leviathan; and down those interminable corridors, what sudden glimpses of half-remembered figures do I see now, shapes, flittings, processions, strange odours of the sink and of the rose-garden . . . It is like a dream from which one wakes all too soon, in astonishment, and alarm.

There were good Le Bruns here; more drawings, more engravings, grand designs for the Hall of Mirrors, the staircase of the Ambassadors, and the Salons of Peace and War (with its grimacing slaves) but no Perfect Love – and no peace either!

It was all:

'Make way for the Dauphin.'

I was always bobbing up and down; one cannot study in that kind of atmosphere. But anyway, I had seen enough. I now had the scales of expression at my fingertips (all except that wretched lost love). What I needed were the structures, the harmonics.

I returned to Paris, said farewell to my good friend Schobert and the musical Prince whose influence had been so helpful, and wandered back for a last night at my cabinet-maker's.

'Fancy a good time, dearie?'

It was a whore with breasts like brioches. God knows what would have happened to them if she had taken off her corsage. For an instant, as a parting gesture in that city of paramours, I was tempted to take her up on her invitation, but I cannot stand the smell of garlic. She began cursing me without a great deal of conviction; a small crowd gathered; the Parisians are ever ready for a fracas. I rolled my eyes heavenward in vexation. Above me, for an instant, a sublime expression appeared at a window.

I rushed to the door and beat on it. The crowd took my action as some kind of evidence of guilt – or, better still, fear. They closed in on me from every side.

'Putain, voleur . . .'

They were clawing at me now. I could smell that awful metallic stench of old garlic. I backed against the door, pushing them away. Suddenly, miraculously, I could feel it opening behind me. A skinny hand grasped me, pulled me in, and slammed the door on the crowd. I turned to thank my benefactor.

It was a little old woman of at least eighty.

'The face,' I gabbled at her, crazily.

She smiled without teeth.

'Oh yes, the face,' she said. 'You had better come upstairs.'

She led me aloft and there, in a small room overlooking the street, was a painting set up to catch the declining sun, standing on a chair beside the window. It was a portrait of a young woman; radiant, satisfied, innocent, complete. I had been saved by Le Brun. I have noted since then that the dead whom you champion can still do you favours.

'Perfect Love,' I gasped.

(It driveth out fear.)

'Grandma,' she replied. 'She always liked the sun. She was his mistress for a while. The drawing-master gave it to her, you know. They had an understanding. I put her in the window because I loved her, and she enjoyed the sunset.'

'Will you part with it?' I asked without hope.

'Why no, sir. I could not part with Grandma.'

There was no reasoning with her. She had no chalk or paper, so I could not copy the face. I committed it to my mind as best I could while the crowd outside slowly dispersed, and at last I slipped away, muzzy with the memory of that expression, suffused with that peculiarly Parisian smell of good cooking and bad drains, waking with dribble on my pillow.

Next day I tried to find the place once more before I left; I thought I might reason with her again; but it was lost. I have at last reproduced that look of singular benignity. You will find it in my Man with a Stool Long Harboured, Presently Despatched, No. 42 but it took me many years to bend my features to it. Meanwhile I had an appointment in Angleterre.

From Paris, I travelled by coach to Calais and from there took ship to Dover – oh, for the gentle waves of the Danube! – arriving in London early on a fine May evening.

Anybody from Vienna who has visited the place will tell you that everyone in London seems to be wearing fancy dress. The ostentation is remarkable if initially ludicrous. I purchased a florid English coat to look less conspicuous, and took lodgings with a tailor in St Martin's Lane.

The day after I moved in, my landlord told me (I had naturally taken the precaution of mastering a little English as well as French) that there was to be a hanging at noon. These events are only celebrated in London eight times a year, and it is always the occasion for a holiday.

I decided to postpone my other business and attend the affair, though with some misgiving – for I had no wish to see an unknown fellow-human suffer – but the expressions that might be recorded both on the unfortunate creature and the crowd served to override my hesitations. Though we have executions also in Vienna, I had never brought myself to attend one. The fact that this was a foreign country seemed to me, in some way, to lessen the distaste I might feel. I was wrong.

The prisoner was a young woman who had strangled her two-year-old daughter, newly clothed at the workhouse, in order to sell the garments for gin – a liquor that I was told used to be even more freely available than it was now, though God knows it seemed prevalent enough.

The hanging, attended by a crowd of several thousand people of which at least half was female, was a wretched affair. The woman appeared to be in a stupor, well-nigh expressionless (which is of course an expression of its own). I felt a certain relief about this.

It would have done her no good to have been sensible of the throng which gambolled about the scaffold as though it had been a maypole or a hurdy-gurdy with a monkey upon it. The expression most to be seen was that of (what is now) my No. 33, The Lustful Peeping Tom. Respectable tradesmen were standing on chairs to get a view.

The crude platform on which she stood finally being yanked from under her feet, a ghastly kind of groan went up from the crowd – not of sympathy, but like a sound of sex. She twitched and kicked. Matter dripped from her body, the gross stuff of life, and her face assumed a series of expressions: a look at first of hatred and rage (of the Costive Man), relaxing for an instant through a sickly half-smile (which was new to me and which subsequently became the Unctuous Tattle-Tale), and at last back into a terminal gaping not unlike her initial expression (of the Simple Loon). There was no sign of the soul's exit.

The crowd slowly dispersed but I stood for a long while, not wishing to be part of it, ashamed that I had been there yet not able to go; fascinated by the miraculous transition I had witnessed from life to extinction. The memory of that gradation of expression stayed with me as I slowly made my way back to the tailor's.

'A good hanging?' he asked me.

'Fearful,' I replied.

'Come, come,' he advised me, 'you mustn't brood. London is a peacock with its feet in its own shit. Sit down, sir, and have some wine.'

He was a cultured man and dressed many of the beau monde, both English and visitors.

'Some say we are a quite exceptional nation. And I heard

a Frenchman the other day call us "un peuple naturellement paresseux, ivrogne et brute". Take your pick. It's not your problem. You are just passing through.'

It was good advice, and I directed my thoughts to the prime object of my visit; viz, to try and see the famous anatomist, John Parsons. This man, I had heard, only a year or two back, had endeavoured to show how the human face changes in reaction to different experiences. He had accomplished this 'by particular reference to the physiology of expression through his work on corpses'. He was cutting under the face.

Feeling that I had had enough corpses, however, for one day, I desisted from enquiry as to Mr Parsons's whereabouts, and drank wine with the tailor until bedtime.

'You are a quite exceptional tailor,' I told him. 'Let us drink to good measure.'

He was a quite exceptional landlord, too, for next day he was able to discover for me where I might find Mr Parsons. I sent a note round to the hospital where he was working, explaining my visit and asking if I might call upon him. Sure enough, a reply came back saying that he would see me at six o'clock that evening at his house in Brook Street.

I walked round, as appointed, with the strange feeling that I was being followed. Once or twice I turned round on my heel to catch the offender, but there was only a flutter in a doorway.

'Come out, man,' I called in German. 'I know you're there.'

Passers-by looked at me curiously.

'God save the King,' someone jeered.

Mr Parsons greeted me with the utmost courtesy, and showed me into his library where he pulled out a large volume in which he had recorded his investigations. He made some excuse and left me alone with the drawings. I cannot describe my excitement as I turned the pages. Here was matter for months of deliberation. Le Brun had shown me the possibilities of expression, but Parsons was showing me their mechanism.

I studied and sketched until darkness and a man came in with a lamp. Parsons returned – he had kindly given me pen and paper – and now he asked me to sup with him.

Over a modest meal, he told me much of his experiences, the difficulties he had encountered, the risks that are incumbent on opening up the dead. I confess it made me a little squeamish over my cold mutton. As I left, he invited me to return as often as I liked to complete my record of his findings.

I was overwhelmed with such kindness from a stranger, and promised, in due course, to send him one of my heads in return (alas, he died of an infection caused by a small cut, in the pursuit of his profession, before I could show my appreciation).

Thereafter, scarcely a day passed but I was not at the house in Brook Street, poring over his anatomies. What engines lurk beneath our elastic surfaces! I could not have done what I have done without the insight of Mr Parsons of London.

My other purpose in coming to this city was to see more of the work of Roubiliac – in particular his bust of my fellow German, Georg Frideric Handel, in Vauxhall Gardens. This had achieved considerable notoriety, even as far away as Vienna, for being the first great public statue of someone who was neither a prince, a general nor a saint. A bust of a musician, a mere artist! In Vienna it would have been unthinkable.

I went along to the Gardens early one evening. The weather was at last clement, and there were already many ladies and gentlemen gathered to hear the music which was very fine – songs by the Doctors Arne and Boyce, and by a Mr Avison – and of course Handel himself, only seven years dead – and another German, the 'London' Bach, Johann Christoph, who had come to hear some of his own music.

On his being pointed out to me in the Gardens, I approached the great man. He addressed me warmly and introduced me to a family from my part of the world, he said. He assured me that the boy (a pale little sparrow-face, slightly bulging at the forehead), only nine years old, would be a better musician than all of them. The father stood by like a fussy little bantam. The mother said nothing. This was my introduction to the Mozarts. They were performing before the King and Queen again next day. (I subsequently spent several pleasant hours at Bach's house, playing my flute – for I was by now tolerably proficient – and listening to the boy and his sister performing with somewhat vexing bravura on violin and harpsichord.)

Now, however, I asked them to accompany me to see the silent harmonies of stone. The great Handel stood at a crossroads of avenues, as an artist should – benign, strumming his lyre, a little preoccupied as if his mind were buzzing with fugues – a monument for which Germany can feel duly proud – so natural in attitude that his shoe is half off! Indeed, little Mozart whispered in my ear that Handel looked as though he were stifling a fart. It is the French way.

Meanwhile, in the shadows thrown by the illuminations, under the trees, half-glimpsed, there, there was something.

Headings from the London copybook: Reynolds, Gainsborough, Hogarth, Hawksmoor (churches in the manner of Fischer von Erlach), Wren very well, Burlington's watery Palladianism, curious exercises in the new Gothic . . . A headlong sort of city, everybody mad for money . . .

Bach told me that the English are relentlessly convinced of their own superiority in everything but music and art.

'Why then,' I asked him, 'do they have a German for a king?'

'Oh,' he replied, 'kings don't matter in England. Anyone will do. It's the bigwigs who matter here. They cut off their king's head a hundred years ago, so nobody here wants the job.'

Stupidly, towards the end of my stay, trying to shake off a flicker at the corner of my eye, I strayed into an area of low streets and courts, and was robbed. Three rogues took my purse and some sketches that I had with me. It was clever of them to take the purse when it was really the sketches they were after; but I can read between the lines.

Some say the Soul is lodged in a gland, but Mr Parsons is not of that opinion.

33

When I returned to Vienna from my travels, I went into a little retreat for a while, experimenting with the new styles. The annual exhibition at the Academy of Visual Arts was coming up, and I wanted to cause a little stir. At the same time, I wished for my work to be accepted for permanent display at the Academy – an honour that was accorded to few living artists. I had taken a studio in the Kollnerhofgasse, near the Fleischmarkt, an area of narrow streets and sudden little courtyards billowing with flowers. Here I worked tirelessly away on a figure which was, if you like, my idea of greatness – not a figure surrounded by trappings but almost literally stripped bare – a modern Marcus Aurelius. I had hired an out-of-work blacksmith whose wife and daughter had died of typhus. He possessed a face like a god. I met him on a bridge when he was about to jump despairingly into the water below.

'Don't do that,' I told him. 'You are about to be immortalized in stone.'

I noticed in fact that he had a bundle of stones tied to his feet.

I'm afraid I could not do much to comfort him. It is shitty being an out-of-work bereaved blacksmith even if your face is 'one of the most enlightened works of our time'. Yes, that was what the critics said! It amused me to note that Stadler's offering was almost totally ignored.

I called my idea of greatness 'A Pioneer Piece of Work' in order to ingratiate myself with the critics. I knew it would not do to be too arrogant. An essay could be forgiven by the professors so long as it was labelled 'Experiment'.

I was odiously pleased by my success. I used to drop by at the exhibition and listen at the back to the comments of the little crowd that was always gathered round my blacksmith.

'How expressive. You almost feel he is going to speak, to say something sublime . . .'

'He must be of royal blood . . .'

The new commissions flooded in. I was invited to take up the post of Assistant Lecturer at the Academy of Visual Arts.

The blacksmith jumped into the Danube, stones and all, poor bugger.

34

Hair – and I will include eyebrows in this – might be one of the things you'd think sculptors wouldn't have much time for. After all, you can't recreate every strand. You certainly can't match its colour. All most sculptors do is put in some wavy blobs and ridges, and hope people will take it as read.

And yet how much is hair (and we mustn't forget eyebrows) part of our impression of character in everyday life. How much is hair part of our own impression of ourselves.

That is why people get so upset when they lose their thatch. Of course, with a wig it is not so bad in public life – though I note a considerable falling off of the fashion – it is only the old farts and baldies these days who cling to their perukes. But, in private, when the wig at last comes off, what a moment of truth is here. It is like a shorn lion.

My own hair is still mostly in place, though it is losing its hue and becoming more dull-metallic, but there it is – shaggy, botchily cut by Johanna, and very much part of my impression of myself. Johanna thinks so too. She calls it my wire wool.

'Just like wire wool, it is. I could scrub the grate with it.'

How can sculptors treat this individual personal curtain as though it were a mere series of squiggles? I am giving a great deal of thought to hair, I can assure you.

I knew a girl whose hair was everything to her. She was in many respects unremarkable. Her face was sharp and pointed, her skin white and freckled, her stature on the low side, her bosom nothing to write home about – but she was beautiful because of her hair. It was a lovely titian-gold and it hung in a great golden waterfall down her back or, more formally, it soared and towered in a gorgeous sunset cumulus high above her skull. She worshipped and glorified her hair. She combed it and addressed it and washed it and preened it; and in the end she died for her hair. On a cold winter's night she was combing her hair by the fire when a spark leapt out and it burst into flame. Her mother, with great presence of mind, caught hold of a pair of scissors and made to cut the tresses off at the roots; but the daughter waved her away and tried to muffle the conflagration lower down. She just could not bear to have her pride and joy destroyed. And so her clothes took fire and she was burnt alive.

That is how important hair can be. And let us not forget the eyebrows. How much are the eyebrows part of our expression! We raise them. We bend them. We lour through them. They help us express surprise, disapproval, fury, gloom. How can such individual features be considered so peripheral that they are reduced by sculptors to a mere ridge above the eyesocket? And how individual they are! Sometimes flat and sleek; sometimes running across the top of our noses; and have we not seen them furry like caterpillars; or scrawny as a strand of couch-grass? The eyebrowlessness of statues and busts is why they so often look skinned.

My own eyebrows are a law unto themselves. See! This hair curls like a corkscrew. At one time I used to try and tame them with tweezer and scissors but I confess I have given up. Why should I seek to tame my eyebrows when I am trying to understand the nature of myself? Let them grow unconfinedly. Let my nose hair sprout. If I could render it in bronze I would, but I fear it might be misinterpreted. I have done the Blithe Nose-Picker (No. 19) and even for that I held back on the bogies.

35

I wonder whether what we are really is not simply a collection of elements – as in a beehive or ants' nest. Perhaps our 'self' does not really exist at all, it is an idea propounded or aggregated by these various elements of which we are made; it is an approximation. And should our 'self' be confused with character? Character is after all what gives rise to characteristics. I have heard beekeepers say, 'That is a bad-tempered hive' or 'It was nervous before the honey-flow but you never saw a happier hive in August.'

Those hives have characteristics, but they haven't got self. Or have they?

I have been constipated for some days. At the moment, my bowels are uppermost in my personality. They make me glum. The honey-flow has stopped.

She looks at me from the chaise longue, looking at me looking at her caressing her knee, waiting for the honey-flow; while the Egyptian watches us both.

Proportion is the key, of course. All our various parts, in proportion, make us what we are. It is the proportion that matters; like the eggs in a cake, or the secretion in a gland, too little and we are dry and costive; too much and we are fiery and bellicose. We are beehives.

And now I began to see why Mesmer had been so interested in my heads; for is not Proportion very much at the centre of his own philosophy? I have read his Twenty-seven Propositions; he must think me a fool if he thinks I have not. Everyone in Vienna has read his Twenty-seven Propositions though of course they don't talk about it to doctors or their doctors would not treat them. His Ninth and Tenth Propositions run as follows:

> Properties similar to those of the magnet are found in the human body; different and opposite poles can be distinguished which can be excited, changed, destroyed, or reinforced; even the phenomena of attraction and repulsion are allowed in it. The property of the animal body, which makes it susceptible to the influence of the heavenly bodies, and to the reciprocal action of those that surround it, has led me, from its analogy with the magnet, to call it Animal Magnetism . . .

Is not this a description of Proportion in other words? And will it be that when I have stripped away every covering of expression I will find nothing but a Magnet? And that instead of an immortal soul I shall discover a Model, a mere Cast or Proportional Representation, an Electric Idea elected as it were by the various members of the body which has no more claim on God's Bosom in eternity than an ant-hill? Or has it? Perhaps indeed it is just that iota of Proportion in us which joins us to the Whole.

The Egyptian is full of magnetism: that I am sure of. Mesmer has given it to me as part of some bizarre test, I shall throw it out presently . . .

36

My 'experiment' proved so popular that I was soon urged to incorporate elements of classicism in almost all the work I undertook – not the Court busts, of course – the Court still wanted heroics – and so would I if I were a great fat white royal super-ant in the middle of a wriggling hill of courtiers, timeservers, nobles, petty artists, merchants and scurrying fickle little Viennese. The Emperor, if you like, is the 'I' of our society, just as I am the I of the wriggling elements of me. You follow me? I am glad.

For friends, for more bourgeoisie commissions, and en-lightened nobles like the Princess of Savoy (granddaughter of the great Eugene), I concentrated ever more on character. The ponderous richly-draped bust disappeared to be replaced with a simpler, contemporary costume, carried on by an abbreviated and understated socle (the whatnot we put beneath a bust to carry it). It was the expression, however, that was perhaps the hallmark of my newer style.

I wanted, even then, to try and explore the quality which accounted for the different 'me-ness' in each individual. I now see, of course, that it was but a preparation for the great task ahead, the conquering of those gleaming peaks – like the distant vistas from Vienna of the white mountains to the west – which has been beckoning me all these months.

At the time, however, it simply seemed a new and inter-esting development of my trade. (You see! I sometimes still use the woodcarver's word. I never once heard my uncle refer to his profession as art in all my life.) What I had done before – the attitudes of my subjects – the poses – the rhodomontades – seemed now to me more and more rigid and lifeless.

Surprisingly enough, but not surprising if you have made any study of the skittishness of taste which prevailed in those years in Vienna (to say nothing of London and Paris), my new style continued to catch on, not just with the princes and the public but with the professors themselves. I was elected to full membership of the Academy of Visual Arts. (I could not help noticing that Stadler, who was also up for membership, failed to get in at the time though he wriggled through soon after.)

Fortified by this election, admired by my peers and encouraged by my friends, I started to take pupils. I now had the necessary space and privacy in which to conduct my lessons, for I had – with my new-found success – accumulated a little money, and purchased a house in one of those flower-and-vine-trailing outlying streets of Vienna, the Dornbacherstrasse, with a garden and sheds where I could model and even cast my work.

For a time all seemed to go well. These were truly days of wine and roses; indeed, I even had my own wine made from my own grapes and we would sit in the garden, my students and I after our lessons, sipping and discussing the world and art, and love, and Vienna, and 'the ebb and flow of great ones who rise and fall by the moon'. Or at other times I would go to one of the countless little Heurigen gardens to drink the new wine with Johanna. She had reappeared, her husband having expired of sympathy and frustration, and then we would trip back through the lanes to my house, and lie down and look at each other. (For her that was still pleasure.)

Meanwhile I was working away at the commissions which kept flooding in, and even began to lecture and teach at the Academy on the prompting of another of my old teachers, Jakob Schleterrer. He was a splendid old fellow, half genius, half Falstaff, around whom stories gather like mussels round an effluent. He it was who remarked, after interviewing a potential model for a Hercules, and noting the man's magnificent, indeed protuberant pectoral physique, 'Tell me,' said Schleterrer aside to an assistant, he had an actor's hammy way of talking, 'Tell me, if that fellow were judiciously buggered, do you think he would give forth milk?'

To tell you the truth, he was more Falstaff than genius, but it was Schleterrer who had introduced me as a student to the disciplines of Le Brun. His heads had been a pet subject of Schleterrer's even then; but now it seemed his enthusiasm for them was greater than ever.

'As scales and the study of counterpoint are to music,' he told me one day, 'so the undertaking of these character heads is essential to the making of an artist. Set your pupils to 'em. If you seek for the truth, it is there.'

I did not like to tell him that I probably knew more now about Le Brun than he did.

At any rate, I set my students upon the heads although of course they jibbed. I lectured upon the heads; and it was on one of these occasions that I caught sight of Stadler jibing and gesturing outside the half-open door at the back of the lecture room. I ordered the door to be shut but not before half the class had turned round and seen his mocking gesture, finger to his head. I learned afterwards that he had at last been elected to the Academy.

I received the news with misgiving; there was something about the fellow that was more than merely mischievous. Who would pursue a student's slight over a dozen years? I dismissed the fellow from my mind, persisted in my enthusiasm for the heads, and even began to pursue my own experiments with grimaces and a mirror in my own garden. I knew instinctively that there was something there.

I could not yet tell what. Soon I started to notice students in the Academy slyly pointing to their heads when I was half-looking. One day, Schleterrer took me aside.

'Franz,' he said, 'my boy.'

'Yes, Professor?'

'Perhaps you have been working too hard.'

'Working hard, yes, but not too hard. I enjoy my work.'

'These heads of yours . . .'

'Yes?'

'They seem to have become, well, over-dominant in your curriculum. They are becoming a laughing-stock.'

'But you yourself commended them, Professor.'

'Commended, yes. But not to the exclusion of all else. There is colour. There is light. There is movement. Stadler now is doing some very interesting work on leaping horses . . .'

But I would not, I could not give up my heads. Was it not Mozart who the other day commended 'expressive gusto' in music? That is more like it. No wonder he is so unpopular with the brittle and the bloodless.

His music, it seems to me, draws together the popular and the erudite. That is what the academics and the buggers cannot forgive him for. They like something that is 'difficult', arid and infertile like their practices; they pride themselves on their ability to appreciate what is beyond the patience of most people. Gusto is not part of their vocabulary. Their expressiveness is tight and dry like their sphincters.

I have heard that Mozart personally is now a bit of a prick. It probably means, knowing Vienna, that he's quite a character. I wouldn't mind doing a head of him but I cannot spare the time. I am still only on Head No. 35, The Wistful Dreamer. Sorry, Mozart.

37

It so happened at this time that my fancy fell on a strange tumultuous girl called Johanna – dark-haired, impatient, volatile and yet at times exquisitely, meltingly gentle – daughter of a certain Herr Blieschies who was a prosperous druggist in the city. Doubtless through his connection with chemicals, he was also involved with certain others who had what I shall describe as alchemical interests. He was also, I believe, a Freemason.

Johanna led me a merry dance, but I was so infatuated with desire for her quicksilveriness – her father's chemicals had got into her brain, I believe – and her wondrously slim little ankles that now jumped this way and now that – that I did not enquire too closely into her father's friends.

I now believe that I should have done, for it was at one of their soirées that I first encountered Mesmer. Oh, I had heard of him, of course. What person in Vienna had not? The place was rife with rumours about any who could claim to cure or influence Nature. Indeed, they were still hanging witches in those days.

Anyway, it was the custom at the Blieschies establishment for Johanna, her mother and brothers to entertain the groundlings while her father took his cronies to an inner room decorated – from what I could interpret from a footman – with Eastern symbols, and smelling of laudanum.

At one of these parties, the man I now know to be Mesmer emerged and made a beeline for me. He somehow knew who I was and what I did. He came up to me and said I could do a head of him if I cared to. I did not like the look of the fellow. He seemed, though half-glazed with some drug, wholly to know me – and not just a social knowing, if you take my meaning – right through me. I made some demurral, that I was too busy, over-commissioned at the moment. He did not like that.

'I won't ask a second time,' he lisped (his tongue was too big for his mouth), 'but you'll be sorry, depend upon it. I warrant you'll come round to it in the end.'

But I had spotted Johanna slipping off with a shifty-looking Hussar, and I hurried away paying no heed to his menaces.

It was only later when someone told me laughingly that it was not wise to refuse Dr Mesmer that I realized I might have made a mistake; but by then it was too late.

Vienna was full of people it was not wise to refuse. One could not accept everybody. The art of survival in Vienna was to be selective in one's enemies.

38

Two heads that I did that year stand out particularly in my memory. They illustrate (why not?) the collision of styles that the new thinking, as they liked to call it, had unleashed on Vienna; of course all the cronies assign the responsibility of the vogue to Winckelmann and Stadler, but Winckelmann could not even draw. He simply went to Rome and raved about 'noble simplicity' as if he were the first one ever to commend the classical. (He ended up knifed by a sailor he was sodomizing in Trieste.) As for Stadler, we know all about him – a derivative, envious sucking-pig gorging at the tit of other people's talent – that's what we know about him. I am sorry if I am extreme.

I had been to Rome. I had travelled to Paris and London.

They had both rediscovered classicism long before Winckel-mann. What else was Burlington all about? Or come to think of it, Jones?

These two heads that I did, then. The first was of the Baron Van Swieten, a Dutchman originally, very popular at court, statesman, Physician to the Empress, doyen of medicine and devotee of the arts (whose son is that miserable skinflint and enthusiast of Handel who gets Mozart to play the continuo for nothing at his private Sunday concerts). I was commissioned to do a bust of the old buzzard by no less a person than the Empress herself. I was, however, given to understand that nothing newfangled would be tolerated.

So, as far as I was concerned – for I grew to like the Baron – his statue would be one of the last great expressions of Austrian baroque with all the majesty and pathos that I could bring to cold marble.

It just shows what actors we artists were required to be in those days. None of your heroic I-will-not-compromise. Look at old Gainsborough! I was told, when I was in London, and I have heard it since, that he hated doing portraits because he disliked the toffs and nobs who were his main customers. He was propping up their bigwiggery, their sense of self-importance, every time he turned in a decent job. But did it stop him doing them? Of course not. The business of the artist is to do the best he can in impossible circumstances, and come up with a masterpiece. It is sometimes the disciplines which create the opportunities. What would the game be without goalposts?

So when I had finished the good Baron's bust, I really believe that it showed the good humour, the sapience, the benignity of the man as well as conveying a measure of his importance, even perhaps of his self-importance, in a manner that no other style than Austrian Baroque, perhaps with a whisker of classicism and a pinch of Nature, could possibly lend itself to.

And I was pleased. And the Baron was pleased. And the

Emperor and Empress were pleased. And if you go to the Imperial Collection in Vienna, I absolutely guarantee that you will be pleased too.

It was the last commission I received from the Empress, as it turned out, but it is satisfying to recall that I said goodbye to the Court and the old style on a high note.

39

The other head that I did that year deserves more than a passing mention for it was done as a result of an episode whose effects upon me were as incalculable as its origins were mysterious.

Perhaps because I had been working so hard upon the Swieten statue as well as the various teaching projects I had at the Academy, or perhaps due to an inexplicable injury, I underwent a brainstorm.

The term had just finished and I was looking forward to taking a holiday with my sketchbook in Thuringia, when I suddenly found myself waking up in the sick-bay of what I learned in due course was the Capuchin Order whose church and catacombs lie at the very heart of the city.

I enquired of the Brother what I was doing there and he told me with some surprise, noting my failure of memory, that I was a Capuchin Brother on his way from Westphalia who had been brought in unconscious with a bump on the head probably occasioned by falling down – this mischance being either a result of attack or of sunstroke – I had anyway been found lying in the sun – and that I would be allowed to continue on my travels in a fortnight or so.

Foolishly, I remonstrated. In point of fact, a couple of weeks recuperating in a Capuchin infirmary would have suited me very well. But when somebody tells you you are somebody you are not, your first instinct is to correct him.

The Brother looked grave and sent for another Brother.

'Well, Brother,' said the second Brother to me. 'How are you doing?'

'Very fair,' I said, 'but I should like to go home now.'

'You are still weak,' said he, 'and Westphalia is too far for you. Besides, you were going to Budapest.'

'Budapest nothing,' I said. 'I live in the city here.'

The two Brothers looked at each other. 'I see you are still far from well. You have only just recovered from your fever. Rest awhile.'

I stopped him.

'Tell me,' I said, 'what makes you think I am a Capuchin monk?'

'You were found in a Capuchin robe lying by the wayside. You had certain papers within your scrip – the money had been stolen – that told us the rest.'

I fell back exhausted. The story was such arrant nonsense that my power of denial required more strength than I possessed. A modest unlikelihood I could have coped with. Total fantasy needed sterner stuff.

After lunch, however, I felt more vigorous and reverted to my theme.

'I am Froberger, Professor of the Academy,' I told them. 'Check up on me if you like.'

Alas, the Academy was closed for the summer – and I had given my manservant a month's leave to visit his mother in Carinthia – at least that was what he had told me he was going to do – though conceivably he was going to spend the four weeks fucking himself into a stupor, not that much fucking was needed to do that as far as he was concerned.

The two Brothers sent for a third Brother who introduced himself as Brother Fessler. I repeated my story. I was by now becoming agitated. It was like a nightmare. I had heard that the Capuchins did not easily tolerate anyone leaving

84

their order; also that they had somewhat stringent ways of dealing with their malingerers.

Brother Fessler gazed at me curiously. He was a young man with unusually thin lips. A high forehead was balanced by a long sharp chin, while his pale eyes glimmered under eyebrows that sprouted like little blond cauliflowers.

'I hope you are not having a joke with us, Brother Martin,' he said. 'We don't like wasting time with that kind of nonsense. God does not like fritterers. The devil is busy. He does not fritter.'

'Surely,' I chafed, unwisely, 'that would be an argument for frittering.'

Brother Fessler narrowed his eyes.

'Do not chop logic with me, Brother Martin. You are well aware of my meaning. God requires a vigorous virtue from us all. I will take the charitable view that you are still not yourself, but I must warn you that we have stern measures here for those who evade their religious duties with a pretence of aberration. I advise you to recover with due despatch.'

I tried another tack for I was feeling both panicky and affronted.

'Forgive my curiosity,' I said, 'but are the Capuchins in Vienna so short of recruits that they must press-gang innocent citizens into their order?'

Brother Fessler's eyes blazed with an immediate and chilly ferocity – a passion which would have done credit, I thought, to a Grand Inquisitor. I saw that my question had been ill-timed, if not ill-considered.

'Do not presume to think, Brother Martin,' he replied, 'that we would be interested in recruiting such a poor specimen as you are showing yourself to be. We must suppose, charitably, that you are still physically incapacitated. If, however, it appears that your problem now simply resides in your mind, we have remedial treatment here that has proved effective against the most stubborn devils.'

I shuddered as he said these words; there was a certain fanaticism about those eyes which spoke of cruelty, and his next remark confirmed my fears.

'Tie him into the bed, Brother Adam,' he ordered. 'We do not want him to come to harm in his ravings.'

I complained bitterly as they tied me down in the bed like a pupa in its casing until they thrust a pad in my mouth reducing me to incoherent mumbles and at last to silence.

Several days passed while I pondered my predicament. It was clear to me that the Capuchins were a brotherhood of the deranged but I judged it prudent, when my pad was removed so that I might take nourishment, to say nothing to the young monk from the kitchen who signed to me that he had taken a vow of silence.

The problem, as I saw it, was that it was now only the beginning of the summer vacation. Most of my colleagues would have gone away. I had few close friends – my work was my friends – and what acquaintances I had knew that I lived a fitful existence, travelling here and there as the commissions took me. In short, I would not be missed until my manservant returned – if he ever did – in August. It was now late June. Anything could happen in the interim. If I persisted in my claim that I was Franz Xaver Froberger, sculptor of this parish, I would be delivered into the care of Fessler and his draconian measures. If on the other hand I admitted, falsely, that I was Friar Martin, I would surely be permitted to carry on my journey – at which point I could of course return to my home in the suburbs, having lodged a full complaint with the Prefect of Police.

This was indeed how things worked out. I motioned to the Brother in the infirmary that I wished to speak for I was not yet allowed out of my gag, and over he came.

'Yes, Brother?'

I motioned to him to undo the pad.

'I am not empowered unless it is an emergency.'

I made signs of dire importance and he loosened the gag.

'Well, Brother?'

'I have remembered who I am.'

'Praise be to God.'

'I am Brother Martin travelling from Westphalia to Budapest. I must have been beaten and robbed.'

I added that for indeed it seemed the likeliest explanation for my presence there. There was a great deal of beating and robbing on the roads into the city. Perhaps some poor Capuchin had equally been assaulted, stripped and left to die, and in the shemozzle our clothes had become mixed up. I had the uncomfortable feeling, indeed, that the Capuchin might have taken over my life, as it appeared I had taken over his.

'I will fetch Brother Fessler,' said the monk, and hurried off to impart the good news of my recovery.

He reappeared ten minutes later with Fessler beside him, pursing his lips and looking as if he had a bramble up his bottom.

'Well, now,' said Fessler, looking me over with his cauliflower eyebrows. 'It is true? Have we a good, whole Capuchin in his rightful frame of mind?'

'Yes, indeed, Brother Fessler. No doubt about it. I am myself again. It has been like a sojourn in Purgatorio. Such a bang on the head I had . . .'

I thought chattering naïvely would probably fill the bill.

'It often results in a fever,' chipped in the infirmary monk whose name was Brother Silvester. 'Indeed, I have known cases of total amnesia. Brother Martin got off lightly when all's said and done. He could have been a case for Saint Jude, Patron of the Impossible.'

It is a strange fact of life that monks have a tendency to talk like old women. Not so Brother Fessler, however. He talked with sharp teeth.

'I know who Saint Jude is, thank you very much,' he sneered at the poor infirmary monk who cowered back into his dispensary.

'Now,' he resumed to me, 'I expect you would like to continue on your travels. Where exactly are you going?'

I had thought about this one, and luckily I had the answer pat for I knew Budapest tolerably well. I had completed a statue there for one of the squares.

'Our monastery, of course, in Buda,' I replied, 'on the right bank of the river.'

This seemed to satisfy him, but he was the sort of man who is never satisfied for long.

'And can you repeat the Capuchin prayer?'

'The Capuchin prayer?' I stammered.

'The Capuchin prayer. Come on, man.'

'But everyone knows the Capuchin prayer.'

'That is as may be.'

'You cannot seriously wish me to recite the Capuchin's prayer.'

'It is precisely my wish.'

He was scenting victory now.

'Why? Don't you know it?' I asked.

It was a feeble ploy and it made him lose his temper.

'If you do not recite the Capuchin prayer instantly, I shall have you thrown into the vaults.'

'The vaults? What vaults?'

'You had better pray that you never know the vaults,' he said, as though he had let slip a secret. 'The prayer, if you please.'

As it happened, the infirmary monk had recited it every night of my captivity so I was able to repeat it with expedition and accuracy.

You could see how cross Fessler was. He was really looking forward to whatever it was he was looking forward to. However, I was provided with a habit, a scrip, enough money for my journey, and given permission to depart as soon as I liked. Before I left, I nipped up to exchange farewells with the infirmary monk who had unwittingly so assisted in my release.

'Goodbye,' said the infirmary monk, 'go in peace and not in pieces.'

'I hope that's the last gag I get from you,' I replied, and he laughed so much he broke a retort full of urine.

40

As soon as I left the monastery, I went straight to the Prefecture of Police and reported my enforced incarceration. I had decided during my days of speechlessness that this would be the best thing to do, in case of any subsequent problem with the original Capuchin monk. I considered that he had either been found dead with my garments lying around him; or that he might have taken up, as I feared, the threads of my own life, a human hermit crab. I usually carried a labelled key in my pocket for I never knew whether my manservant would be there to let me in and now of course he wasn't. Supposing the monk had found it, usurped my residence, traded on my goodwill with neighbours, tradesmen – not of course that there was much of that – but he might have done untold mischief. Besides, I was badly shaken. It is nightmarish to have one's identity doubted, especially when one has spent so much time trying to discover it in the first place. This is what the police are for.

'Yes?' said the office I was directed to.

'I have a complaint to make.'

'Complaint? Is it something of an ecclesiastical nature? Can't do nothing with an ecclesiastical nature here.'

'It's not an ecclesiastical nature. It's kidnap.'

'Kidnap? Are you sure? That is a serious offence of an unecclesiastical nature.'

'Of course I'm sure.'

'Who's been kidnapped?'

'I have.'

'You can't be kidnapped. You're here.'

'I was kidnapped.'

'Can we start again? I hope you're not wasting my time, Father.'

'Brother.'

'I beg your pardon?'

'A monk is a Brother not a Father.'

'Ah. And you are Brother . . . ?'

'I am Mr Franz Xaver Froberger.'

'I thought you just told me to call you Brother.'

'I did . . . this is a Brother's habit.'

'It is not yours?'

'That's right.'

'You are wearing a stolen habit?'

'No.'

The officer heaved a sigh and gazed at me bleakly.

'Would you like to start again, sir?'

'I woke up in the Capuchins' infirmary and they have been holding me against my will. It's quite simple,' I said. 'I'm really sculptor to the Court.'

'And I'm his Grace the Duke of Bilgewater,' said the fellow, facetiously. 'Won't be a minute, sir.'

His face had cleared and he seemed quite to have regained his humour. I sat and drank a glass of water while bureaucracy took its course.

Twenty minutes later, who should march into the Prefecture but Fessler and two brawny-looking Capuchins I had not met before. I almost asked their names for they would have done splendidly for a commission I had from Prince Windisch-Gratz for the adult Romulus and Remus.

'That's him,' I cried to the officer. 'He's the one.'

'Mad as a hatter, I'm afraid, officer,' said Fessler. 'Thank you for alerting us. Leave him to me.'

'No,' I shouted to the officer. 'You're making a terrible mistake.'

'We do get 'em from your lot, Brother,' said the custodian of the law. 'Religion is strong meat for a weak brain.'

'There,' said Fessler, 'you have put your finger on it, officer. And they say you have to fail a stupidity exam to become a policeman!'

41

I struggled but I was a mere rag in the hands of the muscular Capuchins who threw me on to a stretcher they had brought, and tied me down upon it with a sort of straitjacket, placing a gag in my mouth as they did so. They then lifted me up and took me through the streets back to the church.

What an indignity for a man in my position! Anyone might have passed by and seen me. I was torn between conflicting emotions. One, a desire to be recognized and presumably rescued – though the Capuchins seemed to be impervious to normal human contact, and there was no guarantee that, even then, they would release me. Two, a wish to be hurried away from my humiliation before anyone of importance saw me; for it was certain that the scandal of a Court sculptor being dragged through the streets like a booby would reach all the important ears in Vienna with a corresponding blighting effect on my commissions. At any rate, the latter dispensation was the one I was granted.

The church of the Capuchins was built just after the beginning of the last century. Other monastic buildings have sprung up subsequently nearby, but the central pile, flamboyantly constructed, rides alone like a promontory. The cloisters, the refectory, the infirmary and the library with the dormitory overhead are situated at a respectful distance across the way.

I had thought they might take me back to the infirmary,

or into some office for further discussion on my identity, but not a bit of it. Fessler made for the church itself, opened a massive oaken door behind the north wall, and I was carried down a long flight of steps into what I thought was going to be a place of meditation. That was what they told me. Imagine my consternation when I realized that the walls were lined not with improving books but with stone sarcophagi whose contents I had no need to guess at. The air was full of the stench of damp and decay.

We were, I guessed, in one of the crypts. We progressed through another massive door hidden behind a false buttress, along a slight incline, down a flight of steps, through a short tunnel and into an interminably long low chamber lined from floor to ceiling with coffins. I realized now the true nature of my whereabouts and my heart filled with horror, for I had heard vague stories of this place, never dreaming that I should one day inspect their source at first hand. We were in the catacombs.

At the end of this chamber, the passage turned to the right, there was another flight of steps and we entered a smaller room divided on one side into barred cells. One of them was inhabited. A melancholy monk with sad eyes got up and peered out at us hopefully.

'Why aren't you kneeling, Brother Michael?' enquired Fessler, as we passed. 'Down on your knees and pray to God for mastery over lust.'

The wretched monk sank down beside his bars and turned an imploring gaze upon Brother Fessler but it was met with the coldest impassivity.

We stopped beside another cage at the end of the dungeon – which now I saw the chamber to be – and I suppose I must have indicated in my expression that I expected this to be my destination. But Fessler read my look and laughed.

'This is not for you, my mad friend. This is the luxury wing. Oh no, for you we have rather more remedial quarters.'

He opened another door, low set in the wall beside the last cage, and a waft of charnel effluvium rose up to greet my affronted nostrils. Even the Capuchins who carried me muttered an oath of distaste.

'Bloody hell. It smells like an opened graveyard.'

'Don't complain, Brothers,' laughed Fessler. 'It is a concomitant of the driving out of devils. Stench is the sign that the devils are leaving. Not all of them, of course. Some of them are very stubborn. We must wind them out. But this odour you complain of, to me it is as sweet as Arabian gum if it means we are rescuing a soul.'

They did not look entirely convinced, and clattered me down a narrow flight of spiral steps whose walls, in the guttering lamplight, shone with noisome black slime, relieved here and there by pale half-balloons of fungus.

At length, I was deposited on the floor of a chamber cut out of the living rock, some sixty feet, as I guessed, below the surface. Along this grim corridor I now discovered cavelets cut into the stone, each fronted by an iron grille. And, inside these, nightmarish figures waved, gesticulated, capered, crouched or lay huddled in mindless apathy. A ghastly medley of sound filled the air – humming, buzzing, mewing, shrieking, mumbling, and inconsolable sobbing – jumbled and reverberating on the comfortless limestone.

Fessler stepped forward, unlocked the door of an empty compartment, and I was thrust unceremoniously inside. The bars rattled shut behind me, as the two guards turned and, showing more humanity than they had so far manifested, put their hands to their noses as they hurried back up the stairway.

I was left with Brother Fessler. We gazed at each other while I massaged my arms.

'I cannot believe this is happening to me,' I told him at last. 'There has been some dreadful mistake.'

He remained silent, his eyes glowing like clinkers. I tried again.

'I am not a rich man,' I said, 'but . . .'

I stopped, for I realized that had I had all the wealth of Suleyman at my disposal, it would avail me nothing.

'Please,' I implored. 'You are a civilized man. I am an artist. I have a God-given talent. I must exercise it, you know the parable of the talents . . .'

This at last moved him to speech.

'You are a devil,' he told me. 'Do not speak of Our Lord's words in the same breath as yourself. You are Martin the Capuchin possessed by Beelzebub. I command you to come forth.'

Here he raised his voice as he called again.

'Come forth, Beelzebub.'

As he cried there was a confused whining and mewing from all the caves around me.

'Ah, the pretty lady . . .'

'Legs and hands, legs and hands . . .'

'Cacacacacacacaaaa . . .'

'Oh my sweet Jesu, help me . . .'

The sounds seemed to cause Fessler the greatest satisfaction. I even think he enjoyed the smell – compounded of human sweat, excrement, suppuration, vegetable ooze, rat droppings, rancid foods, and damp – whose noisomeness, even familiarity could never reconcile to my own nostrils.

'You are the devil,' I told him.

'That is what they say at first,' he replied. 'But it is typical of Evil to turn order on its head. I am your friend, Brother Martin. I know you are within, imprisoned, in a little room, while Beelzebub lords it in your body. Have no fear, we will drive him out.'

'You do not seem to be having much success with my companions,' I told him.

'Half the cells are empty,' he replied. 'You should have been here last year. We had a positive epidemic. I have never had so many cases.'

'Doubtless many of them were removed feet first,' I observed.

'Some die exhausted,' he agreed, 'their mortal frames over-taxed by the struggle. But the devil, like a rat, leaves a dying vessel and our poor brothers receive the Last Rites and proceed peacefully to God's enfolding arms. I never mind a death because death is victory. Oh death, where is thy sting; and so forth. On the other hand, we have many examples of complete recoveries.'

'I should like to be a complete recovery,' I said. 'In fact, I think I'm recovered already.'

'Not so fast, Beelzebub. You have deceived us once before. No, we must mortify you awhile.'

'How . . . how is that accomplished?' I faltered.

'Scourging, fasting, contemplation, prayer. These are usually sufficient. But in particularly stubborn cases I prescribe duress.'

'Duress?'

'The vulgar would call it torture. But in fact it is cure by pain.'

With that he turned and left me in the darkness with my fellow madmen.

Now you must not think that because I describe these events lightly in retrospect, finding something of a sardonic humour in the sheer incongruity of my translation from Court sculptor to mad monk, that I was not at the time horrified and appalled by the situation I now found myself in. Apart from my sense of shock and disjunction, I was considerably alarmed by the physical conditions of the place. I am not an overly fastidious man, but it was apparent to me that the circumstances of this subterranean gaol were such that the most severe disabilities and afflictions, from poisoned rat-bites to consumptions, and worse, must ensue within a matter of days.

The idea of torture I could not encompass at all. We were after all living in the age of the new enlightenment. The thought of torture was ridiculous. Torture aside, however, I was sure that, if I was not mad when I came in, I would assuredly be raving when I left.

I felt something dark and slimy run across my leg, and I cried out involuntarily.

A voice called out from a neighbouring cell.

'How is it with you, Brother?'

'Better dead than alive, I think,' I replied.

'How come you here? Who are you?'

'I am one of the Court sculptors. I woke up in the infirmary and was told I was Brother Martin travelling from Westphalia to Budapest. And you?'

'I am a mountebank working the fairs. I woke in the infirmary and was told that I was Brother Adolph travelling from Swabia to Rome. When I said who I really was, they told me I was mad.'

'What about the rest of them here?'

'They really are mad.'

'Have you thought of escape?'

'Impossible. There are only two ways out. Via the coffin or through the cloister; however, there you are still in prison. They are short of Capuchins in Vienna and have hit upon this method of recruiting. It is the same principle as the press-gang.'

So my remarks to Fessler had hit home!

'How long have you been here?'

'Seven days.'

'Have you been tortured?'

'Only whipped.'

'Are you well?'

'An abscess has formed on my back. I have developed a quinsy.'

'What will you do?'

'I am thinking of becoming Brother Adolph with all possible speed. I advise you to do the same. But you can't do it too fast or they smell a rat.'

'Not too difficult down here.'

'What?'

Someone cried out in pain in the darkness, someone else started singing hymns, while another yet launched into a stream of the most purulent obscenities.

'The moon is a bosom,' said a little old voice, quite lucidly, 'there were once two but it was cut off to make the Milky Way. Next question?'

'Why don't you fuck off?' said the obscenity merchant. 'Why don't you pull your foreskin over your head and vanish up your arsehole?'

Hours later, a light appeared and a thin soup was doled into our mess-tins along with a slice of hard rye bread. We guzzled and the light disappeared. More darkness. I must have slept. When I woke someone was rattling at my door.

'Froberger?'

'Yes.'

'Take him outside, Brothers.'

Two gaoler Brothers I had not seen before seized me and frog-marched me out of my cell. For a blissful moment I thought I was being released, but instead I found myself being lifted bodily towards a door at the far end of the gallery. Inside was a large bare room with various inde-cipherable contraptions lying around it. To one of these, a sort of large X-shaped object, I was tied before I had the wit to struggle – not that it would have made much difference if I had – my monkish habit was torn off, and there I stood, as they say, bollock naked, my legs and arms spread out, in a condition of the utmost humiliation and helplessness.

'Now you are not so proud, Beelzebub,' said Brother Fessler.

'Move your leg, brother cunt,' said one of the gaolers, prodding me sharply with a stick to make me adjust my position on my cross.

The other gaoler, in the pretext of helping him, ran his hands over my genitals.

So it was that kind of brotherhood, I thought.

'Enough of that,' cried Fessler.

Cruelty was his game.

'Leave the Brother alone, Beelzebub,' he cried at me. 'You should know better than to inflame him with rank desires when I am present. You shall have extra strokes for that.'

'And not the strokes like what I was giving you neither,' muttered the gaoler under his breath.

'Now answer me,' cried Fessler. 'Who are you?'

'I am Franz Xaver Froberger,' I cried in return.

'Beat him,' shouted Fessler.

The first gaoler gave me a dozen strokes of his bullwhip. I screamed like the devil himself.

'Now who are you?' shouted Fessler.

'I am Brother Martin,' I shrieked.

'Beat him,' yelled Fessler.

Finally, the fellow desisted. I could feel the blood coursing down my back.

'Now who are you?' asked Fessler, quietly.

'Beelzebub,' I said at last.

'Three persons without God,' said Fessler. 'An unholy Trinity. Beat him for the devil he is.'

When they had finished and I was blubbering with pain, Fessler asked me once more who I was.

'Anyone,' I said. 'Anyone you want me to be.'

'That is better,' said Fessler. 'Before the cure comes the humility.'

42

It is surprising how quickly you can lose your sense of identity if someone is beating hell out of you twice a week.

After a little while, I neither knew nor cared who I was. I merely wanted to stop being hit. The injustice of my presence in the catacombs was now entirely lost on me. I accepted it. I deserved the punishment. I even came close to loving Fessler for caring so much about me. He wouldn't have had me beaten if it had not been necessary.

I lost all self-respect, not simply because I was filthy, stinking, ugly, scarred, matted, mangey, louse-ridden and fungal, but because I had lost my self. You cannot respect yourself if there is no self to respect. My self and I are not all that well stitched together at the best of times.

There was one advantage, however, to be gained from my increasingly disgusting condition. The second gaoler no longer felt the urge to lay his hands on me.

My companion the mountebank was taken away one day, and never came back. He was made of sterner stuff than I was. Indeed the longer he remained, the stronger grew his resolve.

He had sworn to me lately that he would not in any circumstances become a Capuchin. It would demean the reputation of mountebanks, he said. He assured me that beatings for a mountebank were a mere two a penny.

The word was, later, that he had told Fessler he was a Protestant. Vienna had been a great centre of Protestantism in the last century – more from a general desire among the citizens to thumb the nose at the Holy Roman Emperor than from any deep sense of religious conviction – but there it was. It was more than Fessler could endure.

Doubtless he put the man on the rack and snapped his spine like a twig. Of course the proximity of the monk's immemorial resting-place was most convenient for Fessler. Where better to hide bodies than in a catacomb? It was heaven-sent.

43

I seemed to have spent an aeon underground. The terrors of that darkness, alternating with thin diet and beatings, worked upon me so that I became, like my companions, less than a human being. We were a new category, unknown to Linnaeus, something akin to a two-legged dog.

I began to love Fessler as if he were my Master and my God. He was a stern deity but, within his lights, he was fair. I knew why I was being punished. I knew I was not worthy but I yearned to be admitted to the Truth. He had not tortured me. I was only being chastized, corrected. I loved him for that.

'Show me the Truth, Brother,' I begged him.

'Who are you?'

'I am who you want me to be.'

Incredibly, one day, he suddenly stepped forward and embraced me. I dissolved into tears.

'Oh Brother,' he said, 'I can see the good in you beginning to work like yeast. Come, let us see if God has permitted the talent of which the madman boasted to grace the hand of Brother Martin.'

'What . . . what do you mean, Brother?'

I feared this was yet another of his ruses to make Beelzebub show his residency in me yet.

'We have a need for a Brother Sculptor. In a recent great wind, some of our statues have suffered. Let us see now if

Brother Martin can do a head of me. If I deem it good, we shall send you upstairs.'

I was seized with joy and fear. Joy that I should escape the catacombs; but fear that I should fail. Who knew if Brother Martin could take on this art of which he should have no knowledge? Perhaps it was a trick? But even as I wondered, as hope rose in me, I could feel my old madness flooding back and filling me with craft. I was Franz Froberger, sculptor to the Court, a devil's man, I could count on it.

I smiled diffidently, craftily.

'I should . . . so much like to try, Brother. But I shall need . . . tools . . . I'm not sure what they use . . .'

'It will all be brought down here.'

And so it turned out. I had been saved by a great wind. I was transferred immediately to the upper level and given the cell next to the sad-eyed monk who prayed with renewed vigour for mastery over lust when Fessler was present; and who tried to catch at me through the bars when he wasn't.

The bust I made of Fessler was perhaps the best thing I had ever done. The thin lips, the questing beak-like nose, the deep-set eyes, the whole head carried with the grace of a buzzard – yes, there was something beyond even the Roman in it – it was almost an Egyptian head – so easy, so masterful, so wicked. It was a departure from anything I had done before. Perhaps there was, after all, a touch of Brother Martin in it, a new dimension as they say.

I woke up in an infirmary bed.

'Who am I, Brother?' I asked.

Note the question. Not where am I but who am I? A monk I recognized as Brother Silvester was peering down at me. I had that strange feeling one sometimes has in dreams, that one has woken up but is still dreaming.

'Why, you are Franz Xaver Froberger, sculptor to the Court. You are in the infirmary of the Capuchins . . .'

'Why am I here?'

'You have been ill. You were taken to Dr Mesmer's by your friend Stadler who found you lying on the Academy steps. They brought you here. You have had a brain fever.'

I was suddenly seized by terror, and clasped the monk's arm.

'Don't send me down there again.'

'Why, what do you mean?'

'To the catacombs.'

'The catacombs? But they have been closed for years. No one goes down there now except to bury an Emperor.'

I sank back exhausted.

'What about Fessler?' I asked weakly.

'Fessler? Why, he was here, treating you during your crisis. Do you not remember?'

'Tell me about him,' I said.

'Why, he is an itinerant Friar of our Order. He has a most eminent medical degree from the University. He specializes in Oriental languages and the Eastern sciences as well as disorders of the nerves, you know. I understand he studied at one point with Dr Mesmer. Brilliant man.'

'I see,' I said, though I did not. 'May I talk to him?'

'He is gone. He stayed until the worst was over. He even took you to his personal Treatment Room.'

'Where was that?'

Brother Silvester pointed across to a half-open door at the end of the room which gave on to a sunny corridor.

'Just along there. Third door on the right.'

'I never left it?'

'Never. I would have seen. Oh, he said you would have visions, memories. You were going through hell. Some of the things you said! Made me blush! Mind you, you did a lovely head of him. Caught him to a T. Not quite my style, I admit. I like a nice swaggering statue. But you could see it was good. Surely you can remember that? He said it would be therapy for you.'

'He has taken it, I suppose?'

'Oh, yes.'

102

44

There I leave the matter. A mystery, you see. Not an experience I would care to go through again. What feeds the mind with these things? I see now that personality is merely a stalagmite, a drip-drip-drip of calcareous deposit slowly built up over a lifetime and dissoluble with a mere sprinkle of acid.

I am not quite prepared to take Brother Silvester's version, though. The names Stadler and Mesmer must always give us pause. And only a year or two later there was the case of the mad Capuchins, kept in the catacombs until they came to their senses – which of course they never did – an affront to the age of enlightenment and nearly a scandal of massive proportions. Sedulously hushed-up, of course, because in Vienna the Church and the Monarchy are one.

45

The old woman who does for me is laid up again and her daughter Johanna has come with soup. She is a pretty creature and she seems attached to me in her way.

'Oo, Mr Froberger,' she says. 'You are ever so clever. But why are you making all those faces?'

I do not like to tell her that I am trying to lay bare the secret of Proportion. It is not the sort of thing you say to your cleaning woman.

'Practice,' says I. 'I have been waiting for someone as beautiful as you to come along.'

I curse myself as she steps out of her dress and drapes her body over the sofa. I cannot afford the time but there it is. She has an excellent figure and I sketch her from a number of angles. She has a good flat belly. When I have finished she seems reluctant to go.

'Are you sure you've got all you want?' she asks.

I know her game. Show a woman a sculptor's chisel and she starts thinking penis. I catch sight of myself in the mirror looking at her. There is something in the expression that I have not caught before: a degree of lust, a modicum of caution, a sense of *déjà nu*. I start drawing myself looking at her.

It is Face No. 39 and I call it Old Reprobate.

I lie with her for politeness's sake. If I position the mirror rightly, I can see my face as I ejaculate. It is an expression much like No. 17 – A Sudden Toothache but with more panic – and hard to catch. Johanna and I have been through twenty ejaculations together and I have barely touched the problem. The Egyptian's eyes are boring a hole in my back.

46

The rest of the summer passed peacefully enough. I put my illness behind me and started to plan a new series of heads based on some of the ideas in the Fessler bust. Nothing was said of my disappearance. Hardly anyone even noticed. My manservant eventually returned, term started again.

I still had my students, my commissions, my lectureship; but more and more I was beginning to find this very success irksome, unsatisfying. As I worked away on my new heads – I used actors from one of the little low theatre groups with which Vienna abounded in those days – looking beyond their faces as it were into the brightness and darkness of their little actorish hearts, I would forget the time, and often as I worked on, if it was a week-day, I would discover that I had missed a lecture or totally forgotten a student who would be left hammering at the door. (The holidays, if anything, seemed to have inflamed my manservant's proclivities, and he was hardly ever in.)

At first, as I say, nobody minded. A certain eccentricity was permitted. Then suddenly the blow fell. I received news that Field Marshal Graf Daun had died. I was sorry to hear about the old boy even if he had blighted my happiness with his daughter, but I did not at first realize the significance of his demise. And then one day I was sent for by the Council of the Academy of Visual Arts and given a summary dressing-down.

'Froberger.'

'Yes, sir.'

'You are becoming a figure of fun.'

The Chairman was a venerable old josser with a yellowing wig and a face like a flushed monkfish.

'Fun, sir?'

'Yes, fun, dammit.'

I noticed Jakob Schletterer among the bigwigs, studiously avoiding my eye.

'It's your heads, Froberger. People are starting to talk. It's said you are creating monstrosities in your garden. It won't do, you know.'

'Surely, sir, what I create in my garden is my own affair.'

'Not if it is reflecting badly on the Academy. Stop it and work on something else. Allegorical nudes or . . . prancing horses . . .'

'But . . .'

'Do not but me, sir. You must ask yourself: do you have a

future with the Academy or do you not? You arrived as one of our stars. We were grooming you for promotion. Professor Schletterer had even commended you as his successor. And then you go and start making monsters, travesties, a mockery of all we stand for here. Now do you see what you stand to lose by intransigence?'

'Yes, sir. Thank you, sir.'

'Go away and think about it. I will look forward to hearing that your grotesques have been thrown out like the rubbish, the ramblings of a sick mind, yes, like the sick-room detritus that they are.'

This reiteration of the word 'sick' aroused my suspicions. Had someone been blabbing? Stadler? I wandered away, deep in thought. I enjoyed my condition of life, my little house, my position at the Academy, the comfortable Viennese future that seemed to beckon. I could imagine perhaps being awarded a 'von' in front of my name, admission to the petty-aristocracy. How my mother, the woodcarver's wife, would be tickled to become Frau von Froberger! How she would boast to the neighbours about her lad's advancement in the world!

I decided to settle for a compromise. Yes, I knew it was weak of me. I went back to the Council and I told them that I had abandoned work on my heads – at which news they promised fulsomely that Jakob Schletterer's professorship would be mine. But what I did not tell them was that I had hidden my collection of heads in the cellar of a Heurigen tavern which I frequented and whose owner was a good friend of mine – at least a man with whom I spent a great deal of money – at least I thought he was a friend of mine.

All seemed to go well for six months or so, though the commissions were perhaps a shade slower coming in than heretofore and certain students didn't turn up at the beginning of the new academic year. My lectures also seemed less well attended than previously, and I noticed the finger-to-temple gesture being employed on those few who were faithful by others who were going in to Stadler's course on Movement in Equestrian Statuary – a series that was apparently the talk of the Academy with students sitting on the steps hours before the lecture was due to begin.

This I must say puzzled me. I could hardly reconcile the sneering, envious Stadler with the kind of near-adulation that he seemed to be getting from the students. (His latest piece, 'Hercules and the Centaur', shown at the Summer Exhibition, scarcely merited it.) And I was, of course, right. Later I discovered that he was paying them to attend.

At the time, however, I own that his apparent popularity was disconcerting even though my mind was still buzzing with ideas about those confounded heads of mine which seemed much more important. I could not take the petty politics of the Academy seriously, nor could I really believe that Stadler's success should be regarded as a threat. Having opted for security, I was finding indeed that it was dull, stale, flat and unprofitable. It was a pattern in my life.

I began to draw heads again. I could not risk using models so I had to be content with my own. I could sit, locked in grimace, for hours in front of the glass while I studied minutely the effect of the contortion upon my features and indeed upon my emotions. For I began to notice that ferocious expressions engendered an echo of combativeness within me, while, equally, attitudes of anxiety and pathos rendered me soft and pliable. A new twist to Lavater's theory!

It was during one of these periods of self-examination that I looked round and observed my manservant staring at me from the doorway with an expression I should have liked to have captured there and then: horrified, incredulous, mouth agape, but with just a trace of malice and cupidity around the eyes.

'Come in,' I said, 'sit down, Konrad. Just keep looking like that.'

'No, no,' he muttered, backing off. 'I'm not staying here. What you gone, loony or somethin'?'

I should have known that he would have run straight to Stadler with some of my drawings he'd picked up. It was Stadler's maid he had been fucking. Stadler had actually put her in Konrad's way. Would you believe that? There was I with my visions of noble simplicity and the discovery of self, and there was Stadler pimping for his maid in order to put himself between me and preferment. It defies imagination, doesn't it? The mind turns to cheese.

The next day my collection of heads was hauled from the Heurigen cellar and presented to the Council of the Academy as evidence of my duplicity. A month later, poor old Schletterer had a heart attack and kicked the bucket. Was I chosen to replace him as I had been promised? Was I buggery!

You can probably guess who got the job. Yes, it was our old friend of the equestrian nobility. He stopped paying students to attend his lectures that very same day, and pretty sick about it they were too.

47

And talking of Hercules, it is Mesmer's contention that the Ancient Greeks did not think as we do. The idea of self had not fully emerged. That is why in their drama they wore masks. Homer, as far as he can tell, and he has been studying the *Iliad*, never speaks of ideas like 'mind', 'thoughts', 'feeling', or indeed 'self' at all. People, to the Greeks, were vessels, ships at the mercy of external forces they called 'the gods' – Love, War, Healing, Wisdom, Hate, Revenge, Orgy . . . They did not feel themselves to be thinking beings, in full control. They were driven by wind and tide, lust and Apollo.

Where did this notion of self come from then? When did the voices of the gods become the prompting of different parts of the beehive? It was then, whenever it was, that self truly began.

I am an image made by myself. I am my own idea. I look in the mirror and I see skin, hair, eyes, teeth. But that is only the most superficial part of the truth. Somewhere juices are gushing, muscles are squeezing, heat is dispersing, hairs are shooting, motions are forming, nails are growing, bowels are gripping; the whole engine is roaring and pouring and puffing and dribbling; and on top of that curious engine sit I, the Operator. Or should I perhaps say, the Co-operator? After all, the engine came before I did. I have only been elected by the sum of the parts.

And when I sleep, I shed my 'I'. And when I have insomnia, I cling on to my 'I'. I sleep not, therefore I am!

In Buddhism, Mesmer tells me, there is a higher state called 'no self'. It begins to seem to me, then, that self is not necessary, may not even exist; that existence is all one; that there is no 'thing' that is conscious, just consciousness itself. That is the Great I Am; what the Jews call God. It is Proportion.

Ouch. That was vicious. I have not shat for five days.

48

I demanded, and obtained by right, my heads which had been left in the Council Chamber like Exhibit A.

As I was collecting them, this fellow with the thick lips, a lecher's face, great big green eyes like plums, stepped up to me in the hallway of the Academy.

'The name is Mesmer, sir,' he lisped. 'Methmer. We met before.'

'I cannot stop now for, as you see, my hands are full.'

'Remarkable work,' he said.

'You are the only one to think so,' I told him.

He padded along beside me, looking at me intently with his plums.

'I have instructions to remove them from the Academy by noon. The Council thinks they may corrupt the youth.'

'I should like to buy some of them,' he told me.

'They are not for sale.'

'Not for sale? You are not interested in money?'

'I am interested in money, but I am more interested in heads. They are my life's work.'

'Your position here will soon be untenable, you know?'

How did the fellow know so much about me? Even then, there was something sinister in those pale plummy eyes, like a frog who has been to the bottom of the well.

'I do not think so,' I said. 'A minor setback. I still have a lectureship and several connections.'

'All the same,' said he, pressing a card on me. 'Just in case you think better of it. Do not hesitate to get in touch. You would be in good company. I commissioned an opera from Mozart, you know. I could really make you someone. I mean, at the moment, when you come to think of it, who are you?'

I turned my back on him and followed the little cart full of my heads home with a curious sense of foreboding. However, I soon perked up for there was a note waiting for me from Baron von Swabing, the Empress's chamberlain, enquiring about my availability for a series of busts for the palace. The Baron von Swabing! A former patron in his own right! I raised two fingers at the boorish academics. The toffs knew what was what.

I was so elated by this turn-up that I sent a message to Johanna, suggesting we go into the country for a picnic on the morrow. I felt quite dizzy with optimism. In fact, I found it necessary to lie down for the rest of the day. I no longer had my manservant, of course, for I had promptly dismissed him on discovering his duplicity; so I could send no one out to investigate the strange sounds and distant wild music that seemed to be coming from the bottom of my neighbour's garden.

In spite of this distraction, however, I at last managed to sleep and woke up next day as optimistic as a child.

'Glorious morning,' I said to my neighbour as I took the air at my front door.

He was a moody old codger with a rather pretty wife.

'What if it is?' said my neighbour, suspiciously, as if I were going to ask him for money. 'She won't do it, d'you hear?'

I had once suggested doing a head of her. I tried another tack.

'Was that you having a gypsy evening last night?' I enquired.

'I wouldn't let her set foot in your studio if you were the Emperor yourself.'

'Surely it was you,' I persisted. 'I thought the strings would wind themselves round my skull. Laughter and talk, talk, talk. You must have been up until all hours. Your wife's birthday, was it?'

'Here,' he said, 'that's enough of that. You leave my wife alone. I know all about you arty buggers.'

Strange, isn't it? As soon as they know you're an artist all they can think of is sex. However, I could've forgiven his reflex response if he hadn't been so evasive about his own revelry.

'Next time, do ask me round,' I told him. 'I enjoy a party even if I was feeling a bit dicky last night. Tell your wife I so much look forward to her sitting on me.'

It was a stupid slip of the tongue. I meant sitting *for* me, of course. I left him gaping like a booby, and went back into the house to prepare for the picnic. It was early June and the wild strawberries in my garden were already ripening, so I picked with a will, filling a whole kerchief full and pausing only when I became aware of Johanna standing beside me.

Johanna was in the full fig of womanhood now. She must have been thirty-two or thirty-three but – possibly because of her strange predilections – there was something unbruised, unused, unbroken about her. She was like one of my riper strawberries that had left the green and white tartness of youth behind, and was now all perfume and sweetness.

I rose and kissed her. She was wearing a white dress with a broad floppy straw hat and a brilliant blue ribbon that exactly matched the colour of her eyes.

She carried a basket and a bucket covered with a cloth, which I took from her, inserted a bottle of wine and my kerchief of strawberries; and then, almost without a word, we set off down the lane, arm in arm like the old friends we were.

I had thought to have taken her to the stream at Heiligenstadt but instead our steps turned upward and we found ourselves on the old Sommerhaidenweg.

We walked for nearly a mile in silence, listening to the birds and the very faintest gossiping of leaves stirred, not so much in the wind as in shiftings of the morning air as the sun played upon it.

There seemed to be no one else about. To the left the wooded ridges dangled bribes of cooling shade to those vigorous enough to ascend. To the right, the great scoop of valley revealed itself in little bursts of tree-fringed perspective: spires and roofs glinting in the sun, a white road, garden fences, vineyards, fields, an old quarry fuzzy with bushes and shrubs . . . In front of us rose upland meadows, more woods, more heights. Behind lay the city, and the river, and the faraway mountains beyond.

We paused at length beside a little tumbling stream that

bounced puppyishly down a miniature ravine, and there, half in sun, half in shade, on a bed of the softest new summer grass, with the valley spread out before us, we stopped and spread out our picnic.

Did I mention that Johanna was a deaf-mute? Indeed it was this that furnished her greatest advantage in my eyes. What I admired about her most, apart from her patience and her beauty, was her infinite gift of expression. Her eyes were like narrative wells; inexhaustible, ever plenishing; or like an animal's, full of grace and instinct, with the secrets of the forest in their depths. Silence lent her mystery, and encouraged a mobility of lip and mouth, forehead and eyelid that spoke more than tongue could ever say.

Sometimes she liked to see me talk to her but now I could tell she was happy enough. Her great eyes shone like carriage-lamps with happiness. I opened the wine and we sipped beneath the rumour of the leaves.

Later, we turned to the food. She had brought a veritable feast: chicken, those little sausages the Viennese love, Hungarian salami, lettuce, baguettes, butter . . . And when we had done justice to that, we turned to my strawberries for which she had thoughtfully provided a little pot of cream.

After lunch, replete, and a little drowsy with wine, we lay back and watched the leaves leaning across to murmur to one another like stage lovers against the brilliant blue backdrop of the sky. I could hardly have felt more indolent, more peaceful. I experienced a sensation of the greatest affection for Johanna; not love, for my affair with the Field Marshal's daughter seemed to have stifled that hot talent in me; but a warm, enveloping tenderness that prompted the most delicate emotions.

It was precisely at this moment that the violins which I had heard the night before in my neighbour's garden suddenly struck up their Magyar keening somewhere further down the hillside. Once more they were accompanied by crass laughter and talk, talk, talk.

To say that I was irritated would be to put it mildly. I was aghast. What appalling luck to be followed to this idyllic spot by hobbledehoys! I looked at Johanna, but she lay there with her eyes closed, a beautiful smile upon her face. It would be unkind, I thought, to disturb her. With her razor-keen senses, however, she knew that my gaze was upon her and she opened her eyes and looked at me. I smiled at her, trying not to show my irritation, and she took off her dress. We were in a discreet spot, hidden from the gaze of any passer-by. Indeed, we had chosen it with just this in mind, for I had brought my sketchbook with the intention of drawing her.

Trying to ignore the distant whining and jabber, I addressed myself to the paper and started to work. She made the most graceful figure, like a ripe dryad, spirit of the wood but more like a Ceres than mere sylph. Her breasts were large and buoyant, the nipples not with that chewed look that older women get, but perky and quickening in the sun. Her blonde hair streamed over one shoulder, so. Her arms were slim as a boy's, and as I watched her she moved her long legs in innocent lust of the afternoon's warmth, while her bush caught the beams, and threw off delicate little prismatic reds, oranges and yellows.

I started to feel a little dizzy again. The music seemed not so much louder as more insistent.

The coarse voices, laughing and jollying, seemed somehow not merry but evil.

I could not explain these sounds; I still cannot. They were a cause but not an excuse for what I did next. I uttered a groan. Something must have alerted Johanna for she made a little movement as if to get up. I leaned over and kissed her passionately on the lips, putting a hand over her breast and caressing her nipple. For a moment she responded. I put my hand between her legs, scattering prisms. She looked wildly, piteously at me. There was no doubt in my mind that she did not wish me to pursue the matter.

114

The violins thrummed in my head with that insistent paprika rhythm; the voices, foul-mouthed, lascivious, cries of old whores and panders, jeering, cheering, egging me on . . .

I pinned her down and rode her like the devil. At the end, I was thousands of miles from where I had started. An evil deed to a friend is an evil deed, indeed. How could I have done such a thing? Was it I who did it? Or the sum of the parts? Have you never done something you're ashamed of? Why did you do it? Are we not in control? Are we ships for gods to blow on? Or are we kings of our ant-hills oppressed on all sides by restive barons and a tumultuous, pleasure-seeking populace?

One tear stood like a carbuncle at the corner of her eye.

As she got up, it started to slide down the side of her nose. She stepped into her dress and turned to me.

The violins and the voices had mysteriously ceased.

'I'm sorry,' I said.

It was totally inadequate.

She smiled at me and put her hand on my shoulder. I gathered up the picnic things and we walked home.

When I think of all the bad things I have done in my life, that was the worst. I shall never forget the expression on her face.

In fact, I started on a head of it that evening.

49

As if to show that evil must be punished – but why does it only seem to apply to me? – fortune now dealt me a series of hard times.

I was once more summoned to the Academy and told by the Vice-Chancellor that, in view of my obdurate behaviour over my 'grotesques' and the fact that my name was now a by-word for indiscipline, I no longer had a position on the teaching staff. Because they did not wish to seem unduly harsh, I could have a small pension (200 florins, as it turned out, not enough to feed a cockroach). I told them to stick it up their bottoms.

As I wandered alone, locked in thought, I began to hear the music again. It seemed singularly inappropriate at eleven o'clock of a weekday morning – a sound more suited indeed to low estaminets down by the river or on the edge of Simmering Heath. La-la-la-lalalalala-laaa. Where could it be coming from? I scanned the windows of the dark little street attentively.

'That's the great Froberger,' I suddenly heard an infinitely coarse fishwife of a voice sneer. 'Great, I don't think.'

La-la-la-lalalalalala-Laaa.

'Great big booby,' another bloated voice chimed in. 'He's all fucked up.'

Hahahahahahaaa.

'Stop it,' I shouted. 'Come out of there. What is the meaning of this?'

One or two windows flew up in the street. A pompous-looking old noddy leaned out.

'What is the matter?' he shouted.

'Gypsy music,' I yelled at him. 'Low women. Sneer-ing.'

'This is a respectable neighbourhood,' he cried back. 'Be off with you or I shall send for the police.'

I walked on, puzzled, the music seeming to keep pace with me from some kind of parallel side-street. I thought it must be some trick of Stadler's to try and drive me mad, hire some strolling players and a couple of foul-mouths and I'd crumble like a Sacher cake. Well, I would show them. I twirled my stick and marched round the corner in a regular tantrum. To my amazement, there was nothing: a mangey dog, a pinafored child with a hoop; and that was all. No sashed moustachioed Magyars, no whores with cock-suckers' mouths, no violins and squeeze-boxes, no leering sneering Stadlers . . .

I investigated to see if there were any new or hidden turnings; still nothing. I could not believe such tangible noises could have so elusive an origin. I turned on my heel and went back to the street whence I'd come, looked up and down again; and after a little walked on.

I had not gone past more than two or three intersections, when I came across the fellow Mesmer hurrying from the direction of the Medical Faculty.

'Ah, Froberger. Changed your mind yet?'

'Not yet, Dr Mesmer.'

'The fellows up there,' he said, pointing at the Faculty, 'can't seem to get it into their noddles that there is more to medicine than leeches, purges and the knife. Last month I restored the gift of sight to a beautiful blind young woman, a pianist called Mademoiselle Paradis, to the satisfaction of her father and Professor Barth, specialist of the eye. And yet the Faculty, obstinately refusing to admit that there might be something to my magnetic treatment, have persuaded her father she would forfeit her pension from the Empress if she ceased to be blind. So for the record she is still sightless. Can you believe that?'

'I can believe anything in Vienna,' I replied.

'Ah,' he said, with a quick look, 'You too have had a bad morning? Come, let us have a drink at a little place I know and you shall tell me about it.'

I liked the man no more than I had previously but I was interested in his talk of the pianist. Perhaps if he could cure the blind he might also be able to do something for the deaf and the mute. In which case, I might cancel out the guilt I felt at my disgraceful conduct of the day before. We sat down over a bottle of wine and I put the question to him.

'It is possible,' he said at length. 'My method, as you

know, is magnetism. All living things are subject to magnetism. Each of us is, in our way, a magnet. Different and opposite poles can be distinguished which can be excited, changed, destroyed or reinforced.'

'But how does that help us?' I asked.

'There exists a reciprocal influence between the heavenly bodies, the earth, and animated bodies,' he continued, as if quoting from a life's work.

I watched him attentively, absorbed as much in the expressiveness of his pop-eyed features as in what he was saying.

'A fluid universally diffused, and so continuous as not to admit of any vacuum – and the subtlety of which does not allow for any comparison – and which by its nature is capable of receiving, propagating, and communicating all impulses – is the vehicle of that influence,' he continued.

'How does it operate? What are its laws?' I asked, having been brought up in the empirical school of woodcarving.

'I cannot tell you. The reciprocal action is governed by mechanical laws at present unknown. All I can tell you with certainty is that alternative effects result from this action, effects which I term flux and reflux. These are more or less general, more or less particular, more or less composite, according to the nature of the causes that determined it.'

'Ah,' I said, not altogether understanding, and hoping he'd get to poor Johanna soon.

'It is by this operation, the most universal of those that Nature presents to us, that active relations are established between the heavenly bodies, the earth, and its constituent parts, right down to the smallest atom. The properties of matter and of all organized bodies depend upon this operation. The animal body experiences the alternating effects of this agent, and it is by insinuating itself into the substance of the nerves that it directly affects them.'

'But hold on,' I said, thinking that I had allowed him to

ride his hobby-horse too far, 'where does this all connect with your magnetic treatment? I have a friend who . . .'

'The property of the animal body,' he intoned, as if nearing the heart of the litany, 'the property which makes it susceptible to the influence of the heavenly bodies and to the reciprocal action of those that surround it, that property has led me, from its analogy with the magnet, to call it Animal Magnetism.'

'Ah,' I said again, hoping that I was appearing receptive if not reciprocal, and pouring more wine. 'Animal Magnetism. I have heard people talk of that. But how does it work?'

'The action and virtue of Animal Magnetism can be communicated to other bodies both animate and inanimate. This flow of a matter whose subtlety penetrates all bodies can take place at a great distance. It is augmented and reflected by mirrors, like light. It is communicated, propagated, and augmented by sound. It can be accumulated, concentrated, and transported . . .'

'Will it cure a deaf-mute?' I blurted at last.

'My system will furnish new ideas about the nature of fire and light, and throw light on the theory of attraction, of the magnet, and of electricity.'

'Yes, but . . .'

'It will show that the magnet and artificial electricity have an effect upon maladies similar to that of several other natural agents.'

'Deafness? . . . Aphasia?'

'This principle will cure immediately all diseases of the nerves and in due course all other diseases. Where is the lady?'

I had not told him the sex of my patient but it was clear that the man, as well as having a bumble-size bee in his bonnet, was a person of considerable intuition.

I told him that she lived not far away.

'Bring her to my house tomorrow,' he said. 'I will cure her within the month.'

He gave me his address and we finished our wine. I was about to get up from the table when he stopped me.

'One thing,' he said. 'About payment . . .'

My heart sank because I knew my funds, already low, would not bear much of a fee. And yet I was in honour bound to pay for her. Somewhere, outside the tavern, that damned music started again. I gripped the table. Mesmer looked at me.

'Something wrong?' he asked.

'That music,' I said. 'I can't stand gypsy violins.'

'Music?' he frowned.

'Please continue,' I said. 'Your payment?'

'Yes, I should like three of your heads.'

That brought me up sharp. He really had me by the balls.

'Three?'

'It's your decision,' he said.

Of course I knew I would have to let him have them some time.

It would be like giving part of myself away.

50

I went round immediately to the house where Johanna lived with her mother. I was agog with the hopes that I had for her condition – for, in some curious way, Mesmer's gobbledegook had convinced me of his powers.

At the same time, I was half afraid of the reception I would get from both her and good old Mrs Mohler. Apart from considerations of nicety, rape was still technically an offence in Vienna – and how particularly offensive to society the ravishing of a deaf mute would seem. How could I explain about the effect of those violins winding round my temples? I could hear the judge now, 'Why, if everyone in Vienna started raping as soon as they heard a gypsy violin, the whole place would grind to a halt,' and he would wink on the word 'grind' because judges love a little joke.

Arriving at the house, I paused for a while to compose myself. Finally, I took the plunge and knocked on the door. A little maid admitted me, and I waited in the hall while the girl went off up the stairs. I heard a door open, and a momentary hubbub of voices break out stilled by the doors. I waited on.

It was dark in the hall, shuttered against the heat of the day. There was a little side-table against the wall with two books upon it which I examined. A novel called *The Casbah* and a tome on Home Economy entitled *Curious Ways with Fruit*. Beside them, there was a Venetian fan, a little silver bowl full of comfits and a silver tray with a visiting card on it. The name it bore was Doctor Ingenhaus with an address in the Herrengasse.

Heavens! There was a doctor here already. He had doubtless been called to attend the tormented girl. How my heart filled with self-hatred and yes, fear! It was too late for me to break in upon the scene with my hopes for an unconventional deaf cure. Her problem was evidently more immediate. She had doubtless had a profound delayed shock. Perhaps she was even dying. I twirled my stick in agitation and it fell to the floor with a clatter. As if at this signal, I heard the door open again upstairs. I hung my head in shame, waiting for the worst, noting my expression in the mirror which was somewhere between woebegone and hangdog. It was too late to advance, too late to fly.

Feet came hurriedly down the stairs. I did not dare to look.

'Oh, Mr Froberger, it's you. I'm so glad you've come . . .'

It was Mrs Mohler. But what was this? No recriminations, no beating at the bosom, no scorn and fury, no Sturm and Drang.

'Glad?' I ventured, not daring to hope.

'It's a miracle,' she cried. 'A miracle.'

'What is a miracle, Mrs Mohler?'

I did think it was a miracle, knowing my tendency to duck and weave, that I should have turned up at all.

'Johanna, of course.'

'Ah, Johanna,' I said. 'What about Johanna?'

'She can speak, Mr Froberger. She can hear.'

And she flung herself into my arms and kissed me fulsomely.

'Speak?' I faltered.

'It was your idea, wasn't it?' she asked, drying her eyes.

'My idea?'

'To give her a shock. To surprise her. Confess, you surprised her.'

'I did surprise her.'

'You shocked her.'

'I'm afraid I did.'

'Don't be afraid. Whatever it was you did – Johanna wouldn't say – but whatever it was you did, it worked. She woke up this morning and she could speak, she could hear! The doctor has just been examining her. He says it's all true. Oh, my little girl . . .'

While I waited patiently for Mrs Mohler to finish with my shirtfront, I was experiencing the most profound readjustments. I had arrived with mingled hope and fear, I had tasted despair, and now I seemed to be a hero. What fresh volte-face had the afternoon in store for me? I was soon to learn. An ugly cracked little voice called me from above.

'Come here, you wicked man.'

I looked up. It was Johanna smiling down at me, archly, crooking her finger with a possessiveness I did not at all like the look of. At the same time, it was undeniably an expression I should have to commit to paper. It reminded me of a Hogarth engraving I had seen somewhere.

'Johanna!' exclaimed her mother, pretending to be shocked.

'Franz doesn't mind, do you, Franz?'

I walked up towards her, holding the bannisters. That giddy feeling was back. Was that a hurdy-gurdy out in the street?

'So you're the lucky man?' said the beaming little old fellow who I took to be Dr Ingenhaus, bounding out of the bedroom. 'The most remarkable recovery I've come across in all my days. How did you do it, sir?'

'Come on, Franz, show him,' called Johanna.

She sounded exactly like those voices I'd heard in the street. It was a travesty. My lovely, graceful, statue-girl with a voice like a tart on a windy night.

'I . . . don't think it's . . .!' I floundered.

'Never mind, my boy, never mind. It's not how it happened that matters. Let us all rejoice that it *did* happen. I hear you are to be married?'

I saw a quick look pass between mother and daughter. The gift of speech seemed to have debased the girl utterly.

I swallowed.

'It is true, sir, there was talk of . . . No, that was wrong . . . there was an understanding between us, but alas I have just lost my post at the Academy and . . .'

Again, the look between mother and daughter.

'He has a lovely little house,' said the mother.

'Well, congratulations to you both,' said the doctor. 'A happy day indeed.'

I had to clutch at a chair and sit down.

'He's overcome with emotion,' said the doctor. 'A manly symptom.'

'Could somebody please send the hurdy-gurdy away?'

51

When I finally got away from the house, the sun had wandered well to the west and the inns were already plying their evening trade. All the world seemed merry except me. My sleeping beauty had woken up to hoydenhood, there were unequivocal designs upon my bachelor status (and a sort of veiled threat that I detected in Johanna's eyes if I tried to wriggle out), my job had gone, and – most of all – I realized that I must be ill.

There had been no hurdy-gurdy man in the street – this had been demonstrated to me by the doctor – and now, I realized, no gypsy violins and raucous voices on all those other occasions. I was feeling giddy too often for coincidence. And there was a constriction about my forehead that was more than a passing headache.

Lying down in my room that evening, too tired to eat or sleep or even to work – my usual solace – I resolved to go to Mesmer on the morrow in place of the patient I had been proposing to send him.

I forgot altogether about – I know this must seem strange to those for whom a royal commission might appear to be like a summoning to God, but perhaps you never met the Hapsburgs? – I forgot altogether about the note from the Empress's chamberlain. I had, as you see, a number of other things on my mind. Sorry.

52

Next morning, I woke unrefreshed but I stirred myself to pack up three of what I considered to be my dullest heads in a wooden crate. And later I sent them round, with a pang, to Mesmer's house. Even my dull ones left a horrid gap in my family of faces. However, I persuaded myself it was all in a good cause, and at the appointed hour I presented my person at the house in the Singerstrasse.

A flunkey opened the door and led me into a spacious hall where I was shown a seat, and left for ten minutes in a state of some confusion. Would Mesmer after all treat me if he were expecting a young lady? What manner of treatment was this anyhow? I had heard rumours of convulsions.

Finally, just as I had almost determined to go home and ask for my faces back forthwith, the flunkey returned.

'Dr Mesmer will see you now.'

He showed me into a small study where Mesmer was seated behind a desk.

'Ah, Froberger.'

He stood up, extended his hand, and indicated a chair. I sat. We looked at each other. He was wearing a strange silken robe that made him look like a eunuch, though that was by no means his reputation.

'The young person is better, I understand,' he said at length.

'Yes.'

'A miraculous cure.'

'Indeed.'

How the devil did he know? It seemed he had the trick of omniscience!

'A jolt sometimes restores due proportion to the animal

magnet,' he said. 'It is a dangerous game but it can work. And now you have come in her place?'

'I have been feeling giddy at times. And there have been sounds which . . . I cannot account for . . .'

Ordinary doctors, I knew, would scoff at such fancies.

'Sounds.'

It was not a question. He knew about the sounds, I could swear it.

'Gypsy violins . . . coarse voices . . . a hurdy-gurdy . . .'

'All these are sounds that one hears in Vienna. Annoying though they may be, they are scarcely indicative of sickness.'

'I hear them when there is no one there to make them,' I told him. 'I have witnesses to their absence. These sounds are in my head . . .'

'Or you are picking them up from the ether . . . ?'

'Either way, I do not want them. They seem to me to have a troublesome, a menacing quality. The voices have addressed themselves to me directly in a most uncomplimentary manner. I believe I may be going mad. Make me not mad, sweet Heaven.'

'I am glad you have the comforts of literature as well as your art,' said Mesmer. 'And now you shall have the comfort of magnetism. You are not going mad. You are simply out of proportion. Flux and reflux, Froberger. I should like you to take off your garments and wear the shift which you will find behind the screen. I have others also waiting to be treated. You will not mind company?'

This was something I had not bargained for.

'I am something of a public figure,' I said. 'My statues are in the Imperial collection. I hope there will be no goggling.'

'No goggling, I assure you,' replied Mesmer. 'And no giggling either. My patients are all too busy with their own problems. But I commend a little goggling on your own account. There is a veritable feast of expressions in the Baquet Room. You may change while we talk.'

He waved me towards the screen, and I began to undress.

'What is the Baquet Room?' I enquired as I struggled out of my shirt.

'The baquet is a device of my invention,' he replied. 'It contrives to stimulate the flow of magnetism and electricity to specific areas of the body. The baquet is basically a small iron bath full of magnetized water in which I place a number of bottles, also full of such water, well corked up and disposed in radii with their necks outward. Into the water, I throw filings of iron to heighten the magnetic effect. The vessel is then closed with an iron cover, pierced through with many holes, from each of which a long, movable rod of iron protrudes. It is one – or perhaps two – of these rods that you must apply to your afflicted parts. My other patients will be doing the same.'

'But what is my afflicted part?' I asked, clambering into the cotton shift and feeling like a ninny.

'Your head is your afflicted part, Froberger,' he advised, taking my arm and leading me to the door. 'Haven't you got that into your head yet? It is your greatest source of strength and inspiration, and yet, you see, there is an imbalance. But have courage, for this is a disease of the nerves which, more than any other class of afflictions, can be alleviated immediately. There may be a stage of crises or convulsions but it is natural and not to be feared.'

He now propelled me along a passage at the end of which he opened a door into a long, well-proportioned chamber at the back of the house. This I guessed must have been built out into the garden for it was extensive.

A sound of music and singing emanated from within, and as I listened, I was able to distinguish a fine female voice singing an aria which I recognized as being from Mozart's little pastoral opera *Bastien and Bastienne*.

'Yes,' he said, reading my thoughts, 'I commissioned it from Mozart myself. He already fulfils the highest demands of the laws of art but delights the simplest understanding. Even cows milk better, I have it on authority, when Mozart is played. His music is the ideal communicator and stimulator of the universal fluid. I recognized that in him immediately. You too have something of his quality in your art. I collect genius.'

'Oh, really? If you say so,' I said weakly, feeling a fool in my shift as I caught sight of several rows of other people sitting or reclining around a vessel in the middle of the room from which stuck a number of iron bars, the effect being rather that of a sparsely prickled porcupine.

'No more talking now,' enjoined Mesmer, urging me forward with a hand of iron on my shoulder. 'The rule is strict silence here.'

I advanced towards the baquet where, I could see, a couple of rods had been reserved for me, and allowed my gaze to wander, as Mesmer had suggested, across the ranks of my fellow sufferers.

There were, I suppose, about twenty persons present, roughly ten of each sex, old and young. Some were obviously lame, others twitched, others still had partial or even total paralysis. There was a child with a wobbling head, a man with the most dreadful psoriasis, and a girl who seemed to be in an appalling state of fear. It was like coming across something out of the New Testament.

All these people were arranged around the baquet. Those that could hold the rods were gripping them for all they were worth; others too feeble had cords round their bodies connecting them to the magnetism of their neighbours. Meanwhile the forte piano played and the voice warbled behind a screen, diffusing the magnetism in the air, while mirrors on either side of the room concentrated magnetism upon the sufferers. Placed judiciously round the walls, on special plinths, were already my three heads – whether as decoration or magnetic auxiliaries I could not establish.

Various men, also in silk shirts, moved about the chamber, making slow cryptic passes with an iron wand before the faces of the patients and then laying hands on their diseased parts (or what I imagined them to be) but always, it seemed, observing the position of the baquet's holes, which every now and then they would stop and fix their eyes upon. Then back they would go, finger and wand; before the face, above the face, back and forth; and then the pressure of the fingers upon the head, the lungs, and over the regions of the abdomen . . . and so on . . .

I let my head be advanced towards the rods as Mesmer guided my hands to hold them in place. I had a good vantage point at the further end of the baquet so that I could continue to see all that went on. I felt, or I thought I felt, a kind of tingling that passed into me where the rods touched my temples. I was now left for the best part of two hours.

Meanwhile my fellow sufferers, in their different conditions, presented a very varied picture. Some were calm, tranquil and seemed to experience no effect. Others coughed, spat, appeared to feel slight pains, and sweated. Others again, while I watched, became agitated and even tormented with tremors, spasms and convulsions.

These convulsions seemed to affect at different times at least half the people present, and were remarkable for their force and duration. One young lady seemed to go into an extreme rictus, followed by frothing and foaming until she had a white beard like the effigy of Saint Nicholas at Würzburg, and then the most violent flailing, kicking, spitting, and bounding for a full hour before she fell back into a state of almost boneless languor. Others prefaced their convulsions with a kind of depressed reverie or drowsiness. With others still, this was the concluding phase of the crisis. I noticed indeed that there was a door marked 'Salle de Crise' into which those were carried who seemed about to do injury to themselves or their neighbours.

What struck me most about the whole affair was the

power of Mesmer and his assistants, the Magnetisers, to induce a crisis. No matter in what state of drowsiness the patients were, the sound of a voice, a look, a motion of the hand, was enough to bring them out of it. It was also their skill, at the last, to bring their tempest-tossed charges safely back to harbour.

As I lay with my rods, watching the room, and drowsing, and reflecting upon these matters, and listening to the musicians, and peeking at my heads whose grimaces seemed to accord most fittingly with the activities being carried on below, I was suddenly aware of the approach of Mesmer. He had a short iron stick in his hand which he began to wave about rhythmically in front of my face. I felt the most delicious softness in my bones as though, if I had stood up, I should have tumbled to the floor and melted like a junket. Indeed, I found now that I could not speak or move. Not that I wanted to! My only desire was to rest.

I remember thinking what a pity it was that we sculptors cannot faithfully convey the eyes in our work, for Mesmer's were eyes that cried out for some kind of rendition. Have I said they were green plummy? They now seemed to have the most brilliant mineral quality to them and to shine like steel, shooting out sparks like a tinder-box, and starting to light bonfires of all the detritus within me. At this point he put his hand upon my forehead.

The effect upon me was, literally, electrifying. A great bright light not of pain, but of power or force shot through me. It was painful but it was not pain. I flapped about madly like a loose sail in a high wind, and yet I was not aware that I was making my body do anything at all. The effort was purely reflexive: or indeed quite possibly refluxive.

Two men came and picked me up and took me into the Salle de Crise. There I was strapped to a bed while my paroxysm showed no sign of abating. I was told later that I cried out, begging them to shoot me, to put me out of my misery. I swore hideously at Mesmer. He meanwhile sat calmly by my bed as I bucketed about, holding my hand and occasionally sipping a little water, doubtless magnetized.

It was strange that I was both conscious of all this and, at the same time, somewhere else, somewhere that I can only give you the most tenuous description of because it was like no place and therefore no terms of description could do it justice. It was perhaps more like a limbo, for it seemed to contain parts but no whole, it was like being chopped like a carrot into a soup pot, and each bit wondering where the rest of me was. It was a place without faces but full of sliced wills. It was like being drawn into a great engine that needed me more than I needed it. Indeed the thought crossed my mind that I wasn't so much being cured as that my disorder was feeding something. It was like one's worst vision of an after-life. Suddenly, when I thought I could bear it no more, Mesmer let go of my hand and held my foot.

On the instant, my paroxysm started to subside. And then, when I had quietened, he took my hand again and I was off once more, flapping and swearing and crying for mercy.

After enduring this alternative magnetism and demagnetism for a further hour, Mesmer at length desisted. I had a brief sleep, was woken with a glass of hot water, and directed towards the room where I had left my clothes.

When I had dressed, Mesmer appeared again.

'You are cured,' said he, 'at least for the moment. You will inevitably have relapses and you must come to me again. How do you feel?'

'I feel rearranged,' I replied.

It was a curious thing to say, but that was exactly how I did feel. I felt sound in the head and light in the foot. And yet I felt that something might have been taken from me that I needed. Or that I had given something that in some way I could not afford. Cured or not, I resolved to see Mesmer no more.

As I left, I saw him go to a small boy who was sitting in

the hall, and hold him by both ears. I followed, concerned for the little fellow.

'What is the matter with you, little boy?' I enquired.

'Six weeks ago,' the child replied, 'I lost my hearing in a great wind. This gentleman is giving it back to me again.'

53

I walked home thoughtfully, unaccompanied by violins. When I arrived at the house, the first thing I saw, of course, staring at me in the face, was the card from the Empress's chamberlain instructing me to visit the palace forthwith with a view to an 'important commission'. It was dated three days ago. A three day delay was tantamount to lèse-majesté. But it was too late to do anything about it today, and I scurried around instead trying to find dapper clothes and a clean shirt; everything had gone to pieces in the absence of my manservant who, while being the most disloyal of knaves, was in many other respects a non-pareil and a wonder with the linen.

I suddenly realized I had not eaten all day. There was no food in the house. I would have to go out to a tavern. I discovered I had no ready money. However, I shifted as best I could, obtained credit from an innkeeper I knew, and after a bottle or so of wine and a plate of sausages, returned home in rather better humour. It was then that I discovered a second note which, because no one had answered the door, had been slipped through and had lain unnoticed half underneath my stick-stand.

It was a letter from my bankers advising me that my balance was minus 100 florins and would I be so kind as to call in and see them at my earliest convenience.

What had I done, I asked myself, to deserve such a con-catenation of ill fortune? I should have to lick polish off their shoes at the palace tomorrow to try and stop that commission going elsewhere.

54

There, I have put the Egyptian out. I would have broken him if I could – but destroy such a work? It would be like destroying the square on the hypotenuse.

Even so, I feel better already now I know he is safe in the workshed. Let him brood at the logs.

Johanna came in with some kind of earthenware as I sat at the looking-glass, pulling faces, unable to work.

'Oo,' she said. 'Franz Xaver, don't do that. The wind might change. You look like a regular gargoyle. I brought you some goulash. Look, your favourite, with dumplings.'

I cannot abide dumplings and she knows it. It is not the dumplings themselves. They are harmless enough. Little globules of flour and water swimming in orange grease. All right if you like that sort of thing. No. It is the word dumplings I cannot stand. It makes me squirm.

'Take them away,' I said. 'I cannot eat those words.'

She took no notice, and looked around disgustedly.

'This place is a pigsty,' she said. 'You ought to let me clean up a bit.'

'Bestiality,' I informed her, 'is a state crime punishable by castration.'

She gaped interestingly.

'If this is a pigsty, I am the pig. You have made love to me. Therefore you have been pleasured by a pig. Quod erat fornicandum. There was a lady loved a swine; honey, said she; honey love, wilt thou be mine? Hunc, said he.'

'Hunk,' she said, unbuttoning her blouse. 'Let's get on with it, then. I don't like such talk.'

'Leave me,' I told her. 'I cannot think with all these breasts flying around.'

'I've had enough of your faddiness. Eat up like a good boy.'

She lay down and spooned some lukewarm stew on to her bare belly. I knelt down, enjoying the loathsome indecorum. Even the beasts would not so intertwine two of life's greatest urges. I wondered whether some new expression might not be gleaned from the situation, and contrived to jiggle my mirror across.

I made a good dinner, though the meat was inclined to be chewy.

There is a kind of madness in carnality. Even the anatomist Parsons had not depicted such a grimace.

Many were the days when Johanna and I wallowed at the trough. I had never known such a foul delight. We were all ooze.

Later, I called Johanna, and she had gone.

I had not noticed her go. She had taken everything with her – goulash, dumplings, breasts, bill of hair – it was as if she had never been.

It wasn't even her day, now I thought about it. What could she mean by coming when it wasn't her day, and then going again as if she had never been, leaving a taste of gravy in my mouth?

Today in Parliament, the Prime Minister being taken ill, Herr von Penis, Privy Councillor, was sworn in as Leader of the Government during the crisis.

55

I cannot work without the Egyptian. It is like hopeless love. I cannot live with him. I cannot live without him. There is a god as well as a devil there.

This muck, this filth, this sewerage simply will not do. Proportion does not lie this way. Put a girdle across the lips. There. They are stopped.

I have now put him back in the corner where I can see him as I embark upon Face No. 47, The Panting Satyr.

I have noticed before that every time I put a new expression down, from the gamut of expression of which I am capable, I get the sensation that I am losing my face.

It is he who is causing the pains. That I am sure of.

56

I presented myself next day at the Schönbrunn Palace by the tradesman's door, as usual. This is where the nuisances, the minor petitioners, and the artists come; Mr Haydn and Mr Bellotto, Mr Mozart and Mr Blumauer, Mr Paisiello and Miss Storace; along with Mr Bootmaker, Mr Tailor, and Mr Master of the Royal Shithouse; one door up from the servants and one door down from the petty gentry who'd get their 'von' for squeezing a Minister's blackhead.

The first person I spoke to was Baron Schreiber, one of the Assistant Comptrollers, who I knew as a complete dead loss.

He looked at my card for some time as if hoping to spot a printing error.

'Ho, hum,' he said at length.

Then he stopped and thought about it for a while.

'Froberger,' I said when the silence seemed to be getting embarrassing.

This jolted him into action.

'Ah, yes, Froberger. Froberger. That isn't a Viennese name.'

'No,' I replied patiently, 'I have lived here for sixteen years, but I originally came from Wisensteig.'

'Well, well, well,' he said, pouting his little cherry lips and wobbling his white thighs. 'I'm not sure you should be here at all. There is quite a groundswell here, quite a groundswell, that says we should encourage our own native artists. You say you are not a native artist?'

'No. I came from Bavaria originally.'

'Well, my dear fellow . . .' he paused while he took some snuff, and sneezed and mopped himself with a yellowed handkerchief. '. . . Bavaria, you say?'

'Yes, Baron.'

'Well, my dear fellow,' he exclaimed triumphantly, 'you should go back there.'

'But, Baron, I have a request from the Empress. She is interested in my availability for a commission. See, here it is.'

'From the Empress? Are you sure?'

He again inspected the card I gave him as though it were the most dangerous kind of subversion.

'It appears genuine,' he agreed, at length.

'I assure you it is genuine. Now, may I be permitted to have an audience with Her Majesty?'

'Her Imperial Majesty,' he reproved me. 'Just because you're a foreigner doesn't mean you should forget your manners.'

I learned later that he had obtained his barony by selling cheese to the Court at a small discount. I swallowed hard, glad at least that I'd had my session with Mesmer the day before. Those gypsy violins would have been fiddling away like the devil's consensus by now.

'I would like to see the Empress. Her Imperial Majesty has expressed a desire to see me. I have four busts in the Imperial Collection already. I am sure that she would not like to be kept waiting.'

This last remark of mine was a mistake. It played right into his hands.

'Ah,' he said, giving that cunning little smile of the really stupid when they think they're being clever, 'but you have kept her waiting, haven't you? This Imperial note was sent to you four days ago. Why have you not answered it before?'

Of course, I had thought that this charge might be levelled against me, and I had an answer. I had considered merely saying that I had been away. But one never quite knew in Vienna if one had been seen, or overseen, and I did not wish to be caught out in a lie. I had even contemplated the possibility of saying that I had been ill, but I thought it might predispose the Empress against giving me the work if she thought I was going to make a practice of infirmity. (It was said that she had a horror of disease.) Instead I simply said that I had been working night and day to finish an existing commission on time so that I could the better give my whole attention to the Imperial undertaking.

It was clear that he did not believe a word I was saying, for he rolled his little lips up into a shape that resembled a dog's arse, and left the anteroom with a 'Hmph'.

I meanwhile composed myself for a meeting with the old girl. Contrary to some popular opinion, she wasn't a bad old trout – somewhat inclined to believe that the sun shone out of her bottom – but you do if everyone tells you so all the time. Apart from that, she had a good idea about, and a liking for, solid, middle-of-the-road, baroque statuary with not too much pomposity about it – stuff that I could do standing on my head and let 'noble simplicity' go twiddle its fingers for a while.

Finally, the Cheese Baron returned. His face was a picture which I should have been proud to have executed. On the one hand there was disappointment, probably that he could not prevent me from seeing the Empress. On the other, there was something that looked rather like satisfaction.

In the first part, at my rate, I was right.

'The Empress will grant you an audience,' he said, and motioned me to follow him.

We passed through a couple of double doors and ended in a pleasant well-proportioned room, looking out on to the park, which seemed to serve as some kind of study. I had not visited the Empress here before. She looked up, as we entered, from where she was seated at her desk.

'The sculptor Froberger, your Imperial Majesty!' intoned the Fromage, bowing like a ripe Camembert.

'Thank you, Baron. You may leave us.'

His Cheesiness was clearly rather irked at being invited to go, but he did as he was instructed. The doors closed.

'Mr Froberger,' said the Empress. 'The Baron has explained why you were inconsiderate enough to keep us waiting for a reply.'

'Inconsiderate is not the word I would use, Madame.'

'Silence. Do you bandy words with me?'

I could see there was not to be a revival of the old 'bien aise' which had characterized our earlier conjunctions.

'I apologize, Madame.'

'I would hope so. I am disappointed in you, Mr Froberger. You showed great promise. We gave you great work to do for us. You could have risen to the highest rank among our artists. I was even about to give you the greatest of all commissions you have had so far . . .

I did not like this use of the past tense.

'You *were* about to give, Madame?'

'Certainly, until I heard things . . .'

138

'Things?'

'Things I would rather not repeat.'

'What things, Madame? I cannot defend myself if I do not know the charge.'

'Very well, then. It is said that you are becoming disreputable, that your work has changed out of all proportion, that you are at work on grotesques which link you to revolutionaries and diabolists, that you are a consort of Dr Mesmer, that you ravished a deaf-mute, and that I am obsessed with a shameful love for you. Even if half of this were true, it would present an insurmountable impediment to any future commission. You see that, do you not?'

'Well, Madame . . .'

'Well? Is even half of it true?'

Some of it was, some of it wasn't. As for the last item in her litany of my crimes, I could hardly ask her for authentication. I wasn't even sure that she had said it, or whether it hadn't been a quirk of the infinitely subtle fluid that permeates all. If I was beginning to have doubts like these, it meant that Mesmer's cure was not yet fully effective. He had intimated as much. I should have to return for another paroxysm.

'I am waiting, Mr Froberger.'

There was nothing I could say.

'Your silence proclaims your guilt, Mr Froberger. I am sorry, for I have been the most constant of your patrons. But in the teeth of this obdurate behaviour, I shall have to take off my dress.'

There it was again. Mesmer, what had you done?

'No,' I cried.

'No?' she queried, her cheeks showing a degree of colour. 'Is this what it has come to? Leave Vienna and return whence you came as soon as possible. You are no longer persona grata here.'

She rang a little bell and Lord Gruyère ushered me out. As we passed through, I noticed Stadler waiting in the vestibule. He slowly lifted his finger and applied it to his temple with a boring motion.

57

Before I left Vienna, I had of course to honour my undertaking to Mesmer that I would do a head for him. It was not simply a matter of honour. That counts for little in Vienna. It was a matter of money, for he had agreed to pay me cash rather than offset the portrait against my further magnetic treatment as he had at first suggested.

I entered his house again, full of misgiving for there was something about the man which, while it might heal, could also injure.

'Ah, there you are, Froberger,' he said, extending a magnetic hand, 'zinc, I think.'

He had mentioned zinc before, though I favoured bronze, for zinc is a soft deceitful metal which, liquefied, gives off a hellish fume which can poison the lungs and even melt the brain. I had, of course, mastered the art of casting in this dragon metal, but I was not anxious to use it simply on what I took to be his whim.

He insisted, however, upon zinc, just as he selected a place in the curiously draped chamber into which he led me – I learned later it was used for certain rituals – though it was customary for even my most illustrious sitters to ask where I should like them positioned.

Not a bit of it for Mesmer.

'I shall sit here,' he announced, fixing me with those curious underwater eyes of his.

'As you wish, Mesmer,' I said as carelessly as I could, but inwardly my heart was sinking.

While I got out my things, and started to sketch a first

draft of his head, I received strongly an impression that it was I who was sitting for him, and that my self was being sucked out of me as for my own portrait.

Be that as it might be, the place he had selected was admirable, the chair or throne framed with silver drapes which threw both light and a mirror-like sense of dimension upon the subject, the fold upon fold of reflection almost like a mist into which one could pass into strange countries . . .

'You can begin now, Froberger,' he said.

I can give no very direct account of the sittings for they seemed to slide by almost as if I had been dreaming. Indeed I sometimes found myself ending sentences with no clear idea of where they had started, and would rub my eyes and apologize as if I had been sleeping.

I also received the impression, at other times, that Mesmer had left his body in the chair, and had simply gone off on other business.

I feared, in short, that the head would prove but a poor thing, that I had not concentrated sufficiently upon it; and I could hardly believe at the last, when it emerged from the grog – I could see through all the octopus tangle of runners and risers – that it was, as it turned out to be, a triumph. I had made him a veritable Prospero.

Like him or not – and I did not – there were strange arts in the man; and the money helped pay off certain creditors who would otherwise have been an embarrassment.

At least I could leave Vienna as I had entered it, with my slate clean.

58

I sold my house in the grape-hung suburb – it was a bad time to sell but it would be, wouldn't it? – paid off my debts, squared up my accounts, dodged Johanna and her mother, and shook the dust of Vienna from my feet. (To be honest, I believe the Mohler family would have been much more adhesive had Johanna not been so busy making up for lost speech. A woman without a tongue is like a dog with three legs.)

There were few to whom I felt obliged to say goodbye and most of those – I could tell – were relieved to see me go. Only two poor students of mine seemed distressed. Michael Straub and Anton Waldner had been coming to my house for two years for instruction in the arts of drawing, modelling and casting. I used to let them prepare the plaster of Paris, heat the lead, and do useful jobs around the studio, fetching supplies, keeping the fire going in winter, making the sandwiches, buying the wine – menial tasks which they performed diligently in return for lessons in anatomy, physiognomy, composition, proportion and whatever else I could impart – including, of course, the exercises of Le Brun.

Their appearance at my house was irregular for I believe they found work, when it was available, at a variety of odd jobs to provide the rent for the garret they shared while they attended the restorers' course at the Academy.

They were the best of friends – which was odd, for while Michael had the makings of a great talent, Anton was at best derivative. However, I chivvied them along as equally as I could, for it is none of art's business to come between friends.

They could hardly have provided a greater contrast in their appearance either, for Michael was slight, dark and quick as a trout, while Anton was a big blond lad from the mountains, only losing his expression of utmost good nature when he was wrestling with a problem of technique – at which point he would frown massively and stick his tongue out as he worked like a booby.

These two, it had been, who helped me cast my newest heads – which, I liked to think, bore as much relation to the standard exercises as Bach's Chromatic Fantasia does to a set of arpeggios.

Michael was, of course, much the more excited with my new work because he could see in it horizons that he might one day himself explore, but it gave poor Anton what he called the heebie-jeebies.

Once, going into my little gallery next to the studio to fetch something while we sat in the darkening garden, he gave a loud exclamation and dropped his candlestick.

'What is it, Anton?' we cried.

There was silence.

We got up and hurried into the gallery, almost running into the bulk of poor Anton as he backed out from the shadows shaking his head in disbelief.

'What is it?' we repeated.

'As I went in, I heard this noise, it was like low voices but I couldn't hear what was being said, and I thought that's funny, and I held my candle up, and then that head at the end, it turned its head and looked at me. It sort of winked at me, if you take my meaning.'

We looked at Anton. We went back into the gallery and lit the candle. Everything was just as it had been. Anton scratched his head. The head in question grimaced innocently at the wall.

'Well, that's darn funny!' said Anton.

'Yes, the wine is rather strong,' I agreed.

Michael and I laughed. Only poor Anton looked puzzled still. He wouldn't go into the gallery again after dark. They're a superstitious lot in the mountains.

Funny about him hearing the voice, though. I'd forgotten about that till I mentioned it.

Anyway, young Michael and Anton were gratifyingly distraught to see me go, and I must say I was sorry to say goodbye to them. There is a freshness in the young that, after a day full of hierarchy, and jaded politics, is like a walk under the trees.

'We shall meet again, I dare say,' I told them.

'Where are you going?'

'Back to Wisensteig. It is not far from Munich. I was born there, you know. My mother lives there still.'

'It is expensive to travel,' Anton said, 'but we shall save up and come and visit you.'

'Meanwhile, what shall we do for lessons?' asked Michael.

'You could try old Donner – only I think he may be dead. Or there is always Stadler if you're keen on horses.'

'Stadler! He charges 10 florins a lesson,' said Anton.

'And *he'd* be learning from *us*,' said Michael.

I gave them a few more names, more in helpfulness than optimism, and we left it at that.

It was somehow helpful, as I departed, to know that not everybody in Vienna had been mesmerized.

59

Eyes have always been a stumbling-block for the sculptor. What could be more dead-looking than those blank, smooth lozenges of stone or bronze that lie in the sockets of our statuary?

There they stand, our great men, noble of feature, grave

of expression, and yet so hopelessly vacant as they stare out at us through the pigeon-droppings.

But would it be better if we gave them simulated irises, glass eyes balanced finely and harnessed together so that they swivelled in the breeze, fixing the passer-by with a gaze both magnanimous and coincidental?

Certainly it would be more lifelike, but the effect would be grotesque for it would be particular. By that token, if we swivelled the eye, the cheeks should blush, the brow should ripple, the lips should move and the hair should ruffle in the gale. We should need necromancy not art to make statues, a spell like that cast in *The Winter's Tale* when the statue is warm to the King's kiss.

> . . . If this be magic
> Let it be an art lawful as eating . . .

You remember the passage? Not a dry eye in the house.

But sculpture is not about recreating life. If it were we should indeed be in a pickle, for nothing is more alive in a living face than those two gaps which show us the brain between the bone.

When we think of those we love, we think of eyes. Literature is full of them. You cannot describe someone without reference to eyes. Look at Homer with his ox-eyed Hera. Stadler has little narrow piggy eyes, a description Homer himself could not have improved upon. My darling Johanna's eyes sparkle. Your darling's eyes are violet ringed with indigo. April is in my mistress's face, and July in her eyes hath place.

So what is sculpture about? It is an evocation, an essay, a memorial, a tribute; but it is not a resurrection; not, that is, until we understand the true and perfect nature of Proportion; and then who is to say what is, or may not be?

145

60

My mother was underjoyed to see me.

'What?' she exclaimed. 'Back so soon and without a "von" to your name?'

She did not mean it unkindly, but she had her own life – she had moved back to Wisensteig from Munich only a year or so before – and she had been rapidly sucked into a busy little whirl of cakes and coffee and former friends and charming new acquaintances.

She had, of course, boasted as mothers do about how well her son was doing, how he was going to be a professor, how he was getting all these Imperial commissions. And now here he was without a handle to his name and hardly a penny to his pocket. I could see that it made her look rather silly but there really was not very much I could do about it.

'I'm sorry, Mother,' I said. 'Things just didn't work out.'

'Not work out? But they had been working out so well. Don't tell me you went and got into one of your silly moods, and threw the baby out with the bathwater. And what in heaven's name is that?'

She was staring at one of my heads that I was unpacking; the Guilty Sinner, it was.

'My head?'

'Not your head. That horror.'

'That's one of the damned,' I told her. 'You like it? It's lively, isn't it?'

'Take it away.'

'What?'

'Take it out of my house. It's horrible . . . disgusting. Is that what you've been doing? I'm not surprised they wanted you to leave.'

Though saddened by her censure, I was not altogether surprised. In art my mother inclined more towards the cosily ethereal: buttocky little cherubs and simpering virgins.

I could understand that my tormented souls might be rather strong meat for her.

'Where shall I put them, then, Mother?'

'Melt them down into a cross and pray aloud for forgiveness.'

'I can't do that, Mother. They're my work, don't you understand? They are actually astonishingly, wonderfully good, Mother. They're so good I don't want to sell them. They are me.'

'Ugh,' was all she could say.

At least it provided me with an opportunity of renting a studio to work in – if not to live. I found one, curiously enough, right next door to my old grandfather Johann Georg Straub's workshop. And so the wheel had come full circle, and the chip had come back to the block.

61

It is strange to return to the town of one's childhood after a long interval. The hope, the possibility of happiness, the memory of the child's-eye-view of each day still lingers in the air. It is like a smoke that one sniffs at street corners. And now, as I write, as I reach nearer to the secrets of Proportion – which I am forbidden to see – as I bring the fire down from Heaven or wherever it is kept – the memory of that irrational, infantile, hopeful happiness, strong as a seedling, returns to uplift and at the same time to fill me with sad longings.

My stay in Wisensteig was not an altogether happy one. It pains me to have to confess it, for I had great affection for my mother who was by no means as silly as she made herself out to be. But my love for her was best expressed at a distance. When I had been in Vienna, I wrote to her regularly but now, somehow, our communication dried up. To be honest, I think she was worried about me, which made me nervous. Frankly, I was worried about myself. All I wanted to do was to continue with my heads, but I had to live. Besides I was now thirty-nine. I was in my prime. My career couldn't simply stop.

Then one day I chanced to meet a local bigwig whom I had known passingly in Vienna – one Count Elsdorf. He prided himself upon his enlightenment which included, of course, a general interest in the arts. And, on seeing me, he asked if he could commission me to do a bronze of himself, his wife and his two plain daughters. I agreed, of course, but before I started I asked to see round his castle. The house, you see, throws light upon the sitter.

Anyway, this old boy first of all conducted me round the treasures of his Schloss, which were agreeable if perhaps somewhat predictable – a minor Dürer, I recall, and a cranky Albrecht Altdorfer – and then he showed me his library.

I had never been a great one for book collections. They just tend to sit there in their calf coats with their back turned to you, and someone says: 'That's a first edition, actually. Molière, don't you know?' And you say: 'Oh really, how interesting,' and you turn a few pages of yellowed paper full of dull-looking print with broken serifs and old-fashioned S's, and you think you'd rather have a little Bronzino or a Rembrandt any day.

All this was going through my mind when I saw, in pride of place, on a sort of lectern, laid out ready to impress, a great tome full of finely executed illustrations of flowers.

'What is this?' I asked the count.

'That is the great Linnaeus,' he replied. 'It is the first

volume of his complete Taxonomy of the Flora, the *Systema Naturae*.'

I turned the pages with quickening fascination.

'You mean that he has set himself to categorize and illustrate every single plant known to science?'

'That is indeed the case. A most enlightened project, I must say, sir.'

I could barely speak with excitement. An idea was welling up within me. This after all was the age of classification. In France and in England, I knew, great lexicographers were laying down definitions of every word in their respective languages, and putting the results into dictionaries. Why should I not cloak my explorations into the mysteries of Proportion as an exact classification of every possible expression of the human face?

It would of course be more than mere lexicography, for such an endeavour would necessitate the very greatest exercise of art as well as skill and be rewarded with every kind of honour. It would fund me as I worked, and no one need know what I was really after. I have never seen why one should not have one's cake as well as eat it. An essay on the Human Face by Franz Xaver Froberger. No, von Froberger. It would be long, it would be arduous, it must be undertaken in secrecy for fear of envious imitators – Stadler would be the first to gallop on to the scene if he could see a way of snatching my glory. As some men are not happy unless the woman they are sleeping with is another man's wife, so to Stadler glory wasn't glory unless it properly belonged to me. Don't ask me why. That was the nature of the man.

When I returned home, I told my mother about my visit to the castle.

'The Elsdorfs?' she cried. 'Really? They're so enlightened. Wait till I tell Hildegard and Trudi and Lotte and . . .'

She even made no fuss when I went back after supper to my studio and sat till late among my heads, sketching and writing, putting together a first proposal for the great work before me, in the light of a most enormous witch's moon.

62

I was soon immersed in my plans, and my mother began to grow worried again.

'Work, work, work,' she said. 'But where's the money coming from? You turned down the two other commissions Count Elsdorf got you. Too busy, you said. Too busy at what?'

'I can't tell you, Mother.'

I couldn't, either. I knew she'd be bound to talk.

'Can't tell me? Won't tell me, more like. You used to say that when you were ashamed of something as a boy. It's not dirty work, is it? I don't want any scandals. You're not doing hot statues for some decadent artisto, are you? I know what they're like.'

'Not like Count Elsdorf.'

'Certainly not like Count Elsdorf. Nor nice Countess Elsdorf, either. I don't think a smutty thought has ever crossed their minds. In fact, it's a miracle to me how they ever managed to produce those nice young ladies. But that's by the way. If you'd been made a von, you could have asked one of them to a picnic. But now I think we'll have to aim a little lower.'

'What are you talking about, Mother?'

'Girls, ninny. What you need is a nice girl to walk out with. Look at you. Thirty-nine and still not married. You should be ashamed.'

'You need money to get married, Mother.'

'You'd soon make money if you had a nice young wife. That's what you want.'

'She'd spend my money, Mother.'

'She'd stop you mooning about in front of your mirror.'

'Have you been watching me, Mother?'

'Of course not.'

She looked slightly guilty.

'Anyway,' she continued, 'I've arranged for nice Johanna Spethmann to come for coffee and cakes tomorrow and I want you to be here. Afterwards she will express the need for a little exercise and you are to take her down the chestnut alley to the river.'

'Listen, Mother, I . . .'

'Franz Xaver.'

'Oh all right. Just this once. But I tell you, I'm not doing this again. Do you understand?'

'Just this once. That'll be enough.'

That afternoon I sat down and wrote a letter to my Straub cousins in Munich enquiring about the opportunities for statuary in the city.

63

There is something in this Animal Magnetism, you know. Johanna Clara Spethmann was attracted to me rather in the manner that a lamp is drawn to a moth. I fluttered elusively but no matter where I wandered, there was always this burning bright blonde hair flying after me.

Now, I do not flatter myself. I am not particularly tall or gainly. My features are more rubbery than distinguished, lending themselves excellently to the expression of passion both noble and ignoble, but by no means designed to inflict a dart in the heart. I had had my successes but I had had to work for them. But now, somehow, whether it was Mesmer and his iron rods, or the combined aggregation of

my heads which the Doctor has declared were of themselves
Magnetic, or the unusual amount of time that, because of
my trade, I spent working in metal (bronze being highly
susceptible to – and thus charged with – magnetism), I had
in fact begun to find, since I came to Wisensteig, that I was
the object of considerable attention from the young ladies
of the town.

Indeed, it proved (that very evening before I walked out
with Johanna) near to being a considerable liability to me,
since on going home later than usual from my studio, I
found myself surrounded by a gang of young men with
staves.

'What do you want?' I asked them. 'I think you must have
the wrong man.'

'You're a wrong 'un all right,' said a red-headed youth
who seemed to be the spokesman. 'But you're also the right
'un for what we're after.'

'He's right,' echoed various members of the mob.

This was child's play to one who had served his time at
the Vienna Arsenal with the cannon ornamenteers.

'Let's get this right,' I said to them, casuistically, 'I'm
right but you also say I'm wrong.'

'That's right,' said some.

'You're not wrong,' said others.

'In that case,' I said, stepping out, 'I think I'll be on
my way.'

I had walked perhaps another thirty yards when they
caught up with me again.

'Not so fast,' said the red-haired youth.

I turned on him attentively.

'Very well,' I said, 'I'm listening. Spit it out.'

'We don't like foreigners coming in here,' he said, 'poncing
around, and turning our girls' heads. Everything was fine
until you came along. And now they're all for Viennese
manners and lah-di-dah; and when we finally manage
to get their clothes off, it's "Why can't you do a lovely

sculpture of me or something romantic like Mr Froberger instead of pointing that thing at me?"'

I could see his point if not his thing. It's rare to find a lass with a sense of tact these days. What a damn stupid thing for the Wisensteig girls to say. I could've ended up with a fractured skull, half drowned in a horse trough. Anyway, I apologized to the swains, reassured them that I would soon be leaving for Munich if I had an iota of encouragement from my cousin, reminded them that I wasn't exactly a foreigner, merely a protracted exile, and stressed that I was only going out with Johanna Spethmann because my mother insisted on my so doing.

They understood that. Mothers ruled the roost in Wisensteig. It was a female-dominated town – look at the way the girls were treating these young men.

I took Johanna to task about it next day. She was a pleasant enough looking girl with freckles, and a slightly over-large mouth, but with that wonderful coppery golden hair and a hospitable figure. Sir P. P. Rubens would have had her clothes off as soon as look at her.

'You shouldn't treat the young men so badly,' I told her.

'Who says we do?' she replied. 'It's all proportional, isn't it?'

That casual remark uttered under the chestnut trees, twirled at me girlishly like the handle of a parasol, sounded for a moment sibylline, like a great omen. Proportional! . . . Why had she hit upon that word? Did she know anything? The ground seemed to shake beneath me. The trees wobbled like candles in a birthday cake.

'Hh . . . what did you say?' I asked her.

'I said, it's all proportional,' she said. 'I mean what's bad treatment for some may be just the job for the others. And vice versa. The young men of this town like bad treatment before marriage. It gives them an excuse to treat us badly afterwards. Why, whatever's the matter?'

I was grimacing with relief (Face No. 23). It was of course

unthinkable that she could have known that I had set my sights on Proportion's secret, but with Stadler and the professors against me I couldn't be too careful, and there were Mesmer and Fessler dogging my heels to say the least.

'It's your way of expressing things,' I said at last, knowing that flattery has ever been the servant of evasion. 'Perception in a beautiful woman always seems to have twice the penetration – like one of your new rifle bullets, rather than a mere musketoon.'

'Ooo, Mr Froberger, you do say the nicest things. Do they all say things like that in Vienna?'

'My dear,' I said gallantly, taking her hand to help her over the little bridge, 'that in Vienna would be counted as a commonplace. Your butcher says things of twice the style as he hands you a parcel of giblets. The midwife delivers your child with an epigram. Even the public executioner has a line in apophthegms. In fact, you must forgive me for my coarseness, for I have only been in Vienna fifteen years. Those who have sucked it, as it were, at the breast, have an innate politesse which the rest of us can only aspire to.'

I could see that the more I spoke, the more ardent the young lady was becoming but the truth was, my brain was seething now with notions conjured up by her mention of proportion. When I am preoccupied, I have a tendency to babble if I cannot be silent. Her breast heaved expressively.

'The hay is smelling better than I have ever known it this year,' she said as we approached a small barn which lay beside our path. 'Should you not like to make a small detour and sample a little of the sweetness?'

This was becoming dangerous. I had two reasons to decline an invitation which could only lead to mischief. The first being that I badly needed to reflect upon the mysteries of Proportion again and how far along the road I had travelled with my faces to an understanding of its mystery. I was now beginning to guess at the meaning of my search – which I had originally undertaken with no clear notion of an end. For is not Proportion the same as symmetry, and is not symmetry the secret of Creation? Was I searching for the original face of Man which would be, made in his own image, the face of God?

My other concern was that if I accompanied Johanna Clara on her hay-sniffing spree, I would probably end up with my head stove in, floating in a duck-pond, victim of one of her jealous admirers.

'Ahah,' I said to Johanna. 'I'd really like that. The only thing is, I get terrible hay-fever.'

'Oh.'

She seemed really crestfallen. Her very breasts expressed vexation and disappointment – a trait I would have liked to explore in clay.

We turned our steps back towards the town and arrived at my mother's house in time for cakes and coffee. My mother kept up a barrage of banter whose principal import was young love and the desirability of a cosy nest, but Johanna knew the day was lost. I may say that I tucked into the almond biscuits with a will. I had been aware of eyes following every step of our little promenade. But Johanna, whose strong white teeth and strawberry lips were designed for sweeter things than gateaux, merely toyed with her plateful and soon made her excuses and took her leave.

64

My mother was considerably vexed with me.

'What's wrong with you, Franz?' she said robustly.

'Wrong with me, Mother?'

'I lay on the prettiest girl in Wisensteig for you, and all

155

you do is giggle and dither. I hope you're not turning queer like so many of these artists one hears about.'

Two days later the letter from my cousins in Munich arrived. It was not altogether encouraging but, reading between the lines, I thought I could sniff commissions.

65

I was at the height of my powers when I started on my faces. I had princes as patrons. I could have done anything. The only thing that made me nervous was myself. I struggled before the glass to make contact with myself, and every time I could feel the selfness of me slipping away. My face was an artifice of muscles providing expressions for my colleagues, my acquaintances. It was a mime, a mask – useful, of course, in dealing with Stadler and the professors who hated me – I could smile. I did smile. But it was not me. Where was I? Who? In the early days, I thought I could regain myself through categorizing. Yes, I admit, my classification of faces was initially for my own benefit, though later for the good of all. Science was too stiff. I was no Linnaeus. How could I have thought so? But as I worked, I realized that there were mysterious connections. You are amazed? It was after I made these discoveries that I started feeling the pains. Something did not want me to continue.

It was something I realized I would simply have to bear. I could not possibly turn back for I knew that here was the true meaning of my life – indeed the meaning of life itself. This was where the golden apples grew. It would have been surprising if they had not been guarded by a dragon.

What the dragon was, however, remained hidden from me. Vague intimations drifted across me as I worked; and in the night there were moments of remarkable menace. But that was months, even years ago.

Now, in this small house, in the city of Pressburg, only a tile's fall away from dereliction, unfashionably near the Jewish cemetery, I have woken screaming from dreams of unremembered horror.

66

The mouth is, of course, the most obviously expressive feature of the face. You only have to consult Le Brun or Lavater for the classic rundown. A wide mouth equals generosity combined with lust for life. An upturned mouth goes with good humour and optimism. Similarly a down-turned, thin little mouth indicates a depressive miserly attitude. All this is simple stuff though doubtless very helpful for all those slack gaping mouths who can't work things out for themselves. But a mouth is more than this. A mouth houses the darting erectile tongue, organ of speech and seat of pleasure. A mouth is sweet and biteable as an apple, or it is a hutch of hatefulness and foul breath.

A mouth can taste and smell. This is why kissing is a far more intimate act than copulation. The penis has no olfactory properties – a sensible precaution, it seems to me, of the all-seeing Creator.

What then? A mouth is also like a vulva: soft, pink, wet, flexible, receptive, ingestive, welcoming, castrating, drowning. It is an androgynous feature, fringed with hair, at once the most obvious entrée to the body, and yet possessing its greatest weapon: the tongue.

Foul-mouth, blabber-mouth, bee-mouth, mealy-mouth, this squashy aperture has managed to inveigle itself into our minds and our language as virtually synonymous with qualities of character; and yet it is only flesh and muscle, seat of a cold sore.

Here is a curious thing. Animals, which are far more alert to spirits than we are and have no visions of foulness, have no fleshy red lips. Did you ever see an animal with fleshy red lips? I will warrant you did not. Thus it seems to me that fleshy red lips are at the centre of some secret, and I am treating them accordingly.

My faces now have, universally, fine thin lips or they are masked across the mouth with a chaste girdle. It is safer that way for we are dealing here with uncharted dangers as well as opportunities. I am the Magellan of the face. No one has been here before.

The Egyptian trembles as I work. You probably would not notice it but it is palpably stirring, a magnetic frisson which communicates itself to my left eyelid, causing an intermittent tic. My occasional visitors who are new to me think it is a wink, and wink back. It is not a wink. It is the Egyptian, stirring.

67

I took a studio near my cousins Straub in Munich, and for a time all seemed to go well. The Straubs were a merry bunch – perhaps a little too merry – but I admit I had grown contemplative. They asked me over for a meal once or twice but I had taken to dining alone. I did not like anyone to see me eating. Putting things into your mouth seems to me as private an act as excretion, but of course there is a conspiracy of restaurateurs against the notion.

My old uncle and mentor Johann Baptist Straub had died five years earlier and, while I waited for an appointment with one of the King of Bavaria's chamberlains – I had been assured that this would be a mere formality – I started work on a bust which would commemorate my uncle's kindly good humour and the comfort which he always told me he found in religion. Because he was a sculptor too, I wanted to include in the work something of the high nature of our profession – for is not clay that matter from which we were all originally framed and is not the sculptor, in microcosm, a creator too?

So I made, for his grave, in my new 'classic' style, a bust of my uncle scanning a book – the Book of Life – while he chipped away at another block of marble from which a half-realized figure – his youngest daughter Johanna – half mere blockish slab of stone, half breathingly alive – strained out robustly to touch his outstretched finger.

The family did not quite know what to make of it, though in deference to Johanna, who had enjoyed undressing, and to my uncle's memory, they all expressed appreciation, and it was placed in the churchyard where I dare say it stands to this day, a tribute to a good man and to his daughter's bosoms, and a very convenient dropping-off point for the local pigeons.

68

The King of Bavaria at the time, only recently installed after a spot of trouble, was a stout josser who had a passion for little women in pink frocks with ribbons in their hair.

He wanted every day to be a birthday party, and so it was. The snag for a sculptor, as indicated by the chamberlain to me at our eventual meeting, was that the King never did a sitting on his birthday, and so there were few if any commissions available. The only significant bust in recent months had been done by a Viennese sculptor called Stadler who managed to catch the King seated on an equine birthday present which he had arranged to be given to him.

I enquired as to whether the King would feel like repeating the enterprise. No, he said – and I did not know whether he was talking of horses or pink ladies – His Majesty had more thoroughbreds than he could conveniently straddle.

In the end I had to be content with one of the little women in pink, a Countess Gassner, who had a notion to be immortalized as Leda being ravished by the swan.

The swan I had hired to do the job, however, took fright when the full implications of its part dawned upon it, and broke the Countess's arm in its efforts to escape – an accident for which I was held to blame – and so once more my prospects of advancement were blighted for she made sure that all the other little pink women heard about it.

Relieved at the removal of so many tedious commissions at one stroke of a swan's wing, though somewhat perturbed by the commercial implications, I returned to my faces and to a frugal economy.

69

I suggested my Taxonomy of Facial Expressions to Mesmer when he caught up with me (he always does), thinking that he would jump at the chance of further fame as its patron, but he shook his head dubiously.

'It has been done before,' he said.

'Not in this way. Not in such detail. And, dare I say it, not with such skill.'

I had learned in Vienna not to be niggardly with my own praises. But Mesmer, it seemed, had other ideas.

'Oh come,' he said, 'Froberger. There have been other sculptors of excellence engaged in lengthy procedures of this kind. You know, my dear fellow, that I am foremost among your admirers, but let us not become overweening. Linnaeus is collating, with his classifications, the works of God in Nature. You are simply reproducing your own expressions.'

This was monstrous. I mouthed like a goldfish.

'But,' I expostulated, 'but . . .'

'You would be better advised to complete the work,' he lisped, 'and then you can blow your own trumpet. Meanwhile, what need you of further patronage when I am already your friend and protector?'

He slipped me a handful of florins and went his way.

Thank you, Mesmer. I am down but not yet out.

70

My cousin Johanna had taken quite a fancy to me, it appeared. She used to come round to my studio and sit and watch me work. I would never normally have allowed anyone to do this since it involved so much concentration on my part while I defined the expression that I was after, and then disciplined myself to hold it before the mirror for, literally, hours at a time as I put the face straight on to clay.

I was working on the Surly Old Soldier when she appeared unannounced one day a few months after our collaboration on her father's memorial. I had been moulding away with my face fixed in this frankly unappealing grimace and when at last I relaxed my expression and looked round, there she was in the corner sitting quiet as a cat. She said she liked to watch. It reminded her of her father.

She took off her bodice and her breasts were like pretty little balloons heated by tiny points of pink flame. In a few moments we were married, against my better judgement. She had a mind to it and as the sage says, when a woman has a mind to be married, you might as well tell a cloud not to rain. Perhaps, in my weakness, I hoped that company of the right kind might dispel the disagreeable presentiments that were beginning to steal over me. If I did so, I was wrong, and I wronged Johanna in involving her in my life.

My mother did not approve of the match. She was hoping for better things for me. She wrote me one of her long letters anatomizing the disadvantages.

There was, however, a spell of happiness. My aunt was also against the liaison, not because we were first cousins – such marriages were commonplace – but because she said I was already an old bachelor and without prospects. In this of course she was right but it made not a jot of difference to Johanna who proceeded to have two children in quick succession. We lived on air and water. Mesmer appeared one day and looked grave. I told him that I had found happiness at last, that I had discontinued work on my collection. To my surprise, he was disappointed when I told him I had stopped. He had come, he said, especially from Paris to see how I was and to enquire about the progress of my classification.

'But I thought you were not interested,' I told him.

'I said I did not think the world would be interested,' he replied. 'But as for me, I gave you money, remember?'

I told him that I had other commissions at the moment.

That night I could not sleep and I had come down to put the finishing touch to a little commission I had for a fountain cupid when I heard a strange sound emanating from the studio. I opened the door a fraction and peeped inside. All my heads were muttering and mumbling while the Egyptian harangued them in some unintelligible language. Each head was making an appropriate sound for its expression: anger, pathos, truculence, complaint, self-pity, pain, constipation; all were there, and the strange thing was, they were all my own voice – except of course the Egyptian who had a voice like an Egyptian. The effect, horribly, was that the faces were alive and I was a model.

In the morning, my right arm was completely paralysed, stiff as a statue. Paralysed! I ask you, what do you make of that?

Luckily, Mesmer was still in Munich and was able to treat me, much against the advice of my wife (who blamed him for the attack in the first place). He came round to our little house as soon as I sent for him.

'What is the matter, Froberger?'

'I cannot move my arm.'

'Alas, I do not have a baquet in Munich with me. But let us see what my iron rod can do.'

'Shall I work again?'

'We must put the magnetic fluid in equilibrium in every part of your frame. You are sadly out of kilter.'

71

Plato says that the laws of Proportion run throughout the Universe.

God originally created the Universe from fire and earth. But two things cannot rightly be put together without a third. There must be some bond between them; and the fairest bond is that which makes the most complete fusion of itself and the things combined. Proportion is best adapted to effect such a union.

Out of the indivisible and unchangeable, he says, and also out of that which is divisible and has to do with material bodies, God has constructed a third and intermediate kind of essence partaking of the nature of both; and this compound he placed accordingly in a mean between the indivisible and the material world. It is the Soul.

Through Proportion we see the reality of the light of the self and the unreality of Creation.

I woke slowly, swimming up from a deep dream in which strange shapes I could not recognize curved and twisted in an indecipherable gloom.

72

When Johanna told me she was pregnant, I was dumb-founded. I had never intended to have children. Indeed, I cannot see how the child was mine in the first place. I had practised every continence. I knew that my heads were my children and my face was the matrix where they found shape.

'I cannot see how the child is mine in the first place,' I told her.

Her eyes filled with tears.

'How can you say such a thing?' she asked.

I could easily say such a thing, and I could have said a lot more of such things. I sometimes think woman is self-pollinating and she has roped men in under false pretences. Semen is merely a humour. However, there seemed to be no point in arguing about it. The thing was there.

'Let us try to get rid of it, then,' I said. 'No use crying over spilt humours.'

'Sometimes I don't understand you,' she said.

'That makes two of us,' I replied.

Sometimes I don't understand anything.

'Poor little thing,' she said.

'In England they swear by gin,' I told her, 'though I daresay schnapps would pass muster.'

'I shall do no such thing,' she said.

I was interested in the way woe altered her features, and doubtless I presented a pretty picture of anxiety, incredulity and impatience myself. I was suddenly fed up with the whole issue.

'Oh, have it, then, if you want it,' I said. 'But don't expect me to pay for it. I must do my heads. I cannot earn money too.'

73

Mesmer made me sit upon a stool with my shirt off, and passed his hand with fingers extended all down my body, starting with the head, passing over the shoulders and then down my back and my front. I quickened and stiffened. He placed his head on my solar plexus and stretched his fingers towards the hypochondrium. And finally he touched my right arm with a little metal stick that he produced from his physician's bag. I felt a strange, fizzing, tingling sensation beginning to creep up my arm from the fingertips, but still I could not move it.

'Go down now to the studio and start work on your next face,' Mesmer told me. 'I shall commission it myself.'

I could not remonstrate. I was too worried about the paralysis. What would I do to support my family without the use of my chisel and pen?

I settled myself in front of the mirror.

'I cannot move,' I said.

'What is your next face, Froberger?' asked the doctor.

I reflected.

'It is the Childish Weeper.'

'Weep, Froberger.'

I wept and monitored my expression.

'Now start on the plaster.'

I reached out without thinking, grasped the chisel, and chipped away. With a sudden shock, I realized what I was doing. I was cured.

'I am cured,' I told Johanna.

She looked coldly at Mesmer.

'Remember, that one is mine,' he said. 'Keep working.'

I loved my wife and my two little children: little Franz and little Johanna. That is to say, when I call them mine, I am making an assumption. When you do not know who you are, it is difficult to be certain that anything is yours. You may simply be a figment. How can a woman and two children be yours when you are not? These two little people and this young woman had a father and husband who was streaming into space.

I put this to Johanna in a roundabout way but she told me not to be so silly. She said there was more sense in a teaspoon. I must be grateful to her for she provided me with a glimpse of what life is like for 99 per cent of the populace – humdrum, uneventful, mildly happy. She and the children had their little dramas: illnesses, squabbles, burnt toast, scratches on the furniture, head lice: all perfectly normal and harmless. I read them stories and drew them pictures. We went on expeditions. They were so happy with so little. They looked up to me. They needed me. And all the time I was being taken away from them, sucked out like a bird's egg.

Oh, I struggled against it. I tried to put the heads aside, leave them alone, but every time I could feel the numbness creeping up my arm and I was forced to start again. I did not tell Johanna about it. She would have seen Mesmer's influence and she was partly right. He needed the heads for his work, there was something in them that he could find nowhere else; but he did not yet know – of this I was sure – exactly what it was. He was using me like a cow, squeezing me for strange cream, sending the only money we saw that winter.

'Take the Academy's pension they offered you,' said Johanna.

'Never,' I replied.

In desperation, at last I took a job with a monumental mason making foul little angels, which brought home enough money for a while to make Mesmer's remittance unnecessary (except of course for the treats that women and children love). I gained confidence and stopped doing the heads. For a week, a fortnight, my arm was all right. And then one morning I woke and it was numb again.

'It is in your mind,' said Johanna, when she knew.

'The philosopher Berkeley says that everything is in our mind. And does not Rousseau too?'

'Pooh to Rousseau,' said Johanna, and the children took up the cry.

Secretly, I started once more on the Wounded Soldier in Agony.

I lost my job with the mason due to absent-mindedness. To be honest, the only way I could keep my mind on the job was for it to be absent, but he said he found my attitude insulting. Johanna found me another one teaching young ladies how to draw at the local seminary. My fellow teachers were the ones who liked things quiet. I kissed one of my pupils once when she had done about the only passable drawing I ever saw. I was punished and almost expelled.

74

One day I remember in particular. We all went out, Johanna and the children and I, on a brilliant summer's morning, the light sharp as a Canaletto, we all went out for some reason, I cannot recall how we got there, we floated, we were put down, on the shores of a lake where there was a ruined castle and a deserted garden.

We played by the lake, and paddled and ate our picnic, watching swans drifting by like feathered little icebergs. Little Johanna got at my wine when I wasn't looking and swigged it saying, 'Your good health!' How we laughed. I thought: this is how I want my life to be. I can do it. It is only an effort of the will. I am me. There is nothing in the faces. There is no secret. All I want is to grow old happily with the people I love around me and to lie at peace. I told Johanna. She smiled and stroked my hair.

Later we played hide-and-seek in the garden. Little Johanna's grasp of the rules was tenuous but we ran about shrieking with laughter.

It was my turn to hide and, trying to get away from little Johanna so that she would not give the game away to the others, I rounded a hedge at the double. There, in a lonely parterre, a glade approached by four little paths, was a plinth bearing the vilest face I have ever seen.

His head was tilted back so that the features had immediately a nose-in-the-air arrogance about them; and yet there was something dreadfully knowing about the attitude. The ears were low-set, obscene, fleshy; the forehead bulging; the chin long, narrow and bony. But the worst thing about it was the mouth – yes, those lips big as the natives' who put bone in their mouths to produce a great saucerish beak

– this beak thrust upwards and at me – insidious, sexual, succulent, unmanning – the whole crowned with an expression of unspeakable depravity, command and relish. I had never seen it before and yet I had known it all my life. As I watched, the head sensed me, turned and wagged at me. I thought it would hop down and suck at me with its awful beak.

Little Johanna came round the corner then, and I swept her up, covering her eyes. But she insisted on seeing it. She had a will of adamant.

She looked at it, long and hard, stroked its great pout and said: 'Daddy head.'

She had hit on the truth. The unspeakable thing was a travesty of my own face.

My wife and son now appeared.

'Don't look,' I said.

'Why ever not?' said Johanna.

I turned. An old mossy weather-beaten garden god gazed mildly out at us.

'But . . .' I stammered.

'Daddy head,' repeated little Johanna.

She knew what we had seen. Whatever it was, why ever it had been there, I resolved that I would not be subdued. That was what it wanted. Subordination. Total surrender. Fesslerism.

75

When I reached home, I found that the memory of that head would not leave me. It sat in the corner of my brain, pushing out its lips like the mocking of Christ, tilting its chin knowingly at me as if to gauge my weakness and my pleasure. To rid myself of it, I set about the image with my

169

chisel, pulling it out of the clay, giving it shape outside my mind.

When it was cast, in lead, my wife looked sadly at me. I think she had seen the end of my domestic ambitions in those features.

She would not have it in the house. Soon it was mysteriously destroyed.

It was the day that my cold sore erupted.

76

For two days I stayed glued to my mirror looking at the thing. The more I looked, the bigger it semed to get.

'It's no use,' I said to my wife. 'I can't go to work with this.'

Did I say it was like love? It is not at all like love. A cold sore is like a poltergeist whose playground is the lip.

You think I am making too much of it? Let me tell you more about cold sores. If you have never had one, it will give you added reason to rejoice. On the other hand, as a fellow sufferer, you will appreciate my anguish. I am, you must remember, a face man.

It starts, as I have said, with a sort of burning itch, and you think: that's a strange sort of feeling. I haven't had that feeling before. Something must have bitten me. And you wait for a mild swelling; but what you get is a horrible oozing thing. And when it's finished oozing – which it doesn't for some days (meanwhile you've put yourself in a locked room), when it's finished oozing, it forms crusts like apple crumble. And when you try to encourage its departure by picking bits off, the monster responds by spreading ever wider.

It is like one of those horror stories the ladies read. The

Castle of Otranto had nothing on my cold sore. I could put my cold sore in a book and it would frighten the children. I could serialize my cold sore in a gazette and it would make me a fortune.

It would have been bad enough at any time, but after that disgusting Beak Head that I had seen, it seemed to have the direst overtones. They say Rembrandt, looking at himself in his mirror, saw Time at work. I saw only evil and corruption.

'I don't know what you're fussing about,' said Johanna, outside the door. 'Many people have worse things than that. What if you were a wounded soldier with half your face shot away?'

Dwelling on the misfortunes of others has never been a palliative that I have found effective, though I notice it is one that women frequently proffer.

'It's getting bigger,' I told her. 'Half my face is shot away.'

I withdrew with it into my studio and began to paint it. It was not a good sitter. Sometimes it seemed to have the ability to cover my whole face. At others it would crouch at the edge of my mouth, watching me like a malignant toad. I did a number of sketches and several finished portraits of it. I even started to make a bust.

Later, I noticed that my wife and children had left. There was a note in the kitchen: 'Gone to mother.' She had taken a number of things. I was neither surprised nor aghast. Indeed, I was so wrapped up in my sore I could think of nothing else. My sore had been sent to tell me something.

A friend called by – one of my few remaining friends – more of a friend of my wife's actually – I sometimes wondered whether she weren't having an affair with the fellow – in fact, now I think about it, I'm sure she was – on the pretext of dropping in a copy of Lavater's *Types of Physiognomy* but really to give me some advice on the deportment of my life (so he could step into my shoes).

'Your wife cannot take much more,' he said.

'Oh really,' I replied, holding a cloth before my face and looking around. 'She seems to have taken quite a bit already.'

A witty rejoinder, I thought, but he looked grave and took his leave. I am glad to say he did not take *Types of Physiognomy* with him. What a revelation! I knew of Lavater's work, of course. What sculptor did not? I had read some of his earlier treatises and knew, naturally, of his dispute with Lichtenberg and his mock-science of 'pathognomy'. Now, here it was, the fruit of all his learning.

His theme is that all Types are present in each one of us; we are a microcosm; however, one particular Type tends to dominate in each individual. It is like the humours.

I received very strongly from my reading of the book the impression that if I could master or override my particular Type, I would be in a position to grasp the Whole, and thereby the Essence.

You see? It's so simple, like all great Truths.

Subsequent to this visit, I remained undisturbed for some days. I suppose it was inevitable that the few commissions I had should dry up. I was not, I'm afraid, very welcoming to visitors. I put up a notice that said simply 'Out'.

The days passed rapidly in front of the mirror as I inspected my sore, measuring it and trying out all manner of remedies: alcohol, St John's Wort, dandelion juice, witch hazel . . .

One or two people – diehards or merely curious – would come knocking.

'Come out, Franz, it's a lovely day. We're going for a walk in the woods, maybe a picnic.'

'We can't come,' I would mumble, 'go away, have a nice time.'

I thought of me and my cold sore as 'we'. It was like an old enemy whose return I had always expected. It was like an epidermal version of Stadler. We were inseparable in our hatred of each other.

And at the last I came to see it was indeed a manifestation of the daemon, punishing me for the great enterprise that I had started. If so, it had an entirely opposite effect. For when I knew it as a sign of himself, harbouring on my lip, crusting among the bristles, spying on my every move, locking me to the glass so that whole days would pass as I gazed in hatred at my weeping skin, why then at last I stirred and found a new resolve. It persuaded me to take up my chisel again and work on.

I had finished the Bombastic Preacher and the Worried Man when Johanna appeared again.

'I thought we had agreed no more heads,' she said. 'We won't come back if you're doing more heads.'

Something was happening to her. There was a beakish quality to her now. I had to leave. The air was stifling in the city. I had completed thirty-five heads, but there were thirty-four still to be done. I would never manage it here. My brother Joseph lived in Pressburg (not seventy miles from Vienna). He had a large house, a studio – he too was a sculptor – he would be pleased to see me. It would be a breathing-space.

I hired a cart, collected my heads, and moved out, leaving Johanna all the money I had in the world.

I wept as I went, for I loved them and I could not help them.

I had gone over the mark.

We wander into people's lives as if from a fog; the wind changes; and we are lost again.

77

But perhaps the most obvious of the sculptor's seeming disadvantages – when it comes to verisimilitude – and God knows it does if you're dealing with a Burgomaster's wife who shrieks 'That doesn't look like him' when you unveil your offering – the most obvious limitation of our practice is, to the layman, the fact that in sculpture we cannot or do not record colour. And, for colour, you may as well read 'skin' for I have dealt with eyes, hair, et cetera. We cannot, as the painters can, suffuse our subjects with a blush or catch the deathly pallor of consumption.

Oh, we have our advantages; shape, planes, shadows, a third dimension. But skin we do not trade in.

And yet, you may argue, how much of our perception of our fellow humans is based upon their complexion! Hans-Peter is sallow, Johanna is fair, Friedrich is freckled, Willibald is acned . . . (And Franz Xaver has a cold sore, hm? Go on, say it.) And isn't skin the thing that, when we are in love, or making love, we so particularly respond to? Indeed it is. It is the animal covering of the flesh. And with skin, of course, I include the lips. Those ruddy lips, those strawberry lips, those lips like cherries, or blisters . . .

Would you rather your sculptor rendered you in colour? It could be done. We work in wax, you know. Waxworks can record every mole, every wart, every cyst, every pimple. But, at the end, is a waxwork more interesting than a sculpture? No. Is it more lifelike? I warrant it is not. There is nothing more dormant than a waxwork. Once you have looked and said 'How lifelike!', you move on. Is a waxwork more creative, more artistic, more satisfying to have around the house? No, no, and no again.

If you daubed my precious alabaster with rouge and greasepaint you would lower it. You would kill it.

Then we have to admit, again, that sculpture has nothing to do with mere reproduction. What has it to do with, then? Ah, now we are winding in to the truth of the matter.

Sculpture, more than any of the arts, is pure scale. That is why it is a purer art than painting. Indeed, it is nearer music than anything.

Would you like me to play for you upon my flute a little? Perhaps one of the Bach solos? What castles he can build out of sound!

78

What is a rainbow for? Its end is not by any means utilitarian.

Why does a sunflower display such a faithful equiangular spiral? Or a jet of water describe so perfect a parabola? Why are the leaves on a stem arranged in a helix? Or the dimensions of the human head based upon the golden rectangle?

I cannot yet answer these questions.

All of them, and all Creation, show that Beauty and Proportion are one and the same. Beauty and Truth are also, as we know, identical. Therefore Proportion equals Truth. Pythagoras himself would approve the equation.

Now do you see why I must continue?

79

And there was another place, Johanna, remember? Hugel-
mann's, down by the water's edge, by the ferry, where we
would drink and watch the boats float down the river, wave
at the sailors in Greek dress, hiss at the sailors in Turkish,
goggle at the bathers in no dress at all. Do you remember?
And where you could play billiards all day for no more than
the price of a mocha.

80

And so I came to Pressburg which is also known to the
Hungarians as Bratislava: in a cart with forty different
heads, and no money. (The cold sore, which I had thought
would dog me for life, had responded to the change of scen-
ery, and practically vanished en route.)

My brother Joseph greeted me hospitably – we had recently
been on better terms than the day when he had attacked me
with a sword for references I had made to the sesquipedalian
nature of his genius.

His wife, whom I had not met before, was out when I
arrived, and Joseph took me round the house, pointed out
my room, and showed me the large well-lit attic which he
told me I could use as my studio.

Later, he conducted me on a little tour of the city.
Pressburg is a pleasant enough place. It is really an over-
grown provincial town, though once the Hapsburgs were
crowned here. Nothing very much happens these days.

They have a good cathedral, a castle of sorts, a new Archbishop's Palace, a couple of interesting churches. It had been besieged by the Turks, decimated by the Plague, ravaged by the occasional war, and more or less forgotten for the last fifty years. An incongruous setting for the terrible events that I have to unfold to you – but, to be fair, the great cauldron of Etna itself would be inadequate for that backdrop. Brace yourself, then, and I shall proceed.

Joseph's wife, Johanna, arrived back from some expedition while we were enjoying a glass of wine after our tour. She was a striking woman: twenty-eight years old, slender, almost wild, with an electrifying presence and graceful step; her eyes bright brown, gleaming like polished padouk; her nose and chin finely moulded; her face oval; the forehead wide and candid, perhaps wanting half an inch for perfection in height; her voice husky but melodious; her speech animated; her teeth good but slightly gapped; her mouth that rare combination of firmness and promise, small as to the lips (as you know I like them) but so exquisitely shaped that I wanted to run off with them and plunge them into wax on the instant.

All this I took in at a glance and a how-d'you-do. Joseph was pleased that we hit if off so well. I could see he was mad, mad, mad, mad, mad, mad, mad, mad, mad, mad, mad, mad, mad, about her. He told me I would be company for Johanna. They did not have any children which was a great disappointment to her (as I could see it was to him).

I could sense there would be trouble here.

All went well for a time, however, and the three of us got on happily enough. My brother was an honest sculptor of the old school – although he was, in fact, my junior by some three years – and there was more than enough work in Pressburg and Budapest (which he used to visit every seven or eight weeks) to keep his books full for eighteen months ahead.

'Come, Franz,' he said to me one day when I had been

with them for a couple of weeks, 'let me share my good fortune with you. Why don't you take one of these commissions of mine?'

'No,' I replied, 'by no means. I have not come here to poach on your preserves. Besides, they like what you do. They might not want me at all. I have a different way of doing things.'

'You think you are more advanced than I am, is that it?'

It was it, though I did not care to say so.

'No, no.'

'What, then?'

'I just think that I am not a good person to be in partnership with. I have powerful enemies.'

'Fiddlesticks,' said Johanna, entering at that moment.

'You see?' said Joseph. 'We shall form a studio. The Froberger Brothers. We shall be like the Van Eycks.'

'I still think it is a bad idea. Let me stay in the attic and contrive as best I may.'

'But you have no commissions.'

'No, I shall occupy myself with my own work. It is my own commission.'

'Good heavens.'

The idea of anybody working on his own account filled my good brother with amazement.

'You mean . . ,'

'Yes,' I told him. 'For no money.'

'But you won't be able to buy anything.'

'The idea does not worry me.'

I could hear his brain whirring like a clock before the hour.

'What about your materials?' he asked at last. 'Where are they to come from?'

He thought he had me there, but I had my reply ready.

'I will borrow them from you.'

'That you shan't,' said Johanna, weighing in.

'Now, Johanna . . .' remonstrated my brother.

178

'No Brothers Froberger, no materials,' said Johanna.

I could see that I was indeed in a maze without money, and so I agreed; and, as these things go, the partnership was a success. I was forced to suspend work on my heads almost entirely while I laboured away on Burgomasters, heads of police, garden putti, fountain figures, country bigwigs, the wives of country bigwigs, and even a frieze for a bigwig's urinal.

In a year, I could have saved up enough to buy myself a place of my own again; but I sent the money to my wife.

It was strange that in that year I was not troubled once with a bad arm, nor with the dreams and visions that had so affected me.

Meanwhile my brother's wife was becoming impossible to ignore. She was making outrageous remarks about me, interrupting my work with any pretext, bringing me little biscuits and cordials, unbuttoning my shirt, biting cherries meaningfully. My brother smiled indulgently, the silly fool. I was saved from this predicament, if saved is the word, by the sudden appearance of Mesmer. The fellow had an unerring ability to track me down. All at once, he was there, puffing slightly from the ascent of the stairs – my attic was five floors up – his thick lips open like a booby's.

'There's no escaping you, Mesmer,' I cried jovially, though my heart sank.

'You had better sit down while I feel your fluid,' he replied. 'You are looking seedy.'

He ran his hands over me and I had to admit I did feel better.

'Coo, are you the great Mesmer, then?' asked Johanna, who could never endure my having a visitor without wanting to get in on the act. 'I thought you'd have looked different some'ow.'

She affected the local accent sometimes, an affectation she made musical with her husky tones.

'How, different, madame?' enquired Mesmer. 'How different?'

'Oh, I dunno. Burning eyes, lean and cadaverous, make yer knees turn to jelly . . .'

'Would you like me to feel your fluid?'

'Well, I dunno really . . .'

'Go on, Johanna,' urged Joseph, silly cuckoo.

She sat herself down and let Mesmer run his fingers all over her. She seemed to experience the most benign sensations.

'Now, look, Mesmer . . .' I started.

'Belt up, Franz,' said Johanna, 'put a sock in it, will yer?'

I knew that he slept with her that afternoon. I taxed him with it later.

'Leave her alone, Mesmer. I know you and your tricks.'

'I was simply saving you, Franz. She would have had your breeches off otherwise. It would have been a terrible thing to come between brothers. With me, it is all right. I am simply that irresistible Mesmer. Husbands are affronted if I have not slept with their wives. But with their own brother . . . well, I have known fratricide. Why are you not working on your heads?'

'I have no money. I am working with my brother.'

'How dare you waste your time. I need your heads, man.'

'They are not for sale.'

'I will buy you a small house, give you a modest income – I know you have a spare economy – if you will leave them to me when you die.'

'No.'

'Do you wish to see them dissipated, dishonoured? My collection will be renowned. Your name will be ranked among the greatest.'

His dangled glory cut no ice with me. I knew that if my labours were successful, if my search were concluded, I need have no care for the future. My name would be glorified in perpetuity. But there was something to be said meanwhile for his offer of patronage, especially as he had originally shied away from the word. They come round in the end!

'All right, then,' I cried, 'I accept your terms.'

If I were successful in my tussle with the daemon, I should live longer than he. If I lost that battle, it would not matter anyway.

'But you must look after my wife and children in any event,' I told him.

'I am already,' he remarked. 'Did you not know?'

He winds himself tighter and tighter around me.

I had no more trouble from my sister-in-law. She ran away soon afterwards with a furrier from Styria.

81

I had experienced the pains for some years – mainly in the gut, or the rectum, but sometimes in the stomach and even in the genitals. I had thought it due to over-much sitting or standing which is the posture of our art.

And then, one evening, when I was once again disappearing into my eyes in front of the glass, looking once again for that singular oneness that was myself; smiling, frowning, enquiring, ruefully playful, suddenly sneering, dissolving into the Haggard Old Man with Aching Eyes which was my current subject; as I took up the chisel and started working on the alabaster, I stole a glance as ever at the armless statue of the Egyptian in his demi-arch by the window.

Whether it was the perfection of the figure working upon my imagination, or whether it was some kind of challenge issuing from the dimensions of the stone, I know not, but I felt as if it were a flash of premonitory recognition, as if 'I have been there before'.

I suddenly saw, more than ever, with a completely fresh understanding, having only glimpsed before, how the face is directly proportional to the rest of the body. The eyes are the face's lungs wherein it takes the breath of light. The ears are its arms with which it grasps meanings. (For, as the Florentine Ficino tells us in his treatise on Air and Spirits, the world of the spirit, of which the head is the hutch, lives only on airy things.) The mouth and tongue are its organs of gender (the lips being female, the tongue being penis). The cheeks are its stomach and bowels. The chin and neck are its thighs and legs.

As I pondered this revelation,which gave a whole new meaning to my pursuit, I was unthinkingly tinkering with the mouth of the head which stood before me, when all at once I felt a sharp pain in the region of my groin.

It passed in a moment. One occasionally has these little spasms. They meant nothing to me. I had grown used to stabs. One had to in Vienna.

So I picked up my chisel and started working again around the lips of the Haggard Old Man. Again a sharp pain, no random tweak, this one. I stopped for five minutes. The sensation did not recur. I started once more and was promptly jabbed anew.

And now I realized, almost through the pores of my head, absorbently, that Proportion must have a reciprocal effect in all things at all times, like Mesmer's Universal Fluid.

Because I was working on the mouth – and the mouth is reciprocally analogous to the pudenda, I was actually feeling the action of my chisel, though inflicted on dull stone, on the right side of my right testicle!

Was this why Mesmer was so interested in my work? The Universal Fluid? He knew that my exactitude in my art was such (I say it without a boast, it is well known) that some already call me the Orpheus of Statuary. I could almost mimic life. It is not the business of the sculptor, of course. We aim at higher things than mere representation. But I almost could, if I chose, breathe life into clay. There. Blasphemy! But I could. And this head and my own head were so alike that I was able to feel its pangs of birth as might a twin.

Of course, it would be useless for some lumpen artisan, some mere Stadler, to try to evoke such sympathetic reactions. Unless he had mastery such as I now possessed, he could chip away at his stone till kingdom come, and all he would get would be grit in his eye. His testicle would never feel so much as a twinge.

I continued to experiment with my Haggard Old Man. I attacked his chin. My knee ricked agonizingly. I gouged out a fragment of cheek, and suffered a sudden cramp in the bowel. Everywhere I played upon the head, I found painful reciprocations in my own body.

But I still felt, for some reason, that there was more to it than this. I was only halfway to the truth. So I fell to thinking once more. I reflected that Nature is, though cruel, not vindictive. What I was experiencing here seemed malicious rather than sympathetic. Something was bending the Universal Fluid towards torment, not healing. Why should I suddenly be suffering such throes? Back came the response. It was because I was becoming so near to perfection in my art. So what could possibly be inducing these sharp scourges? Not Nature, came the reply.

I could feel the answer pulsing and quivering under the arch at the end of my studio.

It was the Spirit of Proportion, jealous of the secret, guardian of the mystery, angered at my approach, who was the perpetrator.

He is in my hands and in my heart, waiting.

82

There is no evil that they dare not do, for they have deceitful and violent ways as does a man who has forfeited the protection of the better daemons. They often plan savage and unexpected ambushes from which they rush out. When they attack, sometimes they try from the flank, at others they ferociously charge in from the front . . . These and other things they do, trying to turn us away from a right knowledge of the gods and lead us to themselves.

I have been reading from a book of Old Philosophers, touching on daemons, that I found at my brother's. It is strange to have a voice from the past stretch out and talk to one so. But where are the better daemons? What have I done to forfeit their assistance? I am deserted by the better daemons.

83

So the Empress is dead. She died in her sleep after a supper of mixed sausages. She was a thoroughly good person with a penchant which she dared not disclose.

84

And so we enter the last days.

If you have noticed – and perhaps even complained of – a certain irregularity in my narrative up to this point, I ask your indulgence. It has been written at various times; as a journal; a notebook; an apostrophe; and as a retrospective account of my endeavours.

This last category has been penned under conditions of the greatest affliction. Someone who is my enemy is forever trying to destroy my work. He tries to bend my story just as he likes to thicken a nose or slacken a mouth as I labour upon these last few heads.

Pain is his instrument. He stabs, cuts, skewers, turns the blade, and pricks and stabs again.

His attacks, however, have driven me (as necessity often dictates) to find means of defending myself. Having prised from my labours the secret of the relationship between the proportions of the head and the rest of the body, I have now – by close study and empirical research – devised a system by which I can resist and (almost) master the daemon by the use of expression and grimace corresponding to that portion of the body in which he is afflicting me.

So! You see the Doting Husband? Now I have drawn the daemon in. And now I harry him with a sharp pinch – so! – to my side, usually under the right ribs which is the location where he seems most vulnerable to my ripostes, doubtless because the Creator chose the site for his extraction of Eve from our first parent.

Let me show you again. Let us suppose, for instance, that I am working on an eye. I know that he will then attack me in the lung (I have been plagued recently). Now, instead of discontinuing and allowing him the victory, I bind him with a grimace. I constrict my nostrils and glare my eyes – like this. You see? Followed by the pinch under the ribs – so! Bravo.

Bowel cramps, another favourite of his, I meet by sucking in my cheeks, pulling my forehead downwards, and lowering my gaze – so! Pinch . . . so! You recognize in my expression the Glum Moper.

There. I have given you the secret of my heads. They are no longer me seeking myself, or Character Heads such as Le Brun would prescribe. They have soared beyond that and will serve to deliver the daemon into my hand. By this I shall subdue him and unlock Proportion.

It is a system painfully acquired, as you may imagine, but it infuriates my enemy for it negates at least some of his assaults. And though I am by no means always the victor yet in our encounters, it earns me if not his acquiescence, his respect.

But I am going too fast, doubtless at his instigation, for in all my works he wishes to undo me.

If you should chance to see my heads, remember what they are; not exercises; not bizarre and variegated expressions; not a search for the self that lies beneath; but magnetic devices to trap, as Prospero could, a cunning and implacable spirit.

I have not told Mesmer of these discoveries. I think he would kill me for them when they are complete.

85

In spite of the fascination that the casting of bronze exerts upon me – and lead too for that matter, though lead is an easier game being already malleable and melting at a lower temperature so that you can more easily organize a little foundry at home (and lead too has a saturnine quality which only lends itself to certain subjects – indeed Mesmer says lead is used in magnetism to channel the subtile fluid, preventing its dissipation – I have set up a little lead foundry at the end of my shed here), in spite of all this, my favourite medium is alabaster.

The colour and tone of alabaster is so propitious, with its muted shadows and highlights. It glows with a soft, warm, reflective, lucent quality prized among others by Othello of all people who compared it with Desdemona's skin; 'whiter yet than alabaster', which I daresay it was not if I know Italian skin.

And its touch; so smooth, so soft, so almost alive! It is lightness itself, lighter than stone. Sometimes called gypsum but a low name; the man of physics knows it as sulphate of calcium; a sea rock veined with minerals.

I acquired a great quantity of it latterly, provided if you please by Mesmer.

'This is for you, Froberger,' he lisped. 'It is the best quality for magnetism, for the veins run sympathetically.'

Be that as it may, I told him later, it is the best quality of alabaster I have ever worked with.

Alabaster. It is like a word of power such as the Freemasons use. I shall use it to open doors, I doubt not.

86

Mesmer walked with me around Pressburg as I looked for
suitable places to complete my work. The criteria were
very simple. I need the quietest of surroundings and a door
I could lock. In terms of living quarters, my requirements
were exiguous in the extreme, but I had to have enough
studio space in which to work and house my collection.
The place could not be in the smarter districts of the town
for many of the above reasons, but Mesmer added weight
to them by saying 'he was not a rich man'.

Not a rich man! Ha. He has by alchemy and magnetism
amassed well over a million florins. I happen to know that
because it was whispered to me by spirits who do not lie.

Be that as it may, we settled eventually on a little
low house somewhat set away from its neighbours at the
end of the street which led to the Jewish Cemetery. The
house, indeed, had once housed the sexton or whatever
they call him of the graveyard in question. It was an
unfashionable area, for Jews dead were even less popular
than Jews alive. It was supposed by the Burgomasters
that Jews had to be buried somewhere, but there was no
point in allocating to them the choicer meadows or the
more fragrant parterres. The field that had been chosen
some hundred years before had always been known as
the Marlpit, and though it was not of itself too spongy
for burials, it terminated in a series of bogs and marshlets
which had always been known for mosquitoes and effluvium, and now could generally be counted upon to raise a
mist or stinking flatus when all else in the world was fresh
and fair.

It suited me admirably.

The house itself, cheek by jowl with the cemetery railings, was a mean affair but it had an extensive annexe which had housed coffins and accommodated hearses. I saw immediately that it would make a studio.

Even Mesmer's meanness was put to shame by the location, however, or perhaps he was worried about his modest investment. The value of the place could hardly appreciate. At any rate, he tried to demur.

'This is too damp, Froberger,' he said. 'You will become lowered. The magnetism of the place is not conducive.'

'It will serve admirably,' I said.

The solitude of the place was perfect. I would have none but the most persistent and intractable visitors.

'You are not afraid of ghosts?' he queried, smiling.

I paused. I am, I hope, no more superstitious than the next man. When I had been ill, with those terrible visions of the catacombs, it had been the living, or the supposedly living, whatever Fessler and the rest of them were, who had affrighted me. But there is no doubt that we all have certain primitive fears that have their roots deeper than reason, even in the age of enlightenment.

'I am both sceptical and fearful as befits the times,' I told him. 'But it is not the common ghosts of a cemetery that affright me.'

He took a sharp look at me as we walked back to the town.

'What do you mean?' he asked. 'What is it then that affrights you?'

'It is the Spirit of Proportion,' I told him at last. 'That is the source both of my fear and my encouragement.'

I never liked to tell Mesmer too much because I was never sure how he might use it. His lecher's lips pursed as he reflected on what I had told him.

'How encouragement?' he enquired.

'If I were not so near the truth, I would not have aroused

such malevolence,' I said. 'It is ironic that one who has lived his life in the service of Proportion should now be the object of so much spleen.'

I could see that he believed me. It was making him want the heads for himself all the more. He could sense that I was up to something. And I wanted to lead him on so that he would continue to fulfil his office of patron (I needed more materials). But I would not yet tell him that I was putting into them – with all their expressions and grimaces – I was locking into them – all that I had learned of my code which, once the circle was complete, would dominate the spirit, unfold Proportion, and convey inestimable benefits, perhaps another Eden, to mankind. That was a secret which I would guard awhile.

Mesmer was talking again in his lapping lippy way.

'. . . that I should take the statue away if it so troubles you.'

'No!'

I shouted so violently that passers-by turned curiously to look at me.

'You gave it to me,' I yelled at him.

I was trembling, and ready to kill him.

'Calm yourself, Franz, I was only thinking of your peace of mind.'

'Peace of mind!' I exclaimed agitatedly. 'Do you think I would be doing all this for peace of mind? I am uncovering inestimable benefits, perhaps another Eden. What is peace of mind compared with these?'

The man was looking at me, half as though I were deranged, half greedy to possess those benefits if I should fail.

'It is little indeed,' he said at last. 'But you will, you must continue.'

'As long as I am able,' I told him. 'As long as I can have the house.'

'It is yours,' said Mesmer, 'if that is what you wish, though

I fear it may cause megrims. Tell me, this spirit . . . have you seen it?'

'I believe I may once have done,' I told him. 'It had taken the face of a statue in a deserted garden. It was the most repulsive thing I have ever seen. Why I should have seen him there I cannot tell you. He seemed both to beckon and to threaten. Normally he manifests in the form of pain.'

'Pain? You are sick?'

He affected to show concern but I knew he was only after the completed heads.

'I am as well as can be expected,' I replied. 'The pains move about my body though he shows a preference for my gut.'

'And where does he reside, this spirit?'

'In the statue that you gave me. You know that, surely?'

'The Egyptian?'

'Of course. It contains that art of which Hermes Trismegistus was master. It holds the wisdom of the magi, those old masters of Proportion, which I am unlocking. Perhaps indeed it is a portrait of the Trismegistus himself.'

'I think perhaps we should balance your fluid, Franz,' he said, after a pause. 'One thing is certain. Your magnetism is all over the place.'

87

Mesmer tells me that the Earth is a giant Engine which converts mechanical energy into subtile fluid. Earth's magnetism is produced by the subtile fluid deep within the planet, for the subtile fluid produces magnetic effects just as moving magnets induce the subtile fluid. Sometimes he calls the subtile fluid 'the electric fluid'.

He says there is power undreamt of here if we can but

tap it. By 'we' he means 'he'. It is, he says, the secret of life itself.

I have begun to wonder if he is not a little mad.

88

The pamphlets they have in Vienna. They print more every day! And many, it seems, make their way to Pressburg to make us feel more cosmopolitan. I cannot imagine why anybody reads them. From time to time, I collect pamphlets people have let drop. They seem to find their way against the railings of the cemetery.

I collect them because, in their way, pamphlets are the expressions of a city, the verbal grimaces if you like. A random sampling of my pickings would include: Ladies' Maids; Ladies of the Court; Young Girls of Vienna; A Confidential Word in the Ear of Householders; A Word about the Ladies of Vienna Who Wear their Hair High; Is Antichrist Blue or Green?; A Trip into Hell; Remarks about the Devil of Seefeld in the Tyrol; Silver Angels Talking at Mariazell; Mamma Wants to Send Me to a Convent; Are these things so?; Yes, they are; No, they are not; What of that?

That is Vienna for you. It is the way the wind is blowing against my railings.

89

After I had moved into No. 13, Jewish Cemetery Road, I did three weeks of work on the Servile Flatterer (I give them these names to put the inquisitive off the scent, concealing the true reason for the expressions they show).

The pains are, as I half expected, a little worse in the new studio but I curbed them as I knew how. Mesmer had to go back to Paris but he vowed to return in a couple of months. He has an apartment in Pressburg, I discover. Cunning fox!

I was left blissfully alone. My brother, having discovered his wife's infidelity – she had not left him at this stage – was busy forgiving her.

And then suddenly, unannounced, my own wife arrived. At least she said she was my wife. I didn't think she was my wife. I told her so.

'What is your name?' I asked. 'I don't think you're my wife.'

'Don't be silly, Franz. I know you and your games. I'm Johanna, of course.'

'That means nothing. Everyone's Johanna. I expect this child is Johanna.'

'Of course she is. You are frightening her, your own child.'

'You say that she is my child? Is that your drift?'

'Of course it is.'

'I'm sorry. I can't seem to place her.'

However, they looked so doleful I took them in for the moment, though I could not see how the continual miasmas from the cemetery could be good for the child's chest. They stayed two months. Then Mesmer returned. He came round to the house all agog. I had done nothing. Not a new head to be seen. He banged the table in his impatience.

I tried to reason with him.

'This woman and her children arrived. She says she is my wife. I cannot work. She has developed a peevish streak.'

That stopped him in his tracks. He reflected for a while, puffing out his lecher's lips and going 'tootootoo' under his breath.

'Send them round to your brother's,' he said at last. 'His wife has left him to live with a Colonel of Hussars in Pomerania. A wife and family will be just the thing he needs to cheer him up. In the fullness of time, when the secret of Proportion is yours, you can redraft the laws of consanguinity and they can marry without a qualm.'

He took them round himself, and they were overjoyed with their new circumstance. My brother, who had not eaten for days and looked quite haggard, started playing games with the children, and took wine and cake with the mother. Mesmer had surpassed himself. I felt a little pang as if I had parted from the human family.

I was once more alone with the Egyptian, my fifty-one heads, and the ghosts of Jewish Cemetery Road. In material terms I now had all I needed. A pipe of tobacco, a flute – one of my pupils sent me some of the latest sonatas from Vienna – an armchair, a bed, a ewer . . . I required no more for this was no time for luxury. If I was to penetrate the secret, it would have to be soon. I could feel its elusiveness. There had been too many delays.

I was now within nodding distance of my target, and I set myself to complete the last ten heads within two months – a tall order but by no means impossible. (Sixty-nine, I should mention, my desiderated total, represents a perfect proportion in itself being formed of thrice two which is the female number, and thrice three, which is the male – as well as representing a symbolic wheel of the generative forces.)

My studio seemed alive in these later days with forces (generative? magnetic?) that whizzed and bounced and muttered to me as I worked. I had my heads all ranged around the room, their faces turned inwards so they could see me at my mirror carefully selecting my next mask. I was now so expert in my practice that, once selected, I could hold my face motionless almost for as long as it took for me to do the first draft. And as I sat there, motionless, feeling the first of the great pains that my prey threw at me, I thought of them as my children as well as my protectors.

And when I finally went to bed, I could feel the house vibrate and almost lift as the daemon tried to shake off my pursuit. But the powers of protection failed with the coming of darkness. And if I should finally fall asleep, my dreams would be charged with the most fearful trepidations and chimaeras; gaping monsters, trolls, bloodybones; every conceivable childish terror but with a dimension of adult hell; leering sexual figures; female centaurs; succubi whose delight it was to weaken and shame.

Nocturnal ejaculation was so frequent that I was obliged to wash my own sheets before Johanna could get to them.

There is nothing so bleak as cold semen.

I would wake with a shudder and a start from these terrible dreams, almost too fearful to reach for the tinder-box and candlestick. I knew there was something in the room, a presence that wished me no good. It was as if I had opened, or were about to open, a sarcophagus over which a curse had been placed.

Sometimes I would be thrown out of bed with one great wrench of the mattress. Or there would be a whispering. Cold hands across the face, and worse than hands. A serpent slid under the pillow. I would start up, shouting for help, and look towards the window for salvation, only to see the waving tentacles of a giant squid sucking at the pane. Beyond, the cemetery would be lit up with a low, drear, leprous, charnel glow, and the dead Jews could be

195

seen climbing out of their graves and adjusting those little black headpieces that they wear. I assure you, it gave a new dimension to the phrase skull-cap. And they would troop out in shadowy throng, surrounding No. 13, Jewish Cemetery Road, and make melancholy gestures as if they too were afraid of what was inside, rows and rows of them as if they had been victims of some unimaginable slaughter.

In the morning, with the sun, these sombre manifestations faded as they will do, and I would start work again resolved that I should not be deflected or overwhelmed so near to my great conclusion. Even so, through lack of sleep and the lowering effect of these spectres upon my will, I was in a constant state of fatigue which of course sapped the resistance; and when Mesmer came round, having congratulated me upon my latest piece, the Rapt Listener, he commented upon my wretched appearance.

'You look dreadful, Franz. At this rate you will not finish your project.'

'I am well enough.'

'You must eat. I will send your woman again to clean and bring you soup.'

Johanna had stopped coming round for some reason.

'I do not need soup.'

'What nonsense! Everyone needs soup. Lovely rich soup with noodles . . .'

'I detest soup. I was frightened by soup as a child.'

But I could not dissuade him. He was going to send me soup come hell or high water. High water, now you come to mention it, seems a rather good synonym for the rank stuff Johanna sometimes brings.

'You are under some kind of magnetic attack,' he pronounced, rubbing his lecher's lips with the back of his hand. 'Perhaps we should perform an exorcism.'

'No,' I cried, 'for then you would be exorcising the very thing I seek. The daemon and the goal are inextricably

196

entwined. It is Proportion which is resisting me. It is Proportion which I seek to gain, and I must use Proportion to do it.'

His brow knitted as I tried to put into words the truth that is implicit and too great to be encapsulated in crass syllables.

'You mean . . .?' he began.

'Whoever arouses such causes in himself as are superior to the causes in another, must call forth effects superior to the effects of another,' I pronounced. 'Those are your own words.'

'I do not understand,' he said.

'Nor do I fully,' I answered, and indeed it seemed as if the words had been put in my mouth as a lover might pop in a sweetmeat, or a priest a wafer; the sense was greater than the meaning.

He shook his head doubtfully.

'I mean,' I said, and I could feel the certainty, the lucidity gathering within me, 'I mean that the Egyptian's mastery of Proportion is at present superior to mine, as are his effects and powers, but I shall hook him out. It is the secret we are forbidden to see.'

'The secret?'

He lisped the word in his excitement: 'The thecret?'

'The secret of Creation,' I told him. 'What other secret is there?'

'Creation!'

I could see he was impressed.

'Do you not think the seeker after such a secret would be resisted?'

'And punished?'

'Certainly – if he does not achieve superior effects.'

'We shall have a séance,' he said. 'We shall see what we are dealing with.'

I was amused by his use of the word 'we'. He did not have to endure the rigours of Jewish Cemetery Road.

Not another séance.

A séance will do nothing except waste time.

90

I went along to his séance because, after all, he was my patron, and because I hoped that

. . .

[*Several lines of the manuscript are obliterated at this point*]

. . .

but nothing came of it.

As it proved, it was designed by Mesmer to reassure me. I knew his game. He wanted me to continue to the end undaunted. He considered the monsters to be in my head. He now thinks, in short, that I am deranged, and he is quite possibly right, whatever 'deranged' may mean. One would need to be deranged to continue in this matter. It does not stop him wanting me as his partner, though. Oh no. He wants his share all right for his magnetism and his electricity and his fluid; and he will stop at nothing to get me to the finishing-line. And then what? Who will share the spoils? Let Proportion decide.

I enjoyed the music. He had got some fiddlers in to play wild Magyar strains (not unlike my acoustic experience in Vienna but pleasanter) behind a curtain. I wished I had brought my flute. I sat down and held hands with a stout elderly lady and a little man with a beard whom he introduced as Mr and Mrs Stumpf of Ulm. We asked each other how we did, we did very well; we were charmed to make each other's acquaintance.

Incense was burning somewhere. The lights were dowsed. Several raps were heard. Mrs Stumpf started foaming. Then a young woman in a diaphanous dress appeared high up in a niche on one wall, and began speaking to us in an unintelligible language. I rather wished I were holding hands with her.

'Speak to us in German, please,' commanded Mesmer. 'What is your name?'

'I am the Grecian Princess Atalanta.'

'Do you have a message for one of us?'

'Yes.'

'Who is it?'

'The sculptor Froberger.'

'What is your message?'

'We of the spirit world love you. Do not despair. You are unlocking the door. The guardian is jealous of your progress but we will protect you.'

Dum dum-dum dumdumdumdum deee went the fiddlers. I felt drowsy. I believe he had put some poppy in the censer. So powerful was the personality of Mesmer and his strange influence that I was tempted almost to believe in the farrago. The girl, whoever she was, doubtless some local Johanna of his, was pretty in a sort of dark Hungarian way and I could see her bush through the gauzy wrapping. I felt at least she might have shaved for so ethereal a part. It was the bush that suspended my disbelief.

'Farewell, sculptor Froberger,' she cried. 'Success will crown your efforts. Eat the soup.'

'I must get back,' I said to Mesmer as the candles were lit. 'I am full of new confidence. Thank you for the show.'

'No show, I assure you,' he said, slightly mortified. 'You are a fortunate man whom the spirits smile upon.'

He is a cynical fellow. What a fool he must think me!

91

A Frenchman called Desaguillier has proved that an electric fluid will pass freely through metals. Mesmer is not a charlatan, whatever else he may be.

92

I regard the flute – and music – as part solace, part discipline. And it is amusing to note that the great Cellini was obliged by his father to take it up, and achieved extreme skill at it, while finding it a considerable imposition of his parent!

I find no such imposition in the instrument – although it is true to say that no member of my family had ever shown any musical aptitude before, so I did not feel coerced.

Cellini's father had the right idea for, to the Greeks – and who followed the Greeks more faithfully than the Florentines? – music was as important a part of an education as philosophy, draughtsmanship, architecture or the drama.

I am indeed fortunate that there is so much musical material for the instrument, and so many good composers writing for it today. There is the learned Quantz, of course. And Mozart (though he is said not to like the flute which one has to regard as a flaw in the man). There are Joseph and Michael Haydn; and Dittersdorf, Monn, Zelenka, the Benda family; to say nothing of the great Handel and Bach . . . and Bach's sons . . . though I do not care for the over-quirky Carl Philipp Emanuel . . .

I could be awash with music and never work, so it has to be rationed. And of course it is expensive.

When I play, it is the only time that I am free from the daemon.

'Art thou troubled, Music shall calm thee . . .'

It is true, you know. Listen.

93

There was a regular panic among the sextons and the under-takers last month – even the Jewish ones. In fact it brought all denominations together, a rare feat. Our enlightened Emperor issued a Decree regulating funerals and interments. I ask you. Could anything be more calculated to upset the applecart? And he wonders why he's unpopular!

The whole thing was occasioned by a shortage of cloth and oak in Vienna, it seems. So he decides that no one is to be buried in clothes or in a coffin. Every parish is to have stock of coffins in various sizes, re-usable and available free of charge. Once in the cemetery, the bodies are lowered into a communal grave, wrapped in a shroud, and covered with quicklime. There is to be a single ceremony for all the dead of the day.

What a commotion! You have no idea of the interests vested in Death. They seem even stronger than those con-cerned with the other thing. He was naturally forced to retract, leaving everyone in Pressburg to do as they had done before except burying people inside churches. It made him look an absolute booby – a posture, admittedly, that he has never shunned.

And yet, he is right. For what is Death but a comma, or a semi-colon; it is not the end but a pause leading on to a larger sentence.

Johanna says you never saw anyone as pissed as the sextons the night after they heard the news. Next day there was hardly a coffin went sweetly into the hole.

94

There were three kinds of mean employed by the masters of the Renaissance: the Geometric, the Arithmetic and the Harmonic.

These three kinds of mean are expressed as the three chords on which our musical harmonies are based today.

It is the mean by which Handel and Bach and our modern masters, but most of all, I believe, our little Mozart – I forgive him for the flute – are able to convey *the beauty of that which is beyond hearing through that which is heard.*

People talk and talk, but I have never heard of a better definition of Art.

Winckelmann, eat your pudding.

95

I had no visitors in the following weeks. Mesmer, I knew, had gone away on his travels again. He was a Freemason and had many mysterious contacts and undertakings to attend to, apart from his clinics and his practice in Paris. I daresay I should have felt flattered to have had so much attention from such an *homme d'affaires*; but I knew how much he stood to gain from his patronage of me. I was just another one of his projects which he fitted in between trips to Signors Galvani and Volta, and amours in half the capitals of Europe. His lips are too thick. He needs tape lips.

I did, however, take the advice proffered by the Princess Atalanta about the soup. I needed sustenance even though I found soup hard to respect. There is precious little body in a soup. However, a physical failure at this stage would have been disastrous.

So the days passed in work and soup. I would sometimes break off to play some air upon my flute – in these latter days I favoured the Dorian mode, finding its plaintive plainsong most cleansing – or to smoke my old meerschaum as I pondered a new head.

Sometimes Johanna would linger after bringing the soup or skirmishing around the place with a brush; and I would sketch her; and she would draw me into bed; for warmth, she said.

The days were growing shorter. The wind whipped the leaves from the straggling withies that stood like ghost trees around the marsh, perennially half-wreathed in mist, and wagged the sad cypresses beside the low cemetery wall. Doors thumped, windows rattled, and overhead frantic clouds spilled their burden on the ungrateful land as the gales pursued them.

There was less light for my work, more dark in which the spirits could torment me. Yes, they were round me like dark bees. Sometimes in the morning I was so pummelled and pinched, I could scarcely hold my chisel. But, like a beekeeper, I was becoming used to these attacks. They were alarming, yes, but I could endure them. They were almost like a child's fury, malicious but without a full capacity for destruction.

I suppose I was becoming arrogant. I felt I had the measure of my daemon now. And then, one dark day, as I was doing the Strong Smell (and there were strong smells in the Jewish sexton's house; strange strong smells, mephitic vapours, filthy flatuses, charnel-house reeks) and pinching under my ribs – so! – to counter the pain in my gut, I was seized by the most dire, the most appalling sensation.

This, I knew, was going to be an attack of an entirely different kind. I could feel my head being pulled back until I thought my neck would break. I cried out, thinking that this was the onset of a fatal heart attack or some such mortal seizure, but there was none to hear me.

Next, my mouth and lips – the lips that I have so assiduously tried to refine – began to push out so that I could begin to see them protruding like a great foul dish under my nose. There was laughter in my ears that came from within, not without. I suddenly realized that the daemon was in me. I had let him in.

There was nothing I could do about it. No contortion that I could throw my face into, no pinch of the ribs that would avail.

My earlobes became baggy and pendulous. As I felt them dragging downwards, I managed to catch sight of myself in one of my mirrors. A most disgusting look was in my eyes, leering and gloating. My nose lengthened and thickened. And my mouth, my filthy, disgusting lips spread and grew and poked outwards like a great sucking, sneering, slyly smirking, disgusting purse. My chin tilted upwards, narrowing and pointed, probing and crafty.

I knew, of course, where I had seen the face, or something like it, before. It was the face on the statue in the garden: 'Daddy head'. Only this time it was worse. This time it was not going to let me go. My first head of it had been an approximation, culled from memory. Now it was going to be the real thing.

The pain all the while was indescribable. It was like some appalling rigor; the muscles knotting, the flesh and sinews twisting past all tolerance. And yet, though I am sure that I screamed like the devil, all I could hear myself uttering was bloodcurdling chuckles.

After what seemed like an eternity, I knew that the

alteration had proceeded as far as its perpetrator wished. I took my contorted features in my hand and steadied myself before the glass.

To write of the dread, shame, pain and disgust that I felt at the spectacle which presented itself would require a stauncher pen than mine. Here was I, the seeker after Beauty and Proportion, reduced to a misshapen grotesque that would have given nightmares to a hangman. It would have been better perhaps if the picture revealed had been totally alien to me. At least I could have felt that this was a visitation, like a cold sore, or a carnival mask thrust upon me by drunken strangers. But the real horror lay in the fact that, in its distorted features, I could still recognize my own.

In this loathsome situation, I could only do what I have always done; that was, to turn to the tools of my trade, and start making a portrait of the awful thing that beaked and nodded and sneered at me from the glass.

After a while, I became aware of an insistent knocking at the door. I worked on for a while, thinking it was merely another manifestation of my tormentor, but at length a voice that was unmistakably mortal could be heard hollering: 'Froberger, Mr Froberger, are you there, Mr Froberger?'

I put down my chisel and walked towards the door, holding a cloth before my face.

'Who is it?' I mumbled thickly. 'It is past nine o'clock.'

My voice, through those extruded lips, had a curious clucking-clicking quality.

'I am Count Deym, a friend of Mesmer's. He has told me something of your work.'

I doubted whether Mesmer would have divulged to anyone the details of my labours, being far too keen to keep the booty for himself, unless it were part of some plot to wheedle or cajole – but, be that as it might be, the notion of being seen in this disgusting condition by anyone, friend or villain, was unthinkable.

'Please go away,' the beak was making it almost impossible to speak at all. 'Go . . . awayclk.'

'I cannot take no for an answer,' came the importunate reply. 'I have come all the way from Stuttgart and must return tomorrow. I have a proposition for you.'

'No propositionsclk,' I mouthed. 'I am engaged for the rest of my natural daysclk.'

'A thousand florins,' he shouted, 'to reproduce your collection. We shall have an exposition. I work in wax.'

'Not for a thousand thousandclk,' I rejoined.

I remembered his name now. He had a charlatan's reputation. God knows what sort of Count he was. Silly Counts, we used to call them. He had to flee Vienna because of a duel with some Court official, and I had heard that he had acquired the base art of moulding in plaster and wax in some dubious foreign capital. He had made a small fortune out of plaster casts of antique statues. So now he intended to make another with my heads! Ha! Someone had been blabbing. If it wasn't Mesmer, it would doubtless be straddle-legged Johanna, my little baggage of a soup-maker.

I could feel drool dripping out of the edge of my beak, making conversation through the flange an increasing tribulation. It was like talking through a spittle-laden French horn.

'Go away,' I groaned, furiously, 'I'll have none of your waksh-worksh.'

'Have a care, Mr Froberger. It is not wise to look a gift horse in the mouth. I hear you are not so flush with money. Or friends for that matter. But perhaps you are in your cups for I perceive your speech is slurred.'

'What care I for friend or enemy or fair speedge,' I yelled. 'I have better to talk to than you. Be off with you back to Stuttgartclk.'

The fellow at length gave up, uttering the direst imprecations. I returned to my mirror and continued my task till the candles burnt low in their sockets and my eyes filled with blood.

Finally, when I had done, I threw myself upon the couch and, turning my beak carefully to one side, I sank into a dreamless stupor undisturbed by any of the usual assaults of my enemy, or even by the hellish flatus that seemed to have filled the house as a concomitant to the Beak Head. (Ficino writes of the mephitic odours that surround and nourish a daemon.)

I was awakened, shivering, by a ray of sunshine that fell directly on to my face through a gap in the curtains – a gap, I quickly realized, which might well have admitted the inquisitive gaze of my nocturnal visitor. Had he seen my contorted features? If so, I should have all the gawpers in Pressburg here presently; and in due course, when he had completed his wax impression, I should be as famous as a man I once saw in a travelling circus – 'The Ugliest Man in the World' – who had only half as foul a face as mine.

I put my hand to my mouth in an automatic gesture of despair; and it only then dawned upon me that my beak had gone. My hands explored the rest of my countenance. The chin, the cheek, the lobes were all back to normal.

I advanced tremulously to the looking-glass. Yes, my face was my own again. Had the whole thing been a nightmare, born of too much work and too little soup?

I looked slowly towards my work-table. There in the dusty sunlight stood my model of the Beak Head to refute and rebuke my hopes of normality.

It told me that this latest and most terrible of my visitations had been merely introductory.

96

I am unlocking the face of God. It is perfectly clear to me. God made man in His own image, and that image was naturally perfect in proportion. Nothing less would do. Sin and time vitiated that proportion in humanity, but I am – by God's grace and my own infinite perseverance – pushing back the accretions of deformity that have been heaped up like turds before the face of Man. God has given me my skill and the wit to embark upon the pursuit. Why does he then allow these spirits to torment me?

97

Let the head be cast in lead for that is the metal of our condition.

Let the forehead be high to indicate the intelligence that separates us from the brute, but let us not forget our bestial origins. Thicken the eyebrow ridges slightly, so.

Let the skull be rounded so that we may imagine it embodies our terrestrial globe. Europe is my face, and Java is my hippocampus.

Let the proportions be 2 x 3, the numbers representing female and male, then let us cube that figure 6 to find the Human Number that Plato himself describes = 216.

Those who say that 666 is the Number of the beast are wrong. The correct definition is $6 \times 6 \times 6$ which comes to the sum above. It is not coincidental that 216 is the minimum number of days that the Greeks allotted for human gestation.

Let us not forget what Aristotle has to tell us regarding the Golden Mean.

98

More visitors.

Fessler: how did he get in? It appears he has been shagging Johanna. Loyalty, it seems is a thing of the past.

He slipped in with the soup.

No, he cannot have another head. I simply cannot do heads for every jackanapes who comes to my door. Fessler is a disgrace to his cloth. He is on a mission to Bohemia. He has two sturdy Capuchins with him who keep thwacking their staffs against their horny palms.

Ouch. All right, Fessler. Just this once.

Next.

Count Deym? Silly Count, we call you. I know, they all do. How did you become a Count, anyway? If you're a Count, I'm a toasted muffin. And why aren't you in Potsdam?

Night again.

Mesmer, my brother Joseph, my 'wife' and Stadler look in. Stadler wants to learn the secret of Proportion. I knee him sharply in the balls and he flies up to the ceiling where he sticks in the rafters.

'Can I do anything for you, Franz? You have a fever. I have brought you soup.'

It is Johanna.

'Stop shagging Fessler,' I tell her. 'And get Stadler down from the ceiling. He is eaves dropping.'

She drags me upstairs to bed, and lies with me to keep me warm.

In the morning, I am as weak as a kitten. Actually, kittens have always seemed to me rather too active for symbols of weakness. I was as weak as a peeled sausage with vertigo. Johanna had taken away my chisel and mallet, even my charcoal and paper so I could not work. I lay there and drank soup. Believe me, if I could have done anything else, I would have done. It was disgusting, greasy mutton stuff and smelt of armpits.

Because I was not working, the daemon did not come near me. Doubtless he thought that my spirit was broken.

'Would you like to talk to Mr Nicolai?' Johanna asked. 'He has come a long way to see you.'

'Who is Mr Nicolai?'

'Everyone's heard of Mr Nicolai.'

'Ah.'

'Go on, Franz. Even you must have heard of Mr Nicolai.'

'Sorry.'

'He writes in the journals. And books. Such a lot of books he's written.'

'How do you know? You don't read books.'

'Books of his travels. Discourses. Conversations with sundry persons. And now he wants to see you.'

'I'm not some kind of curiosity, you know,' I told her.

'Yes, you are.'

There was a pause while I pondered her remark.

'Oh,' I said, after a while, playing for time.

Perhaps I was indeed a grotesque, something to be visited and gaped at like a rustic shrine, outlandish but curioso.

'Come on, Franz. You might as well see him. You've nothing else to do.'

'Give me my chisel, witch,' I warned her.

'Not until you're stronger.'

'I'm strong enough to put you over my knee.'

She wriggled with mock-anticipatory pleasure. I've never

known such a woman for debunking. She was impressed by nothing.

'Oh, very well,' I told her, suddenly more tired than I cared to admit. 'He can call on me tomorrow.'

99

A prayer.

Come, Perfect Form, and fill my mind and body with the due dimensions of Thy grace. So that what is crooked, I may make straight; what is excessive, I may curtail; what is attenuated, I may amend. Teach me the width of Truth and the height of Beauty. And deliver me from the stresses of imperfection and the impediments of self-doubt. I ask this, not that I am worthy of the goal but that Thou art worthy of the endeavour; and in the hope that at the last I may come to Thy blest courts and see Thy handiwork, perfect in everlasting measure. Amen.

100

Actually, I am not convinced that Perfect Form listens to prayers. Does the mountain bend its head to the climber?

I hate the word handiwork. It reminds me of something we used to have classes for at school. Miss Pfeffer will take Handiwork. Or was it Craft? And is it Art?

101

As it happened, Nicolai was nearly the saving of me.

He was a stubby little man with round innocent-seeming blue eyes which, on occasion, he would fortify with a pair of golden spectacles. At another time I should have liked to have done a head of him. Spectacles provide the sculptor with a number of challenges.

However, as I explained to the little German, on the assumption that he had come about a commission, further undertakings were now impossible.

He waved his hands deprecatingly.

'I have not come for my portrait,' he told me. 'You have been ill, I understand. I have come to talk to you. I came to Pressburg on my travels to see the cathedral, and I heard that you were engaged in strange endeavours. They talk about your genius still in Vienna . . ,'

'Ha!' I interrupted.

'Your genius,' he continued, unperturbed, 'and of your withdrawal from the world. I am sure you have a tale to tell.'

'I am my own man,' I told him, 'and wish to remain so.'

While I spoke I could sense a vibration coming from the Egyptian as if he did not wish the mystery to be profaned. *He* did not want the mystery to be profaned! It was *I* that did not wish the mystery to be profaned. Who was profaning mysteries anyhow? The effrontery of it! It encouraged me to continue in my conversation with the man, for it was now clear to me that in all things the daemon had to be resisted. To thwart him and overpower him must be my exercise and practice.

'What is that statue over there?' enquired Nicolai, innocently. 'I observe that you regard it with some frequency.'

The fellow was no fool for all his moon face and pebble
lenses.

'It contains all that we sculptors seek,' I told him, trying
not to gasp as the Spirit of Proportion lanced me in the
prostate.

'Tell me more,' said Nicolai, mistaking my grimace for a
smile of cheer.

And I related to him something of the tale – without profaning mysteries – that I have here set down, at length, upon
paper. Indeed, it was he who encouraged me to expand and
amplify the story of my life and of my search for Proportion
which has led me such a merry dance, and which – unless
I can wrest it quickly – I am persuaded may soon be the
finish of me. The fever has left me weak, and I have not
the doggedness which once sustained me.

Nicolai heard my story with growing amazement but
without condescension or disbelief. Perhaps because he was
a stranger, I was able to speak to him without constraint,
and my words, unaffected and unadorned, reached their
mark directly.

Of course, at times he asked for clarification – especially
when I related my system for denying and overpowering the
daemon. To me it seems as clear as the daystar, but I always
find that when I try to elucidate the matter, the daemon
takes the words and warps them.

'Come,' I said, 'enough of muddying words, I will let you
see the heads for yourself.'

And I took him to the gallery where the Jews used to stack
their coffins, and showed him my work, introducing him
to each head and explaining the proportional relationship
of each one to the pains that might assail me, while the
daemon plucked at my guts like a zither. (All right, I was
touching on mysteries here. But I had paid dearly for my
discoveries. I would share them with whom I liked.)

Though much tempted, I did not like to screw my features into an appropriate grimace to counter the assault – the Lustful Mendicant would have filled the bill admirably – for it was scarcely a social expression, and I did not wish to frighten the fellow.

'This is astonishing, quite astonishing,' the little fellow kept repeating.

At length we returned to the studio. I could see the man was moved, and I offered him a pipe of tobacco. We smoked in silence for a while.

'Froberger,' he said at length, 'you must give this thing up. Come with me on my travels. I shall write and you shall sketch. You could do a series of Heads of Eminent Contemporaries. We shall make a pretty penny. That cough of yours needs attention. Prosperity is the best medication.'

'I cannot,' I replied, though tempted and flattered by his offer.

Would that I had taken it up! We puffed away for a while longer.

'I was afraid you would say that,' he ventured. 'At any rate, can you not moderate your assault on this daemonic citadel of yours? Reason, beguile, seduce, negotiate; but do not frontally attack.'

I could sense the daemon shaking with laughter. He was not to be fooled with a game of Grandmother's Footsteps.

'One cannot reason with fire,' I told Nicolai.

'You are a brave and remarkable man,' he told me, sadly, 'but I fear you will undo yourself.'

I put a brave face on it for him, for it would clearly make a better traveller's tale.

'That is my motto,' I said. 'Undo as you would be undone by.'

He made no reaction to my weak jest, but asked for pen and ink, and scribbled something upon a piece of paper which he pressed into my hand as he took his leave.

214

'Being by profession a traveller,' he said, 'I am seldom at home. But, given time, this address will find me. Let me know if there is anything I can do for you.'

We shook hands.

'Where now?' I asked him.

'To Vienna,' he told me.

I felt a pang. Say what you like about Vienna – and one does – one can't help missing it. They say even Queen Marie Antoinette misses Vienna.

'I am going to see Karl Ditters von Dittersdorf, the Baron Van Swieten, Count Georg Adam von Stahremberg, and a poet called Blumauer who kept his hat on in front of the Pope.'

I almost changed my mind as he spoke of these things. The mists cleared for an instant and I could see the sparkle, the gaiety, the golden life that once had been mine; the talk, the coffee-houses, the Stephansdom, the Heiligenkreuzerhof, the Griechengasse, the scores of little Heurigen, the Opera, the excursions to the Wienerwald, the pretty ladies in the Prater.

'Wait,' I said, laying my hand on his arm as he turned to depart.

'Yes?' he replied, pausing (I think I am right in saying) hopefully.

And then the mist closed in again, and I could see only the grey shapes of jealousy, betrayal, sickness, persecution and disappointment. The real centre lay here, with me, in an enterprise from which there was no turning.

'Yes,' he said again, not impatiently.

'Just goodbye,' I said. 'And thank you.'

'The gratitude is mine,' he replied. 'Au revoir.'

'Goodbye.'

I watched him climb into the waiting pony-cart, and drive off towards the sunset. Almost out of sight, he turned again and waved at me. It was as if one on the shore had been gesturing at a drowning man. And then he was lost behind a hearse and its nodding black-plumed mares which came rumbling down the hill towards me from the city. (They still occasionally buried Jews here, although the newer cemetery – nearer the new synagogue – was more favoured. Even the Jews had more or less given my cemetery up. That was the measure of my Jewish Cemetery.)

It struck me, with that sombre image, that Nicolai might have been sent by my adversary the daemon – a neat deflection it would have been to pop me off to Vienna where no doubt a giddy whirl would await me!

I was inclined to congratulate myself upon my resolution, though my heart dipped low as the sun at the thought of what travails lay ahead of me.

102

I have disciplined myself in chastity. One does not approach a mystery soiled. I abjure the notion of pudenda. The daemon torments me with visions of Johannas. Games with gravy, the mute model who loved to be looked at, the Empress's sudden lewdness . . . these are the things that make people say 'You are ill, Froberger'.

Perhaps I am ill. We are all ill. Look at our lips; horribly red and swollen.

That is why I accept the soup. It requires a minimum of aperture, being liquid. I do not want 'fish' in my soup, Johanna. It must be all broth.

Sometimes I put a small tape over my lips to prevent any untoward entry. You should try it if you wish to remain chaste.

103

With the departure of Nicolai, my path took me once more into dark and unadopted ways.

Life at the ex-sexton's house grew stern. There were only seven more heads to complete but it seemed that these were to be the hardest of all for me.

Winter was setting in now for good. The first snow fell, and the blizzard added its own squeaks and howls to the yells and gibbers of my tormentors. Sleep became well-nigh impossible. As soon as it was dark – and it was dark by five o'clock these days – the shadows began to move, stirring from the wainscoting like black rats. And as the night progressed, so did the quotient of malevolence. My bed-leg was destroyed and I made shift to put the mattress on the floor and sleep with a rug over my head.

One night, the tallboy fell on top of me, and I received a crack on the head and bruises all the way down my left side.

Another time, the washstand with its ewer and dirty water were shattered on the wall above me, drenching me with ice-cold suds and making my teeth chatter all night.

I dreaded another attack of the fever which I thought – apart from the effects of draught and inundation within the house – must emanate from the marsh or indeed the cemetery which oozed its discharge into it. But still I did not give up. I told myself to be heartened by the fervour of resistance, that I must be on the right track if my enemy were so exercised.

My sixty-third head, the Vainglorious Oaf, was completed in the teeth of fierce opposition. The daemon went for my kidneys this time. Pains of hideous intensity racked the small of my back – which I countered with the Oaf's eyes, wide open and brazenly staring – which correlated with the renal organs, coupled of course with unstinting rib-pinching.

With my sixty-fourth head, I was confronted by an appalling attack of piles which I resisted as best I could by doing a little buttercup mouth – the mouth corresponds of course to the anus – an undertaking that thus begun, resulted in the Simpering Poltroon. This head, with its indrawn lips and its crinkled delta of surrounding cheeklets, together with an expression of unspeakable weakness and decadence, is (I must be partial) one of the pinnacles of the collection.

There was no doubt about it, I was drawing near to the Mystery.

All the while, the Beak Head stood in a corner of the studio with a cloth over its face. I could feel it sneering at me. I was moved to destroy it utterly for it was poisoning the room. But at the same time, I knew that in its way it too was one more step towards the goal. However grotesque, it was a link in the chain, a stepping-stone to the Islands of the Blest, now so nearly attained.

104

Confusion. Today, I picked up a pamphlet. As I walked, tottered – exhausted by the night – towards the cemetery rails, I saw, as I advanced, this paper, fluttering against the rails, I stooped with difficulty, every movement is now attended with gripes, I saw this paper, idly turned it, the words kicked me in the eyes: THE CAPUCHIN MONK WHO DABBLES IN POLITICS or THE FORTHCOMING ADVENT OF ANTICHRIST.

It is about Fessler. My suspicions are confirmed. Someone else knows his evil purposes. But who? And if I could find him, what could be done? And if Fessler and Mesmer are in collusion . . .

My only recourse is to complete the work before the wind can blow the Secret to his ends. It is getting stronger.

105

I have written to Mesmer telling him that, if I die in my endeavours, the heads must belong to mankind. They cannot simply be his.

It was something little Nicolai told me.

'This is too great a thing for one man to carry. It will burn him out,' he said.

He was right. When I have completed the circle – if I am permitted to do so – it will contain more power than Signors Volta or Galvani ever dreamt of, for we shall hold in our hands that perfect Order and Degree from which and in which the Universe was created. Imperfection, Disproportion and Disorder were only added later. This is evident both from the Bible and from *In Principia*.

Thus, I have given instructions in my Will – which I have drawn up, had witnessed by Johanna, sealed, and locked within a subtle place – that all my heads shall go to someone in Switzerland whom I shall not name here, who shall order them for the universal Good of Man and introduce again the Age of Gold.

They are a Thing beyond Mesmer who is good only to himself, and who would employ them to gross ends, vanities and deboshery.

106

'Deeper and deeper yet.'

And now we enter the most horrible part of my tale which, if you have a weak stomach, or are in any way squeamish, or prefer sentimental romances which depict only the daintier things in life, I would urge you to omit – though I have not minced words up to this point and, if you were of that kidney, you would doubtless have dropped out long before. Talking of kidney, perhaps you will forgive me if I adopt the Vainglorious Oaf for a moment.

Ah, that is better.

Beak Head stood in the corner, as I say; and it seemed to me that something – electricity, magnetism, subtile fluid, call it what you will – was flowing between it and the Egyptian.

My studio seemed full of power beside which the efforts of my art appeared puny but which I knew, if I could make these last connections, I could control and use in some manner that I felt sure would ultimately be communicated to me.

The thought that, if I were successful, I might not only be immortal but immensely rich also crossed my mind; a temptation if you like; I was taken up the mountain; but I had no great love of life and no possible use for personal wealth except to relieve others; so it did not in all honesty weigh with me.

You smile? But then perhaps you have never had the opportunity to turn your back on fame and riches, and pursue perfection? And then again, perhaps you have.

Come, then. I have promised you horror and you shall have it in good measure.

I had only five more heads to finish; and of these I had two already planned – the Shrewd Moneylender and the Peaceful Sleeper – the first of which related to the upper bowels and the other to the main body of the stomach where the most piercing of my pains were now located.

I had completed the Moneylender with such resistance as I had come to expect, and was about to start on the Sleeper, when I observed that the daylight was fading once more. It had been a dull day with dun-coloured clouds and a brooding kind of light at the best of times, and it was now no more than four o'clock of the afternoon, but as I say, the day was already over.

It seemed to me, as it waned from twilight to dark, that the room once more, but now more than ever, began to bounce and crackle with power. It flickered between bust and statue making the Egyptian glow with a strange dark incandescence.

I had not slept for seventy-two hours, and I realized that for some reason Johanna – whom recently I had not allowed to enter the house for she disturbed me with her breasts and her inconsequentialities – I took my bread and soup from her through an opened sliver of door – had not appeared for at least two days. I had not eaten and I had hardly drunk for I thought the well was poisoned and there was no wine.

I found it difficult, as I drew the ragged curtains and stirred the poor brands on my fire, to think straight or even to direct my actions properly. I trembled. The power had somehow got into my noddle and my stretched brain trembled and jumped and twitched like one of Galvani's frogs' legs. My head thumped, and now my ears began to thump too.

It was only after some while that I established that the audible thumping was actually coming from the door. I scraped it open a couple of inches, not knowing what kind of bugaboo or daemon might be attending me – and there was Johanna with her soup, wrapped up against

221

the cold and holding a bottle of wine in her mittened hands.

'Let me in,' she said, 'it's brass monkeys out here.'

I did not like to hear her speak disrespectfully of brass which was, after all, one of the metals of the Mystery, and anyway, I suspected a trick, so, fuddled though I was, I did not immediately comply.

'Who are you?' I asked.

'Don't be a prick.'

I must say it sounded like Johanna, but then it probably would. These days the daemon had been serving up all manner of chimaeras – faces from the past, whimsies, flights of fancy, fine ladies, Venetian courtesans, Hogarthian whores, trollops, doxies and catch-me-quicks – to distract and divert me, that I did not know whether I was coming or going.

I decided to play along with the apparition.

'I hope you are clean,' I said, 'and have not been spreading your legs for any young blades. We must have no contamination now.'

'I'm as clean as you are,' she retorted pertly, 'in fact by the look of you a bloody sight cleaner. Do you want your soup or what?'

I let her in and she put down her saucepan and wine bottle. She had some bread in a cloth which she also set upon the table. The sight of it made me realize how hungry I was, though I managed to compress my aperture.

She poured me out a glass of wine – she had already drawn the cork – and ladled soup into a dish for me. The wine was excellent, a rich ruby red that the Hungarians call Bull's Blood, and it coursed through my veins like that invisible fluid of Mesmer's which draws together all shapes and material (and indeed immaterial) forms. The soup too was, as soup goes, very fair – pork with paprika and noodles – and I could feel my powers reviving as I ate. Johanna watched me like a granny feeding a goose. I was so hungry that I ate the noodles which

I would normally have left, sucking them up between pursed lips.

'Where have you been?' I asked her at last, feeling slightly indecent as I always do when feeding in public.

'I was poorly, wasn't I?' she replied. 'I had one of me turns. I shouldn't be out now but I thought you'd be starving. Much thanks I get for it, I must say.'

'Come here,' I suggested, wiping my mouth with one of the rags that I keep for the clay, and feeling a material form in my breeches, 'come here, I will give you a turn.'

Not that I would have, of course, so near completion.

'Oh no you don't,' she said, dancing away out of reach, 'you've got to get busy on your face-aches. How many is there now?'

It seemed to me that she was indeed a devil, for why otherwise should she ask questions that she had never raised before?

'I have a few more to go,' I told her guardedly, 'but now you are here, let us, as Horace says, snatch the moment.'

I saw no reason not to embrace the vision so long as she did not have the upper hand. She was, after all, a vision; that is, not carnal; air.

'Not till you've finished,' she replied, shaking her head, 'you finish your last one and then we'll see about it. We must have no contamination now.'

I was chastened by her use of my own words.

'Bitch,' I said, although I knew she was right.

Johanna never took such an interest in my work unless it were of her own pert body. That proved this creature was a vision.

My very mouth, as I spoke to her, was full of bitterness.

'Goodnight,' said the vision, dancing out of the door into a polka of snowflakes, 'work well. I shall be round tomorrow.'

My powers were quite renewed by the nourishment and wine, and I addressed myself to the Sleeper with a will. The visitation of the mock-Johanna seemed to have quietened the daemon and I was allowed to work on by lamplight undisturbed, my face fixed in a rapture of repose with my eyelids lifted only an iota so that I could just see my hands upon the alabaster as I shaped it. It was the stillness, as I was to discover, before the storm.

I had all but finished this face – there remained only a little refining around the brow which I could do later – when I felt the most powerful invitation to sleep. It was indeed as if the poppy god, old Morpheus himself, had opened his arms and beckoned.

Since there was so little left to finish, I did not even attempt to fight the drowsiness that now enfolded me, but dragged myself upstairs and fell across the bed.

It was the last peace I was to know in this life.

107

I suppose I must have been asleep; but in these latter days, sleep and waking seemed indivisible. Perhaps sleep indeed allows us to peep beyond the meniscus of reality and into that place which Prospero tells us our little world is rounded with. Certainly my waking hours were filled with mist and curious shadow, and my dreams had a strangely gravitational quality as if this was where I belonged.

However it may have been, it appeared to me that I had not, after all, gone up to my bedroom but was still completing the last touch of my chisel upon the alabaster.

I had arranged my heads in a double circle around the studio and there they stood, each one almost touching his neighbours; the lead on the outside and the alabaster within, arranged in a sequence which I may not yet tell you, with the Egyptian and myself at the centre, waiting.

It seemed that I had, after all, got my calculations wrong, and that the Sleeper was indeed the last head I needed to complete the circle. This I held in my hands.

Light was beginning to flicker around us; not the evil livid light of the daemon, but little tongues of blue and orange flame. There were two different sources of sound in my head – on the one side the distant ululations and gnashings of despair – but much closer, the thunderous huzzahs and diapasons of triumph and jubilation. Great chords and arpeggios played on the organ of Heaven's vault itself, accompanied by the massed harps of the seraphim, pealed and redoubled in anthems of joy. Old Handel, I remember thinking, would have given his right arm to hear it. It made the Hallelujah Chorus sound like a hurdy-gurdy.

A circular current of wind that was not wind began to sweep about me, voices sang and jabbered in languages that were old when the world was in its infancy, a fine touch.

Above me, the ceiling and the roof had parted, and there was nothing between me and clouds of radiant glory that themselves were descending and parting to reveal Pure Form. I looked down, and the wretched worm-eaten floor had gone and I was standing on the edge of a chasm that reached down a thousand miles through gulphs of fire in which impure shapes – yes, I have seen the Bosch in the Imperial Collection – and he was right! – buttocks with wings, breasts with tiny spiderish legs, anuses with fronds like jellyfish, scrotums with lobster claws – floated and rose and fell, stinging the legions of the lost which sank in doomed disorder, pursued by daemons.

With an effort that was all will, for mere sinew would have been to no avail, I put the Sleeper in place beside the other heads. The flames began to leap around the circle now, faster and faster, until they were a belt of pure fire. The Form descended from above, and the lamentations and the Pit receded.

The Egyptian and I became One (had we been One all

225

along, had my enemy been myself?), moulded together in a shape of perfection that was all Light. And the Form that was above and the form that was below began to meet as the spiral came down like a waterspout to touch me.

And at this last moment, a voice sounded in my ear. It was the voice of good old Balthasar Moll, my old friend and tutor, who of all people was the one I trusted most.

'Surely,' he said, in that kindly ironic manner I knew so well, 'surely you are not going to leave that Sleeper's brow without the final stroke. It would be all right for Stadler . . . but for you? Come now, boy, where is your pride?'

And I reached out and, as the blue flame whirled ever faster about me, I touched with my chisel upon the brow of my last work. And as I touched it, it shattered into a thousand pieces. And as it did so, the circle was broken, the flame died, the Form receded, and I became as you might see me now – a broken man – and the world, and the future of mankind, is as it was and will be.

I am sorry about that. My fault.

108

Meanwhile, in another part of the wood . . .

Bumpppp. Thumpppp.

I was awakened in total darkness by the house shaking. I thought, this must be an earthquake. They are not unknown in this part of the world. I waited for the sound of falling masonry, or at least a tile or two slipping from the eaves. The noise that reached my ears, however, came from the direction of the stairs, and seemed to take the form of a series of dull thumps of enormous magnitude.

I tried to get up for it had always been my fear that my heads might be stolen. They are worth something for their metal alone; but such a collection, even without its magnetic or esoteric value, would run into thousands of florins for it is unique, and there are those who know its worth.

However, I could not move. I seemed literally to be rooted to the bed. Nor could I cry out. I had no more motive ability than a bolster. I was a sack of flesh, a bag of bones. After all those investigations into who or what I was, I had come to this.

Of course, I had become used to fear. I lived with it. Or, rather, it lived with me. I had ventured upon a forbidden path beside which ran pits full of dragons, hydras, banshees, vampires, scorpions and cacodaemons. But I had always felt, secretly, that if I held to my course, maintained the truth, followed the lanthorn of faith in the cause, that I would – though assailed – win through to the end. I have told you that Vienna had been a great stronghold of Protestantism in the last century, until rigorously discouraged by all manner of Imperial edicts forbidding Lutherans and their like any advancement or privilege. Because it was frowned on, I had even flirted with it myself. I had read the great *Pilgrim's Progress* in German. There were many such books still to be found in the city. It had influenced me at one time, and I still clung to the notion of rectitude triumphant.

Now, at last, I began to have doubts. The power coming up the stairs, shaking the house, wobbling the cemetery so that the gravestones chattered like teeth, juddering the city, rocking the continent, trepidating the terrestrial ball itself, was something that neither I nor any mortal resolution could withstand. This power could have done anything. I could not move. I could not pray. I shut my eyes and waited.

An army seemed to be coming up the stairs, a stone army composed of stone or metal giants, like the statue in *Don Juan* that we hear about. I felt its presence all around me. The last one was in the room. The door banged shut. Silence.

I slowly opened my eyes. It was the only movement that was vouchsafed to me so it seemed churlish not to use it. The chamber was bathed in a low, greasy light; and around me stood my heads, each with a statuary body that was a copy of my own; and they gazed at me with the gamut of expressions that I had laboured so long to provide for them – even the Sleeper now miraculously restored from the shattering.

I wanted to cry out to them; 'My children, my selves, why do you stare at me thus? What do you want of me?'

But there were no words at the end of my straining tongue. The sensation that it was I who was the statue, they who were the living forms returned to appal me. The door swung open once more and I turned fearful eyes towards it, knowing that this was what all the rest were waiting for.

There was a pause. Then in stepped Beak Head with a footfall like the closing of a tomb. All the other heads turned towards him, each in his way attentive.

If it had been possible for Beak Head to be more grotesque and repulsive than he had seemed on his first visitation, it was so this night. The mouth seemed more than ever like a disgusting, knowing, prehensile, sexual beak; a protruded or extruded vulva; while the chin had been sharpened and lengthened to provide an androgyne penis, weak but nonetheless vicious; the eyes glaring with a kind of sardonic mirth that had no humour; the earlobes hanging low like the balls of a goat. And yet, more than ever, I could see myself in it, the worst side of myself; the weak, low, conniving, furtive, grubby, lying, cogging, bullying side that I had always been careful to hide away from the world – except from those to whom I chose to lie or cheat or cog or grub or bully, and then of course it did not matter.

Beak Head now stood over me – I had not seen it move but suddenly it was there – and motioned to the others to crowd around me, speaking to me the while in tones that were as chilling as they were incomprehensible.

'Cha nilgri, cha boson, cha naquama. Quaqua naza, qua neboni na mazum.'

All the heads turned from him to me like birds that had heard it was feeding-time. Indeed the vile beak making its quaqua seemed to me to derive from some ancient hermetic bird-language, perhaps the ibis-talk of the Egyptian hierophants. Hermetic or not, I knew what it meant. It meant no good to Franz Xaver Froberger.

At a sign from Beak Head, I was now seized by these creatures of mine, turned over and stripped (for I had fallen asleep with my clothes on). I prepared myself to be pecked to death, or my heart torn out, or my eyes beaked from their sockets, for these were all the possibilities that now seemed only too imminent; at any rate for extinction however it might arrive.

I made one last prayer to the God of Proportion, that God whose path I trod and whose wrath I endured; and at this eleventh hour he answered me. Suddenly my powers of movement were restored, and up I sprang like a jack-in-the-box, leapt over the head of the Sympathetic Listener, jumped the full length of the stairs, and ran out into the snow.

I could hear the quaqua of the Beak Head as they followed me. Where was I to go? I looked more like a fanatic than a reclusive sculptor, bollock naked as I was, slithering on the rutted track, gasping and moaning as I ran. Who would take me in? I tried a couple of houses, floundering up the steps, plunging at the knocker as I turned my head fearfully for the pursuers, for I knew that just behind, just behind, was that terrible line of dark figures, holding hands as they advanced like Death's dancers. From neither house was there any response.

The road was ice-hard and bitter cold on my feet. My penis felt as if it could shatter like a stalactite with frost, and my balls were so shocked they seemed to have taken refuge in my larynx.

There was no one moving in the town. The Watch had gone to sleep. Even the strays had taken refuge. I ran up to Mesmer's house and pulled the bell. Normally he was the last person I wanted to see, but tonight the last person I wanted to see was better than no one. I saw that the windows were shuttered and I knew I was lost. I could hear, just around the bend, the quaqua and the odious shuffle of pursuit.

'Help me,' I shouted, 'for God's sake, help me.'

But I could only whisper because my balls were in my throat. I started running again, this time towards the cathedral. Surely I would find sanctuary there? Behind me the quaqua was louder and more insistent. I reached the cathedral at last, ran up the steps and pushed at the door.

It was shut fast.

'Help,' I tried to cry again, racketing the massive door-handle. 'Sanctuary for a poor sculptor, the great whatsisname.'

It was true. I could not remember my name. It did not matter. Shadows crowded round me. Quaqua was in my ears. Hands of frozen stone and metal clutched at me and lifted me high.

I fainted, and woke in another circumstance.

I was once more lying spread-eagled on my bed, pinioned by hands of metal and stone, and Beak Head was snuffling at my body. It was parting my legs, showing the rest of them what it was doing, poking its disgusting beak up between me, nibbling and sucking as it went.

Nothing could have been more loathsome than its attentions. And yet, with a feeling of utter shame and horror, I discovered that I was responding to this obscene caress, and try though I might to discourage myself, I could feel that terrible willing sweetness spreading through my loins.

'Don't stop,' I could hear a voice beseeching.

230

It was mine.

To be thus exposed, under the gaze of creatures that I had made, that were in some sense myself, and to watch them gloat over the weakness of their Creator who was now reduced to a twitching, beseeching wriggle of flesh was a matter of the utmost humiliation for me. But I could not deny the filthy thing.

It lipped and slithered and guzzled and nuzzled and lingered and fondled and sniffed and lapped and thrust at me with a tongue like a slow-worm.

'Quaquaquaaaa . . .'

I could see its dreadful leering, gloating face. It knew I was totally lost – a dripping instrument of flesh on which it played with no more feeling than a hack continuo.

Oh, I tried all the tricks. I screwed up my eyes and pulled my mouth so tight it was almost inside out. I pinched my nostrils and put on the Stern Martinet. I tried faces which I had no name for, which according to my calculations did not even exist. I thought of sad occurrences and the House of Hapsburg. All to no avail.

I spilled myself halfway across the bed, and Beak Head quacked and sucked at me like a duck. It was eating its Creator in a blasphemous travesty of the Sacrament. Then it turned me over, and while the heavy hands held me down, it raped me with its chin.

I have to set this down. Please do not read it if you find it upsetting. It hurt me more than it hurt you. A rape is never a pleasant episode, but a rape by a pointed little metal chin must rank as one of the most outrageous. It was doubtless to show me who was master, or to punish me for my behaviour in the Vienna Woods – though the lesson in either case was hardly necessary. It was perhaps for no other reason than sheer malevolence.

Then Beak Had let the others take me. My own faces . . . the Quiet Librarian, the Jolly Tapster, the Constipated Man, the Childish Weeper . . . I was rammed and rodded by three score and more lead or alabaster members, at the end of which my bottom felt like the Regimental Colours at Minden. The pain was excruciating and there was no grimace to relieve it.

I yelled, I whimpered, I cried for mercy, I called upon magnetism, Proportion, Newton, Leibnitz, Voltaire, Maria Theresa, the Academy of Arts, and the Holy Mother of Christ, but it didn't hold them up for one instant.

And then, when the last one had finished – the Rapt Listener rogering away like a noctambulist – they turned as a man, or as a model of a man, and left.

I lay upon my bed and sobbed like a child as they plodded down the stairs; not just at the pain; or the shame; but at the end to my work and to my dreams. After all my searchings and my labours, I had come back to the beginning. I was, as King Lear has it, no more than a poor forked animal.

109

The first murder occurred the same night as I experienced these bizarre phantasms. Indeed, it was almost as if I had picked up from the ether something of the horror being perpetrated in the locality.

Johanna told me the news in the morning. I was still troubled in spirit, sickened by my remembered humiliations, so I was not perhaps as impressed as I ought to have been at the time with the report of the unfortunate boy.

'Head cut off like a turnip,' said Johanna.

I made, I hope, suitable noises of dismay and she went off to get more details of the affair.

The sight of another human being, especially one as robust as Johanna, made me realize just how incorporeal had been my visions of the night before. They faded as dreams do, leaving just a trace of unpleasant flavour in my mind, but I was able to finish the Sleeper and press on with the Wily Machiavel. Indeed it seemed that there must have been something cathartic about my nightmares – for the pains which had been my constant companions – and latterly growing in intensity – were this day quite fallen off, and I now was able to work on without the necessity of continual pinching. I was even able, when the light had gone and drowsiness stole over me after my soup and bread, to go to bed and enjoy a sound night's sleep undisturbed by the tweaking and twittering that had been my nightly portion.

I awoke more refreshed and optimistic than I had felt for many weeks. My journey was nearly over. My piles had moderated. I had assembled sixty-six figures and I needed just three more.

Johanna appeared again, hot with news and carrying veal broth with noodles.

'Have they found the man?' I asked.

'They found a tramp. He was almost lynched. The stupid fool was sleeping in a barn not three miles up the road.'

'Was he the murderer?'

'He had a knife on him. All bloody it was. Said he'd stabbed at a rat with it but no one believed him, of course. Where was the dead rat? Nowhere! They hauled him off and he was half dead by the time they got him in.'

I heard the news with a sinking heart.

'Perhaps he was telling the truth.'

'The truth! You only had to look at him. Evil, he was. Kept pulling back his lips and showing his yellow teeth in a snarl. He can hardly speak. More a beast than a man.'

In spite of my concern, I was interested in his way with his lips. He sounded like my Desperado at Bay, No. 43.

'Did they find the boy's body?'

'Not a sign of it. They keep asking him where he put it and he snarls and says "Pu' wha'?" They'll get it out of him.'

233

This, however, they seemed unable to do although they nearly killed him. Interest in the case was kept at fever pitch by the head's funeral next day. It was buried in a little casket pending discovery of the trunk. The prisoner's trial was arranged for the succeeding week. I worked on.

By the evening of the day after the funeral, I had half completed my Wily Machiavel. Johanna turned up later than usual, just before dusk, with some duck soup.

'Dusk soup,' I said to her, but she was in no mood for humour.

'I got delayed hearing the latest,' she told me. 'That little milkmaid, Trudi Krantz, she's just told them about her escape last week. She could have been the first. She was on her way to the shed last week – you know they live over the fields to the east there – it was almost pitch-dark but she knows the way backwards – and she said she felt something trip her up, throw her down and start scraping at her neck with something . . .'

'Could she not run away?' I asked.

'She was held by these cold, weak arms, she said. The terrible thing was, she said, she felt they might get stronger given half a chance.'

'She was inventing it,' I told her. 'You know what milk-maids are like. She wanted attention.'

'She got attention,' said Johanna. 'There was a great red weal all around her neck with toothmarks deep into the skin. They reckon she was lucky. That girl was a rehearsal.'

What she told me made me think. I don't know why but a little tic of disquiet was beginning to tweak away at the optimism I had felt earlier.

'Tell me,' I asked. 'On what day did this occur?'

'Tuesday last, I think. Why?'

'Oh, nothing. Just a thought.'

'If you saw something, you better tell the police.'

'I saw nothing. What could I see? I never go out.'

'You don't see nothing but your face. No wonder you're such a crackpot. Well, I'll be off before it's dark. I don't like to be out late even though they've got him locked up.'

She went off into the dusk, crossing herself.

I sat for some time, deep in thought. The day before Tuesday last, I had completed another head: the Simpering Poltroon. It was coincidence, of course. What else could it be? But early next morning there had been an attack.

There was nothing I could do about it, however. I must press on. How could there possibly be a connection? That night I nearly finished my Machiavel. It was a masterly piece though I say it myself; the eyes bleak and watchful, the mouth in a thin smile; plausible, yet faintly contemptu-ous; the nostrils narrowed, the forehead furrowed but never worried. Yet I could not quite bring myself to finish it. Not a pinch nor a pang did I feel all night.

In spite of myself – my face furrowed yet never worried – for I find the character temporarily adopted clings for a while – I awaited Johanna's arrival next day with some impatience.

I almost prayed for another murder. The vagabond would be innocent. And my head would be still unfinished. Not that these murders could have anything, anything at all, to do with my heads. It was absurd.

I felt I knew something. And yet I knew nothing.

Johanna at last appeared but there was no further infor-mation. Had there perhaps been a murder that none had discovered? These things can happen. People live alone. Who should know it better than I? I am sure that in some garret there is a head and body waiting to be found.

Pray God let there be another murder. I would gladly offer myself but I have work in hand.

Why should my pure endeavour, the loftiest pursuit imagi-nable, become so stained with blood?

110

I have not worked for three weeks.

The vagabond, one Matthias Kopf, has been sentenced and will hang in a fortnight, a speedy sequence in deference to local sensibilities.

This cannot continue. I must work or the entire rhythm and proportion of my opus will be thrown out. I feel that there is a compulsion for me to complete the matter soon. It is part of some design which is as yet hidden from me.

I shall finish the Machiavel today if it kills me. And yet, if I do, and someone else is killed . . . what then?

At least, Matthias Kopf will be spared.

It seems to me, that either way, I shall be responsible for a death over which I have no control. Can the hands that open the Secret have blood on them? I am snared whichever way I go.

111

God help me, I hear from Johanna that another child has been murdered – a most hideous affair – the head stuck grotesquely on to the trunk of a snowman in the Schwarzallee. Some kind of cord or membrane, hanging from it, had wrapped around the figure like a red scarf.

There is no doubt in my mind that I am responsible. I should never have gone ahead with the Machiavel. Indeed I remember purposing not to, setting my face against it. Why, then, did I continue?

I remember some feeling akin to compulsion, like that which precedes orgasm, a restless necessity from which there was no deflection.

And then busying myself with the wax. 'Let the head be leaden,' I remember saying it to myself, a strange refrain, 'for it is the metal of our condition.'

How can I continue? Yet the goal beckons more shiningly than ever.

The man Kopf has been released, more dead than alive.

112

Later, in the light of noonday, the idea of guilt seemed nonsense. I was making heads, that was all. There could be no question of guilt. Heads cannot kill. I could hardly have an object more noble, in fact damn 'hardly', I could not have an object more noble than that of uncovering the Perfection lost at Man's Fall. These crimes were horrible, but they were, as far as I was concerned, mere coincidence.

I put aside guilt and got out my mallet and chisel, my block of alabaster, and started upon the Winsome Suitor, echoing a pain that I had intermittently observed in my spleen, though now hardly more than a dull ache.

I worked upon this for two days and far into the night. On the second day, Johanna told me that the town was still in uproar looking for the criminal. Few dared venture out after the hour of five except armed bands of men who combed every alley in the town and every barn, copse and gully outside it.

At last my Suitor was finished, and I slept.

113

I am in despair. After so long to be stopped by so cruel a stratagem! I would rather suffer the pains a thousandfold than be the (albeit unwitting) instrument of another's death. And such another. A beautiful young boy – snatched from his life, stripped of his very body. It is too much. I cannot of course go on now. It is unthinkable.

The latest murder seemed to tap an almost lyric vein in Johanna.

'She left the house to meet her lover in the barn. She's only sixteen, and him just a year older. You can imagine her, Franz, tiptoeing to the back door, not wanting her family to hear, lifting the latch nice and slow, creeping out into the yard, past the goose pen praying they wouldn't cackle, her path lit up by the great big moon we had last night, and the snow. Past the sty and the stables, heart thumping as she peered into the shadows. She knew about the murders, of course, so she wasn't taking any chances. At last she comes to the barn door . . ,'

'Please,' I groaned, 'there's no need to act it out.'

'What's the matter with you, Franz. I'm only trying to give you the story. It's not you that's going to be murdered. At last she comes to the barn door. She looks around, nervous-like. No father with his stick, no monster of Pressburg with his garrotte. She pulls gently at the door, creeeaaak . . . in she slips. It takes a little while to see 'cause it's dark in there . . .'

'It's dark in here too,' I told her, 'in my head. This is a ghastly tale.'

'It gets ghastlier,' she told me. '"Horst," she calls softly. No answer. It was where she'd arranged to meet him. "Horst."

She moves on a little and over to the right where a patch of moonlight catches the top of a big round stone her father uses to weight his plough. Only . . . oh God . . .'

'I cannot hear this,' I tell her.

'Be a man, Franz. You're too sensitive by half. Anyway, you're bound to hear it sooner or later. So it isn't the big round stone, is it? It's Horst's head propped against a sack, still running blood into the sacking. She screams. Aaaagh! And even as her father snatches up his old flintlock, she sees a shadowy figure spring down and run across the yard with something in its arms, down the track, between the trees, lit up by the moon, across the bridge and into the wood beyond. Her father tries to follow with his dog but he's lost him, and at last he comes back to fetch help and cover the remains . . .'

'Enough,' I cried, 'enough, enough.'

'What's the matter with you, Franz? I didn't know you was so sentimental.'

My mind was in a tumult but I contrived to remonstrate.

'Sentimental's one thing,' I said. 'But a natural shrinking from gory details is another.'

'I should've thought you'd like to hear the news. You get out so little, don't you?'

She gave me a meaning look whose meaning I failed to catch.

Poor Horst, whoever he was with his hopes and fears, his sweetheart and his expectations, is no more. He is Horst de Combat.

What am I to do?

114

I went down to the cellar last night after a day of indecision and torment.

Unable to work, I sat in front of the glass staring endlessly at my features looking at the daemon in me as I used to gaze at the cold sore; repulsive, evil. And as I sat, all my faces shaped and framed themselves across my features, grinning and leering, frowning and becking, winking and straining, howling and scowling. My face was a kaleido-scope of expressions, changing endlessly and meaninglessly as I watched.

And always, at the back of my mind, was the knowledge that I had to make the decision: to complete the circle and start on Face No. 69 and risk another death. Or to stop on the threshold of Proportion, save another's life, and waste my own. It was a decision I could not make.

I went down to the cellar – I call it a cellar, built low in the ground where the Jewish sexton used to keep corpses cool in summer before burial – I went down for some reason or other – call it a whim – I went down to the cellar to get my umberella.

And there, lying on the ground, propped against the wall, were five bodies, all headless.

I stood appalled, my anatomical eye noting the way their limbs were arranged.

One of them rose to its feet. I started to gibber, holding one arm in front of me to ward off the spectacle. Somehow it had regained its features. It was Mesmer.

'Give me the heads,' he said. 'Now, while there is still time.'

Suddenly I knew what my decision had to be.

'I cannot,' I told him. 'There is but one to do and then I shall have it. We shall all have it. Inestimable benefits will accrue. Forget the Golden Mean. It will be the Golden Age.'

'There is a force stirring,' he said slowly, 'in the heads.'

'My heads?'

He nodded.

'That block of alabaster I gave you is shot through with mineral channels that have become magnetized. By some chance, they lie upon the same axis as those of the human head. Through them the electric fluid travels freely. It is a rare block. Fashioned as the heads are, in lead and alabaster, and arranged according to certain principles that I must not discover to you yet, they contain a power beyond calculation which I alone can tap. If it is wrongly done, with sufficient fluid coursing through them, they can become animated . . .'

'Animated?' I repeated again, only half credulously.

'Not what you might call alive, but full of force, and with an implacable resentment of things that are alive. They will need bodies. A few they have taken already . . . including yours.'

'Mine?' I remonstrated. 'But my head is still in place.'

'You have given them your features,' he told me earnestly, his fat lips now pale and curiously flattened with his intensity, 'and you have lost your head.'

'I must do the last one,' I told him, 'if it costs head, body and soul.'

A shudder passed through me as I said the words. They had been used before.

'What about these bodies?' asked Mesmer.

'They shall remain here,' I told him. 'When I am done, they shall be restored to their owners.'

241

115

I had dreamt about it for so long, I could hardly believe it was now upon me. I was embarking on the final head, Head No. 69, the Wise Philosopher! I had deliberately left this subject till the last, both for its matter and its correspondence. The expression that I chose for it matched a new ache that I had begun to feel, quite unlike the others, around my breast.

I had reserved the finest piece of alabaster for the Philosopher, and I worked upon it for two days without rest. Something beyond me seemed to have taken possession of my hands so that I was no more responsible for the perfection of the result than the beauty of the sunset. And perfection, I could sense, it was going to be!

As I worked, I speculated as to what I should do when the doors of Proportion were opened to me. What equity should I bestow to mankind! I would not destroy wealth but I should make all men wealthy, so that there would be no need for the vicious and time-wasting self-seeking that characterized so much of what passed for human activity. In such circumstance, there would be no need of Hapsburg or Bourbon. Everyone could hang up their vons. Plain Mr would be honour enough. There would be no bad artists. The unequal humours and fluids would be rectified so that sickness and distortion would be no more. In fact, everyone would be beautiful. I was a little concerned about Death which I saw as an aspect of disproportion. On the other hand, if there were no deaths, we could hardly agree to births, and I knew (to my cost!) how much store women set by that kind of thing. Doubtless all would be made plain when the moment arrived.

Finally it was done. The head shone softly, perfect in every particular, the calm light of wisdom glowing from features never before equalled in alabaster. It was a thing indeed for a Golden Age.

As I finished, I could feel the daemon admitting defeat. This was indeed, it had to be, the key. I lifted the head and put it in the position at the top of the inner circle that I had reserved for it, and waited for whatever it was that I was expecting to take place, surprised indeed that nothing had happened already, but there were no precedents.

I waited for ten minutes. Absolutely nothing occurred. I knelt and prayed: 'Oh Perfect Form.' Still nothing. I got up and took another look at the Wise Philosopher, thinking that I might perhaps have left some flaw; but it was perfect yet.

I stepped into the middle of the two circles – lead without, alabaster within – and knelt again. No pillar of cloud, no organ music, no celestial choirs. I lay down on the floor, weary after my exertions, and waited. Presently I fell asleep.

When I awoke, I was running through a wood with four other grimacing variants of myself. This time they were not after me, I was one of them. I held the headless body of a youth in my arms. The other four were also carrying other corpses. We were like a pack of daemons. We would kill the world.

I exulted without pleasure, and fell into blackness.

116

They all stood round me: Mesmer, Fessler, Johanna and someone I did not recognize. I could not move. For some reason, I found it prudent to pretend to be unconscious. Mesmer touched me tentatively with his iron rod (I noticed he had a small baquet on the floor beside him). I could not help myself twitching as the effect of the rod communicated itself. It was like a kick from a mule. But I still kept my eyes closed.

'The crisis is over,' Mesmer told the others.

'You give him too much, Mesmer,' said Johanna. 'Poor old bugger. You put too much poppy in the wine.'

'You are going to live in comfort for the rest of your life, young lady,' said Mesmer. 'Do not get a conscience now.'

'I still don't think you should've done them things to him with that rod. What did you tease him for anyway with all that murder stuff you wanted me to tell him?'

'I wished him to finish his heads but to be unworthy of them at the end,' said Mesmer. 'If he had been worthy, who knows what might have transpired? There is power in the heads, depend upon it.'

'He was a bloody sight worthier than you,' said Johanna.

'I do not aim for such lofty heights as he. He was prepared to risk a youth's death to reach his ends. That is unworthy. It is one of the principles of mystery that only the deserving may be admitted.'

'But if he hadn't done that, there'd have been no end.'

'That was the irony of the situation,' said Fessler.

'Iron being the operative word,' said Mesmer, poking at me again with his rod. 'It was necessary to stir his phancy. His mind is full of wild speculation. We have to play upon it. If he were as others are, we might have had some trouble extracting such a treasure from its author. But his shame and confusion will cloak our stratagem.'

'I expect you are right,' said Johanna. 'You usually are, sod you.'

'But you too are right,' said Mesmer. 'The dose was strong. We do not want to lose him here. You had better go and get him more soup. Soup and brandy.'

She left. Fessler shrugged. He did not mind where he lost me.

'We could bury him in the cemetery,' he said. 'It is very convenient.'

'Have you any idea what observances are required before a Jew is buried? We would have every Rabbi in Pressburg up in arms.'

Fessler shrugged again.

'He is already weak,' said Mesmer. 'Another chill will finish him off. It will be tidier all round.'

117

Oh yes, it was all a dream.

You don't think that kind of thing happens in a place like Pressburg, do you?

But mark this, if you will. Later, I was woken with a pain in my bum and an icy draught that came through my bedroom doorway. I could feel the fever starting up again but I staggered downstairs and found the front door wide open with a pile of snow inside the studio where the wind had blown it.

Of all my heads, all sixty-nine of them, and the Egyptian, there was no sign.

118

I walked round distractedly for a while, and then Johanna appeared with broth (goose, as it happened). It dawned upon me, as I admitted her, that I was still naked.

'Shame upon you,' said Johanna, 'walking about in the buff at your age. No wonder you got fever and your piles is playing up. I never liked those faces of yours anyway, scare you to death they would, if you met 'em on a dark night.'

She would not look me in the eyes. I knew then that she had brought me drugged wine, and that Mesmer had taken the heads.

'Why can't you stick to something nice, like a nice nude or a Virgin,' she continued, warming to her theme. 'Virgins is always popular. I'll be a Virgin for you if you like.'

She busied herself about the studio, kindling the fire and wrapping blankets around me. I had lost the will to argue or remonstrate. I could feel the fever tightening its bands around my head, and unleashing its shakers and quakers in my bosom. I sat and stared at the empty shelves and tried to eat my broth.

'Don't talk if you don't want to,' said Johanna, unnecessarily, 'suit yourself. I know what it's like with a fever. D'you want me to warm you up, then, give you a little chafe? You like a chafe.'

She spoke to me as if I were an infant. I shook my head. I did not want a chafe. I wondered how much Mesmer had paid her. The doctored wine bottle, doubtless suitably magnetized to induce a crisis, had been removed. It had produced a crisis all right. My gloomy expression provoked another bout of guilt in Johanna.

'Cheer up,' she said. 'You aren't dead yet.'

I was sorry about that. I should have liked to have been dead. It is the actual dying that is such a nuisance. Death, say the Freemasons, is the key to our life. It is the putting it in the lock and turning it which is so squeaky.

I gazed out across the scrubland beside the cemetery, normally grubby and unlovely as yesterday's dinner-table, over which today the snow had thrown a careless white damask. The sun was shining. A tree flopped a burden of snow from its branches, almost smothering an unsuspecting robin. A dog lifted its leg against a broken railing, drawing yellow whirligigs with its pee upon the pathway – making a rather better job it, I thought, than some of our modern artists.

I could have found in the spectacle much to commend the world, but now I could summon up nothing.

Johanna was putting her shawl on, half concerned about me – she would probably spend some of the money with which she had been bribed in looking after me – half relieved to be gone. She thought she knew my moods. I was better left alone at times like this. I suddenly saw that, God help her, she loved me. She wished to suffocate me with her lips.

'Goodbye,' she said, 'see you later. I'll bring you some sausages later. That'll perk you up. Sausages and a nice bottle of wine. You like a sausage. Mind you keep well wrapped up now. Ta-ra.'

Ta-ra. I continued staring at the shelves long after the door had closed, until the sun had traversed the little row of sour trees at the cemetery's boundary, and had started its rapid winter decline into the bog. And at last I reached for pen, ink and paper.

I must resist the fever if only to finish my account of the whole matter for Nicolai as he had urged. There will be no more exercise with the mallet and chisel. The furnace and the lost wax have seen the last of me. It is pen-time and look sharp about it.

119

Mesmer's house is shut. He is gone with his thick lips and his lisping ways. There is no doubt that he is behind it. Revenge would be pointless, repossession impossible. The error was mine when all is said and done. Ah my heads, my baby men, my Russian dolls, my sine quaqua non.

My cough was bad last night, so I came downstairs and did some more writing by candlelight. I could not continue long, however, and sat in a blanket beside the fire until cock-crow.

The paper is like a mirror without glass upon which one can only scratch one's expressions.

The odd thing is, when I look at the real mirror, I sometimes have the feeling that I am seeing nothing, that my features have disappeared and that I am looking at a dummy such as I have seen milliners use in their windows. Free of emotion now, I have used up my features. There is no more pain. Only the cough and the soup. No more, thank you, Johanna.

120

Today I am a little stronger, and I have written at length about my life in Vienna. I have inserted it earlier on in this narration. You will already have read it. Thank you. Parts of this account, as I say, are old and were set down years ago but much is newly-collected, or recollected, and freshly penned. I had always had the notion of emulating the great

Cellini, putting down as it were my apologia, ever since I was shown a translation of his autobiography in London.

I started years back, but it was just doors and windows. The brickwork has been left for these latter days,

I started years ago.

I have thought much about the way things have turned out; about destiny and predestination.

I started years ago, and I was finished before I started.

121

'Everyone's talking about it,' said Johanna.

'About what?'

'You know. Don't play the innocent.'

'I do not know.'

'The naked man with no face.'

I sat coughing by the fire, writing and pretending to write. I did not believe her any more. She elaborated on the outrage. It seemed the apparition lacked eyes, nose and gob.

'No face? Any other distinguishing features?' I asked.

'Only a big . . .'

She stopped and blushed.

Johanna could blush at will. It was one of her distinguishing features. I was surprised she was not blushing all the time at what she had done to me.

I controlled myself.

'Who has seen him?' I asked.

'Mrs Rogosky and Mr and Mrs Ferencz, last night, as they were coming home from a musical evening. And one of the Watch saw him the night before running across the square like a monkey.'

'A monkey with no fur, poor bugger.'

'Yes.'

'A poor forked animal.'

'I suppose so.'

'I am surprised it is so big out in the snow. I am surprised it hasn't got frostbite.'

Suddenly she burst into tears.

'It's you, isn't it?' she said.

'I? What happened to my face?'

'I don't know. But it's you. You're trying to kill yourself.'

I coughed for a while.

'I do not think I should need such extreme measures,' I said.

In fact, it was perfectly true. I had been nervous that a recovery might be setting in, and I had the absurd idea that if I ran, as I had run on that other night, I might just hear the feet and the quaqua behind me. In spite of everything, I wanted them back. I could not live without them. It was a desperate notion. As for the featureless face, it was doubtless a trick of the light or a typical piece of Hungarian spookishness. They loved that kind of thing in Pressburg.

'I'm sorry about the heads,' she sniffed. 'There was Mr Mesmer and this monk. I was worried about you. You needed food and warmth, not a lot of daft heads and mumbo-jumbo. They give me four hundred florins.'

'What?'

I was aghast.

'So little?' I spluttered.

She was indignant.

'Little? It's more than you see in a twelve-month. You'd be dead by now if it weren't for them florins. Look at you.'

To be betrayed by someone who loves you, for so little . . . It was too much.

I coughed again. It was odd that they had seen no face. Doubtless it was because they had been so busy looking at my wigwag.

'You're wrong,' I told her. 'I should not be dead. I should be living in a state of Perfect Form and Degree. And so would you.'

'Pooh to that. Perfect Form and Degree don't butter the muffins.'

I was growing bored with the conversation.

'You are wrong,' I admonished her. 'Perfect Form and Degree butter everything and touch us all, or would have done so. And now be off with you. The hour is late and I shall have to hurry if I am to end tonight.'

122

It is finished at last. Rereading it I find that there is much that is unexplained, more that is inexplicable. I am sorry about that. It would be satisfying to give you Reason and Logic. To provide you with an Answer.

You may perhaps think it easier to classify some of the events I have tried to describe as enthusiasm or even madness. You may be right. But madness and her sister nightmare – for nightmare is only another form of madness, rounded with a sleep – these two are circumscribed. They follow in their mad way certain rules. Life is much more disorderly than that. The Academy of Sciences, our sister institution, newly built ten years before I arrived in Vienna, was very hot on Catastrophe, which Buffon shows us increases with time. That is the disorderly law of life. Everything gets worse. Perfect Form, now, is something different. That is of the Beginning, of before the Beginning. But I must not go on about Perfect Form.

I am just going to take my very imperfect form for a run now. The wind is blowing up nicely, and that ghost-finger pattering at the window tells me it is snowing hard again. That should do the trick.

Venio, Creator.

Off with these lendings.

Once round the square and the last one back's a quaqua.

God, it's cold.

Postscript

When we consider that the poor wretch was afraid
of these imaginary spirits, that he was alone, and in
this loneliness strained his disordered fantasy to its
utmost in order to procure a sufficiently vivid mental
picture of these figures that he was so appreciative of,
and even to imitate them in marble, then it may be
widely accepted that he did almost meet his death
for fear. But certain enough it is, that a sculptor
beginning with the purest Antique proportions of the
human figure, then misled by a blighted imagination
and insane hypotheses, should conceive at last of the
spirit of Proportion itself in an embodiment of the most
abhorrent disproportion imaginable by man.

Recollection of a Meeting in Pressburg
Friedrich Nicolai

Froberger is a name of convenience for Franz Xaver Messerschmidt. Messerschmidt's curious life, extraordinary works
and even more extraordinary character inspired this story
– which is in many ways a 'gothic' interpretation of what
little we know about him. Many of the details, however, are
true. Just as many are complete fabrications of my own.

As a matter of interest, there was indeed a scandal about
the Capuchins keeping lunatics in the Catacombs; and the
Faceless Man of Pressburg did become quite a *cause célèbre*
during the winter of 1784–5. It was true that there were
originally only a very few actual witnesses; but somehow
the affair played on the imagination of the town, and what
started as one or two isolated incidents grew to be quite a
ritual. Half the pranksters in the place were soon running
up and down in the buff with pink scarves wrapped around
their faces. It is only stopped when an outraged Burgomaster

253

issued the Watch with fowling-pieces, and one silly arse got peppered.

Messerschmidt himself died of a chest infection on December 6th of that year.

Ignaz Fessler was a mysterious and enigmatic figure who appeared on the Viennese scene in the 1770s, in the first instance as a Capuchin monk. He then obtained a release from the Order and became Professor of Oriental Languages at the University of Lemburg in 1784. Leaving this position after a few years, he moved to Berlin where he founded its first Freemasons' Lodge in 1793. His last recorded post is as a Bishop of the Russian Church in the 1820s. The indications are of a wandering empiricist experimenting with occultism, orientalism, the new physics and the old metaphysics.

As for Mesmer, the good Doctor lived on until 1815 and died both rich and honoured in his eighty-second year, attended by what was described as 'a young priest called Fessler'. Fessler was in his mid-twenties when he was sculpted by Messerschmidt in 1774. Thus the young-looking priest who attended Mesmer was in fact well over sixty.

Did he have some secret formula, an elixir or water of life that helped him to stay young? Or was he master of some arcane secret upon which he and Mesmer lavished untold wealth and care? Perhaps, indeed, he is still alive and will be able to tell us.

It is interesting to note that Mesmer's theory of a universal subtle fluid and its electro-magnetic operation are not so far from today's field theories of particle physics – which in turn have been combined with the symmetry properties of Einstein's ideas about gravity and relativity – to produce the theory of Supersymmetry or Perfect Proportion, as one might say.

Of Messerschmidt's sixty-nine heads (as distinct from his other great works) less than half remain. A show was given in some kind of waxwork pavilion in Vienna some ten years after his death – about the same time that Count Deym was showing Mozart's death-mask – but whether they were actual heads or waxy replicas is not established.

The surviving heads – considered by psychiatrists to be full of sexual as well as other symbolic meanings – are now distributed in Vienna, Budapest, Munich, Nuremberg, Berlin, London and, I understand, New York.

The rest are . . . who knows where?

If you should stumble across one on your travels, try to obtain it at all costs. It could be worth a very great deal of money.

And there could be more to it than that.

ACKNOWLEDGEMENTS

My thanks are due to the Curators of the ICA in London whose exhibition of works by Messerschmidt in 1987 first gave me the idea for this novel. I should also like to thank: William Rider & Son for permission to quote from the book by W. D. Ince, *Mesmer and the Art of Magnetism*; the London Library for its endless fund of helpfulness and bibliography; Anne de Rohr for translating much German; Steve Cox for his encouragement and suggestions; Anita Brookner for correcting some of my more glaring deficiencies in art history; and finally Dennis Burden of Trinity College, Oxford, for his unfailing network of savants in whatever subject I have consulted him upon. That I have not always benefited from their wisdom is neither their fault nor his, but entirely my own.